CHASING
HOPE

Books by Kathryn Cushman

Chasing Hope
A Promise to Remember
Waiting for Daybreak
Leaving Yesterday
Another Dawn
Almost Amish

CHASING HOPE

A NOVEL

KATHRYN CUSHMAN

BETHANYHOUSE

a division of Baker Publishing Group
Minneapolis, Minnesota

Published by Bethany House Publishers
11400 Hampshire Avenue South
Bloomington, Minnesota 55438
www.bethanyhouse.com

Bethany House Publishers is a division of
Baker Publishing Group, Grand Rapids, Michigan

Printed in the United States of America

Library of Congress Cataloging-in-Publication Data

Cushman, Kathryn.
    Chasing hope / Kathryn Cushman.
        p.   cm.
    Summary: "A college student with unfulfilled Olympic dreams and a tal-
ented but troubled teen runner try to find hope for the future in an unorthodox
mentorship"—Provided by publisher.
    ISBN 978-0-7642-0827-0 (pbk.) 1. Athletes—Fiction. 2. Mentoring—Fiction.
I. Title.
    PS3603.U825C43 2013
    813'.6—dc23   2013017368

Cover design by Andrea Gjeldum

13 14 15 16 17 18 19   7 6 5 4 3 2 1

To Jim and Leah Cushman—

*Your courage and strength are
an inspiration to all of us*

Then Moses led Israel from the Red Sea and they went into the Desert of Shur. For three days they traveled in the desert without finding water.

Exodus 15:22

PROLOGUE

A dozen men in ugly white outfits and weird haircuts ran barefoot along the ocean's edge, moving faster, faster, faster, as the music swelled until it filled the entire theater. Sabrina Rice leaned forward in her seat, clutching her bag of popcorn tight to her chest. Her feet tapped against the sticky concrete floor, twitching with the urge to run alongside those men. And then she saw *him*. The man with his head thrown back, arms churning at his sides, and a strange sense of joy shining in his eyes. In that moment, her life made sense. In that moment, she found her hero.

It made no difference to her that this movie was over twenty years old, or that the revival theater was mostly empty, or that it would have been far more convenient to rent *Chariots of Fire* at the local video rental store and watch it at home—as only a few hours ago she had complained bitterly to her mother—or that she'd really wanted to go bowling with her friends today. For the next two hours, nothing existed but Sabrina and the runners on the screen, particularly Eric Liddell. And watching him, face toward the sky, drinking in God's pleasure as he ran, that's when she knew. With absolute certainty she knew what she wanted to do with the rest of her life. As she walked from the theater, she turned to her mother. "I am going to be an Olympic runner and I'm going to tell people about God, just like Eric Liddell. Maybe not China, though. I don't think they allow that anymore."

Mom threw back her head and laughed. It wasn't one of those grown-up kinds of laughs that let a kid know how stupid they were. No, this was one of those "I'm so completely happy I can't hold it in" kind of things. She reached down and scooped Sabrina into her arms and spun around in a circle. "Sounds terrific."

Sabrina was so happy with her newfound purpose that she wasn't really too embarrassed by her mother's public display of affection—thankfully none of the kids from school were anywhere near this old movie theater. "Can we start training now? You want to go for a run when we get home?"

"I think that's a grand idea." And just like that, they became running partners.

Much to Mom's credit, she never balked when Sabrina insisted that they go for a run every single morning, rain or shine. It didn't seem to matter that Sabrina was only twelve years old and according to most grown-ups, "couldn't possibly be serious about what she's going to do with her life." Even long after the point that Mom had to ride a bike to keep up, she was always there and ready.

Every single day.

At five in the morning.

Rain or shine.

For the next six years.

1

10 Years Later

"Is this seat taken?"

Just when Sabrina thought her day couldn't get better, Koen Conner's baby blues were staring down at her. She smiled at him across the table of Campus Eats, Southern Tennessee State's finest on-campus eatery, suddenly grateful she'd decided to stay there and study after her shift was over. "Uh, no. It's not." *Definitely not.* She removed her feet from the opposite chair and sat up straighter, wishing she'd spent a little more time on her hair that morning. She reached up to tuck a tangle of stragglers behind her left ear, very much doubting that it looked as nonchalant as she intended.

"I was hoping you'd say that." He dropped his backpack at the end of the table and instead of taking the chair across from her, he pulled out the one beside her. It made a loud scraping sound as it scooted across the tile floor, causing him to close one eye and pull his head back just a fraction. He dropped into the chair, which rocked precariously forward and to the left. "I'm thinking it's time to get some new chairs in here. Maybe you should tell your boss, hmm?" As if on cue, the chair rocked backwards and to the right. He quirked his left eyebrow. "See what I mean?"

"Perhaps it is time for some new ones."

"Oh, I don't think there's any *perhaps* about it." He stood, exchanged his defective chair for one at the empty table behind them, and then made a show of sitting slowly, as if waiting to see if it would actually hold him.

Sabrina couldn't help but laugh. "Better?"

"If it wasn't, I'd be on the floor right now." He put his elbow on the table and set his chin in his hand, unleashing the full force of his beautiful boyish grin on her. "What are you working on?"

She glanced at the computer screen, pleased with her early progress. "A brochure."

"For?" He leaned a little closer to the screen, which also brought him closer to Sabrina.

"I just found out I've made it through the first round of interviews for an internship with the Grace Rose PR firm in Atlanta. Round two involves an in-person interview. I'm working on something to take with me that will hopefully help give me an edge."

"Atlanta, huh?" He turned toward her, now even closer. It made it very difficult to form an intelligent response.

"It's the biggest PR firm in the country. They have offices in a dozen major cities. Landing an internship there is what we all strive for. It's the gateway to anywhere we want to go."

"Really?" He leaned just a bit closer. "And where do you want to go, Miss Sabrina Rice?"

She looked at him, felt his closeness, and tried to remind herself to breathe. Any other time and for any other person, she could spout out her life's plan all the way down to the minute details. Right now, with Koen this close, it all went a little fuzzy. "I, uh . . ." Her tongue stuck to the roof of her mouth, which was just as well, because any answer she might have given was long since forgotten.

He seemed to find this amusing, because he grinned, then finally leaned back against his chair. "How'd you do on that psychology exam?" He had a dimple in his left cheek.

"I'm feeling pretty good about it." She took a sip of her decaf Earl Grey. "How about you?"

"Well, let's just say—" he unleashed another grin—"I think I could use a study buddy for the next one. You know anyone who might be willing to help me?"

"I . . . uh . . . think I might."

He held her gaze and continued to smile. "I was hoping you'd say that, too. You're just full of the answers I want to hear today."

"Thanks," she sort of squeaked, "I do my best to be helpful." It was impossible not to smile when she looked at him.

"Well, if that's the case, then what if I—" He turned his head slightly toward the window just over Sabrina's shoulder. "Wow, what the . . . ?"

Sabrina turned to see what had caught his interest. A girl was racing through the middle of the campus, her legs pumping at an impressive rate. Her shoulder-length hair was bleached white in the front and dyed jet black in the back, and it whipped up and then back with each stride. She jumped down a set of four steps, landed cleanly, and picked the pace right back up, hardly missing a beat. In her left hand she held what looked to be an aerosol can.

A campus security guard rounded the building behind her. Behind her and losing ground fast. In spite of the fact that he was young and appeared to be in decent shape, by the time he reached the steps the girl had jumped over, it was more than obvious his chase was a lost cause. He stopped, doubled over with hands on knees, gasping for air and shaking his head.

"Did you see that? That girl was *fast*!" Koen's voice grew louder with admiration. "I'm thinking she must have been part gazelle or something. Can you believe that?"

Sabrina looked down at the table. "No, I don't think I can." She started gathering her things. "I've got to go."

He reached over and put a hand on her arm, the warmth of his touch almost managing to restore her to her former mood. "Hey, wait. I wanted to ask, there's a bunch of people watching the Tennessee versus Duke basketball game over at Jared's tomorrow. Do you want to go?"

"I . . . I . . ." Inside her, two opposing forces battled. One would do almost anything to spend a day with Koen. The other, meanwhile, couldn't bear to watch collegiate sports, and most certainly not when it involved Tennessee. A few seconds ago, before she'd seen the running girl, her answer might have been different. But now, well . . . "I can't." She put her books in her backpack, her heart aching in so many places she'd forgotten existed, she thought she might burst into tears—something she hadn't allowed herself to do in years. Three years, to be exact.

She did manage to paste on a smile in an attempt to salvage something of this day. "Thank you for inviting me though."

His eyes narrowed a fraction, as if he was trying to understand what just happened. "Sure."

She threw her backpack over her left shoulder and walked from the table. Just as well. She needed to stay focused on her studies now, anyway. At least, that was what she'd keep telling herself. She'd almost made it to the door when Lindy Stewart and her entourage came breezing through.

Lindy and her pack came to Campus Eats almost every day around this time, ordered fat-free chai lattes, and basked in the admiration of every single male in the place. As the number two tennis player and number one most desired female on campus, Lindy never lacked for admirers. "Look who's here," Sabrina heard her whisper to the girl beside her, then she smiled and waved into the snack bar. In spite of herself, Sabrina turned to see who the object might be, although she was pretty certain she already knew the answer.

Lindy bypassed the line and took the seat beside Koen. She put her hand on his shoulder, and he smiled and said something that caused them both to laugh. Of course he smiled. Sabrina turned to go, wishing she had just kept walking.

So much for her day that couldn't get any better.

2

Saturday afternoon, Brandy Philip ran up the front walk and leapt onto the porch, looking at her watch in midair: 5:59. As much as she wanted to stand outside and enjoy the chill of a Tennessee February while she recovered from her homeward sprint, she only had one minute to spare.

She pulled open the storm door and shoved her way inside, shedding her sweatshirt as she made for the kitchen. "Grandma, I'm home." She sniffed the air, searching for a hint of what might be for dinner—hoping it wasn't spinach or black-eyed peas, but something more along the line of creamed corn or chicken and dumplings. She sniffed again and walked into the kitchen to find . . . nothing.

Absolutely nothing.

No Grandma. No food on the stove or counter, and no smell that either had ever been there. Nothing but the always lingering hint of Grandma's Jergen's lotion.

"You're late." Her voice came from the living room, the same room Brandy had just walked through. She turned back.

"Am not. It's just now six o'clock."

"I asked you to be home by five thirty tonight." It was a statement. Nothing more, nothing less. At least Grandma wasn't a lecturer, which made her infinitely better than most grown-ups.

"Five thirty, really? When did you say that?"

"Last night. I told you we were going to our neighbor's house for dinner, my friend who lives just a couple of streets over."

"Oh, right." Brandy waved her hand dismissively. "Have a good time. I'll just fix some mac and cheese right here and call it good. I'm going to the movie with some friends later."

"Nope. You're coming." The determination in Grandma's voice was unusual enough that Brandy paused to consider. No reason to turn this into a showdown. Just a little bit of reasoning and they would all go their merry ways.

"Why? I'm sure the two of you will have more fun without me around, and I'm plenty able to fend for myself."

"No, you need to come with me. My friend's granddaughter lives with her, too. You two can get to know each other. It's time you found a nicer group of friends."

"My friends are fine."

"We are going. Now."

What was with this newfound bossiness? Brandy hesitated. Would it be best to dig in and fight hard, hoping to avoid a similar situation in the future, or just give in this once and hope it was a one-time thing? Fact remained, she was hungry. And there was no way this dinner could last more than an hour or two at most. Still plenty of time to meet up with her crew later. Might as well give Grandma the satisfaction of believing she'd won this round.

"Okay, let's get this over with."

Sabrina watched until her grandmother disappeared from the dining room back into the kitchen, then continued to listen until she was more than certain she could move without being seen. As soon as the coast was truly clear, she reached into her pocket for the two white pills that waited there. She popped them into her mouth, swallowed them dry, then returned to setting the table. She took care to line up the silverware just perfectly. Tonight meant a lot to Nana.

"I don't know, do you think maybe we should use the fancier plates?" Just that fast, Nana reappeared in the dining room.

Hopefully Nana hadn't seen the Tylenol, because it would definitely tip her off that Sabrina wasn't feeling well. "No, I think these are beautiful. It's just a casual dinner. No reason to be too formal about this, right?" The old lace tablecloth had been around for far longer than Sabrina, she was sure of that. Yet, just like everything in Nana's house, it felt warm, cozy, and familiar.

"Hmm. I suppose you're right. Don't want to come across as pretentious." She walked closer to the table and looked around. "Yes, these will do just fine." She still didn't look quite convinced.

"Mrs. Jenkins is such a nice lady. I look forward to meeting her granddaughter."

"From what I gather from Maudie, she hasn't fallen into the best crowd at school. I'm sure hoping the two of you get along, that maybe she can look to you as something of a role model."

"I'll do my best." Sabrina saluted.

"I know you will, darling." Nana gave a nod of satisfaction, moved as if to turn, but then stopped and jerked back around. "You okay? You look a little pale."

Sabrina had lived there long enough to know what was going to happen next. Nana would put her hand on Sabrina's forehead, make a clucking sound, then go in search of the thermometer. Sabrina was pretty certain the results would show a low-grade fever, which would ruin their plans for the evening. As appealing as it sounded to go to bed, she knew her grandmother was looking forward to this event, so she took evasive action and made for the front of the house. "I'm fine. Just a little tired. You know how I get when I'm working on a school project."

"You don't get enough rest, that's for sure and for certain. You need to take better care of yourself. When you came to live here I promised your mother I'd see that you got healthy meals and enough rest."

"Oh, Nana, grown-ups worry too much. I get as much rest as any other college student."

"Yes, but you're not any other—"

Dingdong.

"I'll get it." Sabrina hurried toward the door, thankful for the interruption from the rest of the all-too-familiar lecture. She turned the knob and pulled the door, her words already forming. "Good evening, Mrs. Jenkins. How are you?"

Mrs. Jenkins had the kind of permanent dark circles under her eyes that declared her a woman who had spent years being pushed past her limits. In spite of this, her smile was bright and cheerful. "Just fine, Sabrina. It's so good to see you again. Your grandmother has kept me updated on your happenings, but I'll be glad to hear the details straight from you."

"Bless your heart, I'll just bet she has. Nana does like to talk about her family."

"You count that as a blessing is what I'm saying. There's lots of people who wish they could say the same." For just a split second the look of weariness encompassed her entire face, all the way to her eyes. She turned to look over her shoulder. "Brandy, hurry on up, now. Sabrina's standing here waiting to meet ya."

Sabrina peered into the darkness, searching for the young girl who needed a nice older friend. Maybe she could be a kind of mentor, the same way a couple of college girls had taken her under their wing several years ago. It would be nice to pay it forward.

Mrs. Jenkins shook her head. "We walked over here. You'd think it would be the old lady instead of the teenager that was lagging, wouldn't you?" She glanced over her shoulder then nodded with satisfaction. "Oh, here she is. Sabrina, I'd like you to meet my granddaughter, Brandy. Brandy, this is Sabrina." She held out her arm toward the driveway, just as the girl walked into view.

"What's up?" Brandy nodded her head back slightly.

Sabrina found that she was unable to respond in any way. Absolutely could not speak.

It wasn't the tiny loop earring that pierced the girl's nose, or the thick line of dark black eyeliner, or the cold hard eyes that left Sabrina unable to speak. It was her hair. Shoulder length, white in front, black in back. There could be no mistaking who this girl was or where she'd seen her before.

"Oh, please do come in, you two." Nana picked just the right moment to arrive at the door. Sabrina took a step back so that the two could enter, but she still couldn't find her voice to speak as Nana ushered them inside. "Now, Brandy, you come right in here and tell us all about yourself. How are things at the high school? You're a junior, right? Is old Mrs. Monroe still teaching chemistry and physics? How is the basketball team doing this year?"

Sabrina attempted to work through her shock and at least fake some interest in Brandy's answers. It proved to be harder than she'd imagined. *Be a good role model. Set a good example. At the very least, be polite.*

In spite of Nana's insatiable list of questions, Brandy managed to answer most everything with a single syllable, two at most. She made no attempt to be sociable or to even appear that she was remotely interested in having a conversation.

Sabrina's initial shock at seeing this girl was soon replaced by a deep and growing dislike. Did she have no concept of manners, or common courtesy? And then Nana asked her the question whose answer sealed Sabrina's dislike into a deep and permanent state. "Do you play any sports at school?"

"No."

"Oh really? I thought I remembered Maudie telling me that you ran track."

Brandy shrugged. "Used to. Not now."

"Oh right, since you just moved here, you probably haven't gotten the chance to get started in all that. I'll bet you'll be involved soon, huh?"

"Nah. Don't much like it. Coaches are a pain."

The circles under Mrs. Jenkins' eyes seemed to darken by the second. She shook her head and stared off in the distance. Nana glanced at her, then back to Sabrina, her eyes wide with panic, and Sabrina swallowed the "somehow I don't think it's the coach who's a pain" retort that'd been on the tip of her tongue.

This Brandy girl might be a spoiled, selfish punk, but Nana was a wonderful lady, and Sabrina would do her best to help. She forced herself to work up a friendliness she most certainly did not feel. "Brandy, have you thought about what you want to do when you graduate high school?"

Brandy looked at her, green eyes cold and hard. "Well, I can tell you what I won't be doing. I won't be living at my grandmother's house while my mother and father are paying my tuition at some lame college. I've never been much of one for freeloading, or for freeloaders, as far as that goes. I'll be doing something interesting, and I'll be standing on my own two feet."

"Brandy." Mrs. Jenkins hissed her granddaughter's name, but offered no words to follow it up.

Brandy continued to look at Sabrina, a dare in her eyes.

"Brandy," her grandmother said again, firmer this time.

Brandy shrugged. "Sorry. No offense intended."

Hate.

The word so seldom entered Sabrina's mind that the initial thought stunned her. But try as she might, she couldn't squelch it.

Hate.

When she looked at Brandy it welled up inside her and poured over into places she hadn't gone in a long time.

I. Hate. Her.

Sabrina saw the absolute mortification in her grandmother's eyes. The evening that she had planned so meticulously was going down in flames, thanks to this juvenile delinquent who had no idea what she should appreciate. It was up to Sabrina to somehow overcome, to be the bigger person for her grandmother's sake.

"I'm sure there wasn't." Regardless of how she was feeling, regardless of how much she wanted to let that little brat know some things about real life, Sabrina was going to salvage the evening. For Nana's sake. She dug deep and pulled out what she hoped was a radiant smile. "Nana has made her famous artichoke spinach dip. Who's game to give it a try?"

3

Driving home at last, Sabrina felt the weight of a long and exhausting day, and the lingering aches and chills of that low-grade fever. At least she had a nice warm dinner and some comfy sweats waiting for her at home. Less than two blocks to go until relief, she saw probably the only person who could make her day worse.

Brandy was standing out on the curb in front of her grandmother's house, leaning against a black muscle car that practically screamed "punk" and talking on her cell phone. Probably planning her next delinquent adventure with her friends. Even today, tired as she was, Sabrina felt her hackles rise. That girl needed to be taken down a notch or three.

Well, Sabrina had neither the time nor the energy to devote one more second of thought in that direction. She pulled into the driveway and had to will herself to stand up and get out of the car.

It had been a few years since she'd felt this way, and back then it was after a hard day of training. But there was no forgetting the complete muscle exhaustion, the worry that she couldn't take another step, the inner voice that begged for just a short rest. That was the voice she knew had to be ignored at all costs. You just dug deep and looked for something inside you that could make you keep moving in spite of the overwhelming desire to stop. It boiled down to the drive to achieve, to be the absolute best you could possibly be, even when things got hard, even when you wanted to give up.

Sabrina made it up the steps and into the quiet of the house. Tonight she was especially glad for Nana's Monday night dinner with her ladies' group from church. There would be no need to expend extra energy to put on enough of a front to prevent Nana from guessing she was ill. And, she could make something small for dinner, something cold that would feel good to her sore throat. A Greek yogurt and berry smoothie would be just the ticket.

She made her way to the kitchen, poured in her own special recipe of juice, frozen berries, yogurt, and a banana, then let the blender grind it all up into a nice pink concoction that was sure to make her feel better.

Minutes later, she was sitting at the kitchen table, feeling the coolness of her liquid dinner. Much better.

She clicked on her iPhone and scanned her list of emails. One in particular caught her eye. The sender was Rita Leyva, a missionary whose newsletter Sabrina had been receiving for the last six or seven years. This wasn't a newsletter though. Instead, the subject line read, "Sabrina—a potential job/ministry opportunity." Out of curiosity, Sabrina opened the email.

Hello Sabrina,

I hope this email finds you well. I'm writing to you now because I often think back to our conversations when I visited with your youth group. I remember how dedicated you were to someday working for a missions organization, and most of all, I remember hearing you speak on the Children of Israel at the youth gathering and the little devotional you presented me. Those words have stayed with me all these years as being so powerful. At that time, I could not only see your gift for inspiring a group, I could also see your heart for missions and following God with all your heart.

As you may remember, I work for Bridges. We are experiencing rapid growth in our efforts to take hope and help into the poorest countries in the world, in the form of job training, food, medicine, and mostly God's Word. Recently, we began looking for someone who could help us spearhead an awareness campaign here in America. Your name kept coming to my mind, so I called my contacts at your home church and found out that you are about to graduate with a degree in Public Relations.

I would consider it a personal honor and favor if you would apply for the job. I've already spoken with Dennis and Susan, the directors of the organization, and asked them to give you serious consideration. They have agreed.

I hope that you will consider this prayerfully, and if you are led as I am confident you will be, send a resumé as soon as possible.

If you would like to contact me with any questions you may have, feel free to email or call my cell, (805) 555–7239.

In Him,
Rita Leyva

Weird. That had come out of the blue, for sure.

It was a nice thought, but Sabrina's life had gone another direction. She supposed she should compose a nice "thank you but no thank you" response—maybe this weekend when she had a little more time. She flagged the email for follow-up and moved on to the next one.

"Sabrina?"

She jumped at the sound of her name. She put her hand to her heart, which was racing from the sudden burst of adrenaline. "Oh, Nana, I didn't hear you come in. You're home early, aren't you?"

"I suppose I am." Nana squeezed the palms of her hands together, then twisted them in a wringing motion. "Listen, Sabrina, I need to ask a favor."

"Sure. You know you can ask me anything."

Nana continued to rub her palms together, her brow furrowed in concentration. "Nana, are you all right? Come in here and sit down."

She waved Sabrina aside. "I'm fine, just fine. It's just that, this favor, well, I know it's going to be something that's hard for you to do. I hate to ask it, I really do."

"What is it?" Sabrina could never remember seeing Nana so worked up. "You know I'll do it for you, just tell me."

"Maudie's granddaughter, Brandy . . ." Nana shook her head slowly side to side.

Well, that explained the angst. And Sabrina thought that perhaps she'd been a little too quick to give her word without knowing what it was all about—or more correctly, *who* it was about. That girl was the least likable person Sabrina had ever met. "What about Brandy?"

"She's gotten into some trouble lately and it seems like the court system is done being lenient. She has a hearing late next week, and it looks like she might end up in juvenile hall. As you can imagine, Maudie is broken up about it. Brandy is the only person she has left, and troublemaker though she might be, Maudie loves her with all her heart."

"Where are her parents, anyway?"

"Brandy's father—Maudie's only child—died when Brandy was just a baby. He was never married to Brandy's mother, who is now a drug addict and has been in and out of prison for most of Brandy's life. Brandy's uncle took her in with his family for a while, but they kicked her out right before Christmas. That's why the poor thing is as messed up as she is—she's never had anyone to really count on. Anyone except for Maudie, who's trying her best to provide a stable home environment for her."

"I guess I'm not sure how I can help her."

"Well, Maudie's lawyer said this judge is a bit of a maverick. He's a stickler for the law, but he is usually willing to employ some unusual tactics to help kids straighten out their lives. Her suggestion was to get Brandy enrolled in some extracurricular activities. It will look good for the court, and hopefully convince them that she'll be too busy to get into more trouble. The lawyer thinks the judge just might give her another chance if she can show she's making an effort."

"Okay?" Sabrina still had no idea how she fit into this picture.

"Maudie says Brandy is a fast runner."

Yes. She is. "Then she should sign up for the track team."

"There's the problem. They talked to the coach, but because of her behavior issues, she won't even consider giving Brandy a chance."

"I don't see how there's anything to do about that."

"Well, you know the cross-country coach pretty well, right? Could you maybe talk to him?"

"Nana, cross-country is a fall sport and it's only February. I don't see how talking to him is going to be helpful."

"Please, Sabrina, just tell me you'll try. I can't bear this for poor Maudie if she loses that girl."

Nana was such a warmhearted person, there was no way Sabrina could let her down. "Sure, Nana, I'll try. I wouldn't expect much, though. Who knows if Coach Thompson will even remember me."

"Not remember you? Sabrina, how many training runs did the two of you make together?"

"He's paced hundreds of runners through the years, Nana."

"That man adored you since the first time he saw you running wind sprints around the high school track. You were visiting during Christmas vacation and it was snowing that day, remember?"

For just a moment, Sabrina could almost feel the featherlike caress of the snow as she rounded the corner, see her mother's mittened hands holding the stopwatch, feel the adrenaline coursing through her veins. She remembered the man who came to stand beside Mom and Nana at the rail.

After finishing her last lap, Sabrina had walked over, curious about this person talking to her mother. He introduced himself as the cross-country coach from the local high school. "I was just telling your mother I'm excited about having someone like you on my team in a year or two. It near about popped my Achilles when she told me y'all live over near Chattanooga and were not considering relocating. Ah well, I guess the good news for me is that you won't be direct competition." He smiled then, nodded at Mom. "That girl of yours is something special. She's bound for greatness."

Sabrina shivered and the memory faded back to blackness, back where she liked those memories to stay. "I remember, Nana."

She'd soon find out if Coach Thompson did as well.

"Sabrina Rice. What a surprise to see you here." Coach Cal Thompson set aside the *Runner's World* magazine, stood, and came around his desk. Even at almost sixty, he moved with the agility of a great athlete and a world-class runner. "How are you these days?"

Sabrina sort of smiled. "Oh, I'm fine."

But the look of sympathy on Coach Thompson's face said

that he did not believe that. Would never believe that, because he knew that she would never be *fine* again, at least to their way of thinking. "What brings you here? This is quite out of the blue." When he smiled, a road map of wrinkles gathered across his face—a face that had spent years in the elements and showed it—with eyes that radiated warmth and genuine concern. And, though he probably wouldn't admit it, pity. She hated that look, hated that others couldn't keep it from their eyes around her. She just wanted to leave. Finish up this thing she did not want to do and then get out of there.

"Well, yes. Actually I have a favor to ask."

"Whatever it is, count me in. You know I could never say no to anything you ask."

"Uh, in this particular case you might want to hear what the favor is before you say that."

He leaned back against his desk and folded his arms across his chest, his smile only broadening. "I must say, I am more than a little intrigued."

"Well, here's the thing. My grandmother has this friend, Maudie Jenkins, and Mrs. Jenkins' granddaughter moved in with her a while ago and she attends school here. I gather she was pretty good at track back in junior high."

The hint of a new prodigy lit his eyes with interest. "Jenkins? I don't recognize the name. She's new here did you say?"

"The girl's last name is Philip. Brandy Philip."

He blew out a long, slow puff of air. "That name I do know."

"Somehow I thought you would."

The interest faded from his eyes. "That kid is trouble on two feet."

Sabrina nodded. "So I gathered. But fast feet, and well, here's the thing. There are some legal issues at hand, and her grandmother has been led to believe that getting her signed up for an extracurricular activity will increase her chances of staying out of juvie. I know that the track coach has refused to take her on, but I was hoping maybe you could, sort of, I don't know, count her as a project for the semester? Her grandmother is desperate."

"Rossina's never been one to take on the troublemakers, so I'm not surprised she refused to take her. Brandy is welcome to give cross-country a try next year. Of course, everyone around here knows that I have a zero-tolerance policy with conduct issues. She wouldn't last a week."

"You're right." Sabrina had no doubt that he was. Well, she'd done what she set out to do, asked the favor as her grandmother had requested. "Thanks for taking the time to talk to me about it."

"You know I'm happy to talk to you at any time." His face grew serious. "How are you, really? Are you . . . you know . . ."

"Good. I'm good. Concentrating on graduating *magna cum laude* in a few months, that's the goal now." She turned to go, relieved it was over. Yet, when she got to the door, she wasn't quite sure why she did it, but she turned. "You know, I actually saw Brandy Philip run last week."

"And?"

"She runs faster than any sixteen-year-old I've ever seen. Her form's not quite right, but I would say the kid has some of the rawest talent I've ever been around." No reason to mention the fact that she'd had a can of spray paint in her hand and campus security hot on her tail. "Nice talking to you." She walked from his classroom, but not before she noticed the glimmer of interest reignite in his eye.

4

I guess we'd better start heading back. I pride myself on making an appearance in at least one class a day." Brandy took one last drag from the cigarette, then threw it to the ground. She watched it roll its way beneath the shiny red convertible parked in the back row of the school's lot.

"Better watch out. Miss Homecoming-Queen-of-the-World would be positively *appalled* to find something so dirty in the vicinity of her beautiful new birthday present." Janie threw her hand over her eyes and pretended to faint. "*Oh, the outrage of it all.*" She feigned a high-pitched Scarlett O'Hara kind of southern accent, a sharp contrast to her own deep voice and country twang.

"Oh, I do apologize, madam." Brandy approached the vehicle in question. She turned back toward Janie. "You got a key? I'm thinking this paint job could use a little . . . customizing."

"Customizing, yeah, I think that's exactly what that car needs." Janie rubbed her chin between her thumb and forefinger. "Yes, definitely." She pulled a key ring out of her pocket and tossed it toward Brandy, but not quite far enough.

Brandy bent over and picked it up. The small metal ring held a large brass J, a miniature Corvette, and a multicolored peace sign, as well as two keys. The first key was blunt and quite thick, not a particularly useful tool. The second one, which looked to be a mailbox key perhaps, was much thinner and sharper. The perfect weapon. Brandy scanned the parking lot, making certain that they were alone.

That's when she saw movement coming from the next row over. A woman was walking down the middle of the lot, heading their way. Brandy pocketed the keys, waiting for her to stop at her own car, but the young woman kept drawing closer. She wore aviator-style sunglasses and a pink baseball cap pulled low, a black ponytail bobbing out the back. She continued to move toward them until Brandy and Janie both ducked behind the convertible to avoid being seen. Peeking over the car door, Brandy saw the girl stop at a blue Prius not ten yards away, then turn and look over her shoulder as if sensing she was being watched.

"What's *she* doing here?" Brandy whispered and dropped back down below the car door.

In a few seconds, the Prius pulled out of its spot, the hum of the tires on the pavement the only clue that it was in motion before it disappeared.

"Coast is clear." Janie stood up and stretched. "You know that girl?"

"Unfortunately." Brandy would waste no other words discussing that stuck-up piece of work. Life was too short.

"All right, then. Are you ready to do some cus-tom-izing?" Janie dragged the word out, making each syllable deep and gravelly, as if she were the baddest girl in town. If she was so bad, then why was she prepared to stand by, hip cocked like she was something, and let Brandy do all the work and take all the risks?

"Changed my mind." Brandy started toward the school.

"Wait, what? I thought you were gonna . . . you know . . . What's the matter?"

Brandy turned. "I changed my mind, I told you. Isn't a person allowed to do that around here? You want it done so badly, do it yourself." She pulled the keys from her pocket and flung them several car lengths back, in the general direction of the red car.

"Hey, why'd you go and do that?"

The bell rang, announcing five minutes until the next class. Brandy sauntered toward the building, not giving Janie a second look. It was time that girl learned to do something on her own.

Inside, Brandy stopped at her locker and got out her math notebook, supposing she should at least make it appear that she was serious about her studies. *Ha.*

When she walked into the classroom, she passed a group of girls huddled at the back of the class. They all seemed to be chattering at once. "Did Bradley ask you to the dance yet?" "Are y'all going to eat at ChaCha's before or should we meet at Langmo's?" Ah yes, the school dance was this weekend. *What a bunch of losers.*

Brandy took her seat in the far back corner just as the bell rang. The girls slowly broke up their conversation, but they were still giggling and whispering as they made their way toward the front.

Mrs. Panneke walked over and took a seat on a tall stool beside the projector. "All right everyone, open your books to chapter 3. Today we're going to talk about—"

"Mrs. Panneke?" One of the student assistants from the office stood at the door, a piece of paper in her hand. "Coach Thompson asked me to get this to you right away." She walked in and delivered the note, then disappeared out the door.

Mrs. Panneke looked up. "Brandy? Coach Thompson would like to see you in his classroom immediately after this period."

Brandy could practically hear the heads whipping around to

face her. She knew what they were all thinking, and for once, she was wondering the same thing. What had she done now?

"Brandy, come in, have a seat." Coach Thompson motioned to the desk closest to his own. He didn't exactly smile, but he didn't look mad, either. Perhaps he'd seen them smoking and this was going to be one of those "smoking is bad for you" talks. No problem. Adult blather was easy enough to tune out.

She took a seat, folded her arms, and waited for the onslaught. He shifted and rubbed the back of his neck, but seemed to be searching for the words. Good, this lecture would likely be short.

"How are you enjoying our school?"

Brandy snorted. "I don't know that *enjoy* and *school* are two words I would ever use in the same sentence."

"So I've gathered." He came to sit in the student desk beside her. "I understand you are quite a good runner."

Brandy shrugged but didn't say anything. The quieter she remained, the faster this would be over.

"Here's the thing." He rubbed the back of his neck again. "I don't allow troublemakers on my team. Period. That's always been my rule. One strike and you're out."

"Guess it's a good thing I'm not on your team, then." Brandy stared directly into his eyes, letting him know she wasn't scared of him or his rules. What did she care what he did for his team?

"Would you like to be?" He took off his little wire-rimmed glasses and looked at her.

"You're kidding, right?"

"Like I said, I've heard you are a good runner."

"Yeah, and like you said, zero tolerance. I'm thinking one call to the school office could let you know that I'm not your girl."

"You are more than correct on that score. I've already talked to them."

"Then why would you even make this offer? I talked to Coach Reznik. She already told me I can't be on the track team. This whole conversation seems a little pointless."

"I know something of your situation, so let's just say I'm willing to give you a break."

"Why?"

"If you must know, it's because one of the greatest runners I've ever known asked me to give you a chance."

"Someone asked you to give *me* a chance? Who?"

"Doesn't matter. It's someone I respect enough that I'm willing to try something that I'm pretty sure I will regret."

Brandy sat there, trying to get her mind around what was happening. She wasn't about to get a lecture for yet another mistake. This guy was offering to help her, to maybe keep her from being sent to who knows where. Not only that, she was actually being asked to do something . . . something respectable. How long had it been since that had happened? "I appreciate the thought and all, really I do, but something tells me we'd both be wasting our time."

"There's only one way we'll ever know the answer to that question, isn't there? Why don't we give it a shot? Who knows, maybe we'll both be pleasantly surprised."

Memories of finish lines and blue ribbons and the out-and-out admiration from the other kids flashed through her mind. For just a moment, she felt the rush that a sideline of cheering fans could bring on. How long had it been? She knew the answer. Too long. "I don't think so."

"Why don't you give it some thought? Per district policy, it's too late to add you to this season's track roster even if Coach Reznik suddenly decided she wanted to—which she doesn't. But I work with the two-milers Tuesdays and Thursdays. You can come work out with us on those days, and start getting geared up for cross-country in the fall. We have several superb distance runners on the team, but we could always use one more."

"I just don't think I'm your girl."

"Probably you are right, Miss Philip. But what are your options?" He sighed. "Here's the thing. I don't usually go out of my way like this, but I'm giving this a chance. For your part, I'd want you to work out with us this week, then come hear the speaker at lunchtime on Friday at the Fellowship of Christian Runners' meeting. She, too, came from a difficult background, but went on to become a college athlete. Now she coaches at the Samson Academy up in Nashville."

"Samson Academy? That's where all the rich parents send their kids, so they'll be on the top sports team and get scholarships."

Coach Thompson nodded. "I think there's some truth to that."

"Makes you wonder, doesn't it, if only rich kids can afford to go there, why do they need scholarships for college in the first place? Why not leave them for the kids who can't afford college on their own? It's one more way they've got it all rigged in their favor. There's nothing left for someone like me."

"Well, I'm offering you a chance to change all that. You come to practice tomorrow and Thursday, and the meeting on Friday, and then we'll talk more about it."

A skeletal memory dug itself free from deep within the graveyard where Brandy had long ago buried such thoughts. It was track-and-field day for Mrs. Tooley's kindergarten class, and Mom was there watching. She was wearing her prettiest pink blouse, and her hair was brushed straight, shining like black silk in the sun. She held open her arms, and Brandy ran to her. She could feel the intensity of her mother's hug. Then she pulled back, eyes shining and so remarkably clear and focused that day. "I'm so proud of my girl, winning all three races." She pulled Brandy close again. "We're going to be all right, the two of us. You keep on running fast like that and the two of us, well, we'll go places, you wait and see."

Just as suddenly as the memory appeared, it evaporated into the darkness and smoke and stupor that covered all her childhood memories. And then Brandy was back in the present, looking at Coach Thompson, still trying to figure out why he was willing to do this, and even more so, why she suddenly wanted to. "Yeah, maybe I'll be there."

He smiled. "Good, that's what I was hoping you'd say."

Brandy started for the door, and as much as she hated to admit it, she felt something like excitement. Someone had recommended her. One of the greatest runners Coach Thompson had ever known. Who could it possibly be? She thought about her junior high track coach, but that had only lasted a few weeks until Ms. Bickers kicked her off the team. No, it couldn't be her.

Brandy didn't bother to exit toward the parking lot. She knew that by now Janie would have left without her. She started the long walk toward home still puzzling about what had happened. For just a split second, the memory flashed through her mind of the girl in the parking lot. No, it couldn't be her. The last person on earth who would ever go out of her way to help Brandy was that chubby-faced diva. Not to mention, she hardly looked like the athletic type.

Without consciously making the decision to do so, Brandy began to jog, then run, then all-out sprint toward home. She concentrated on taking long, sweeping strides, pushing her legs to move faster and faster, long past the point that her burning leg muscles cried out for relief. She refused to give in to the pain, not allowing herself to slow until she reached the sidewalk in front of her grandmother's house. There, she slowed to a walk, gasping for air, trying to make sense of it all. She couldn't. But as she paced back and forth, waiting for her breathing to slow, her mind seemed to work with renewed clarity, and that's when she knew for certain who had made the recommendation. She just didn't know why.

Why would Sabrina ask Coach Thompson to help her? What could possibly be in it for Sabrina? And what did he mean when he said she was one of the greatest runners he'd ever known? One thing was certain. Brandy didn't know any of the answers.

Yet.

5

W hat's the matter, Sabrina?"

"What makes you think something is wrong?"

Sabrina's mother had a mood radar that was uncannily accurate even from over a hundred miles away, through nothing but a phone line and less than a few sentences into a conversation. "Oh come on now, we both know that I know something is bothering you."

What *was* wrong? How could Sabrina explain it to her mother, when she didn't understand it herself? "I wish I knew what to tell you, but I really . . . don't. I'm just stressed out about school and internships, I guess."

"What's new with the internship position?"

"They want me to come to Atlanta for an interview next month. There will be over fifty applicants called in. A maximum of fifteen will be offered intern positions. Grace Rose only hires entry-level employees from their intern pool, and usually only about three of them. So . . . we're looking at some long odds."

"I've never known you to be one who is daunted by long odds, so somehow I doubt the problem is stemming from there."

And Sabrina knew that her mother was right. Those kinds of numbers didn't upset her, they motivated her. Excited her, even. No, her melancholy had nothing to do with her school or internships. "Mom, you remember *Chariots of Fire?*"

"Remember it?" Her mother laughed. "Honey, we've watched that movie so many times over the years that you know we could both quote it."

Sabrina put the phone on her other ear. "Eric Liddell said he could feel God's pleasure when he ran, remember that?"

"Of course."

"Eric Liddell felt God's pleasure when he ran and God blessed him with an Olympic gold medal. I used to feel God's pleasure when I ran, and now . . . well . . . why would God do that?"

Her mother was quiet for just a moment. When she started speaking again, her voice was low, thoughtful. "Honey, I've asked myself—and God—that same question. I wish I knew the answer for you, but I don't. All I can say is I believe with all my heart that God did plant His call on you, and that He did it for a reason. You know that I believe His call is still on you."

This was the biggest disagreement between the two of them. Sabrina's mother insisted that the call to mission work did not end when the running ended. Sabrina saw it differently. "Then why would He take away the means to accomplish the call?"

"Obviously the means He has in mind are different than what we understood. Things aren't going to happen the way we had planned, but the answer is there for us. We just need to keep praying and looking for it."

"Yeah. Maybe you're right." But Sabrina knew her path was in a different direction now. Her shoulders sagged with the onslaught of exhaustion. It was too much. Too much. "Good night, Mom. Thanks for always being here for me."

"Sorry I don't have any easy answers for you."

"Me too, Mom. Me too."

Nothing had ever kicked Brandy's rear quite as bad as the two days of team practice. Her calves burned going up and down stairs, her thighs were tight and sore, and her butt was downright aching. But no way would she let on to any of it. She wouldn't give those other kids the satisfaction of thinking that she might not be good enough or strong enough to run with them. When she left the team, it would be on her own terms, not theirs. And *no one* would say she left because she wasn't tough enough.

But there were some things she wasn't signed up for, like this lunchtime propaganda meeting. Coach had wanted her here, so here she sat—not wanting to get him all mad at her just yet. She'd wait until he was convinced his team couldn't do without her before she pushed back on some of his crazy rules.

They held the meeting in the largest classroom on campus—the only one with auditorium-style seating. There were easily sixty kids there, so it shouldn't be that hard to sign in, get seen by the powers that be, and then disappear without anyone noticing. Brandy printed her name on the sign-in list, then made her way to the far back corner. When the time was right, she'd slip out the back and meet Janie for a quick smoke before their next class.

"You're Brandy, right?" A tall girl with long blond hair came to sit beside her. "I've been wanting a chance to introduce myself since you started working out with us. I'm Erin Methvin."

Brandy nodded. "Yeah, I've seen you at practice." Which was partially true. She'd seen Erin's ponytail at practice. The distance

41

runners were split into three groups. There were the beginners, those who could barely run a mile without puking. They brought up the rear. Then there was the middle group, the ones with fair endurance and speed. The third pack led the way down the sidewalk, around the city block that encircled the school and through the small park across the street. That group moved at an amazing pace, but not only did they never seem to break a sweat, they carried on an almost constant conversation as they ran.

On the first day of practice, Coach Thompson had said, "Don't worry about trying to hang with the front group. Those are experienced runners—we don't expect you to keep up with them. In fact, if you need to run with the group in the back while you're getting started, that's fine, too."

"As if." Brandy walked away from him, directly toward the front, her plan being to blow them all out on the very first day, thereby establishing where she ranked in the pecking order around there.

Instead, she'd learned the hard way that there was a major difference in sprinting distances just far enough to break free of pursuing cops, and running three or four miles at a consistent pace. She'd spent both workouts giving it everything she had just to maintain pace with the tail end of the front group. That first practice, she might have even given up and allowed herself to fall back into the middle group had it not been for Coach Thompson's words. No way was she going to give the satisfaction to some old man who thought he knew her. And since Erin had always been one of the leaders of the front group, Brandy just focused in on her ponytail as they ran. It would swing back and forth with each stride Erin took, somehow mocking her with each sweeping movement. Brandy saw it at night when she closed her eyes.

"I'm glad we get this chance to sit together and chat for a few minutes before the speaker starts. Aren't you?"

"Sure." Brandy glanced toward the exit door, now considerably further from her grasp than it had been just a few seconds before. "It's just that—"

"Thanks for coming, everyone." Coach Thompson looked around the room, his eyes coming to rest on Brandy and Erin. "It's great to see you all here. Why don't those of you toward the back move forward. I know you're not going to want to miss anything that Ms. Ratcliff is going to say. I'm sure you all will find her very inspiring."

"I guess we better move up a few rows." Erin smiled at her.

"Guess so."

In spite of her best efforts to tune out the speaker, somewhere in the middle of her talk, Brandy found herself listening, interested even. This girl had come from a broken home, had to pay her own way to college. Regardless of where she was working now, she hadn't been born a rich brat.

"So, after making the team as a freshman walk-on and then surpassing everyone's expectations for three years, one day a coach pulled me aside with the news I had been dying to hear. They were working on finally securing me a scholarship slot for my senior year. You can't even imagine what that sounds like to a person who had been working, going to school full-time, and amassing a fortune in student loans. Sounds like an answer to that prayer I've been telling you about, right?"

Heads nodded around the room. They all knew where this was going—happy ending for the girl who prayed and didn't give up.

"That's what I thought, too, until a couple weeks later. The same coach came to me and apologized, but said they wouldn't be able to make me the offer after all. They'd found a running prodigy that they were desperate to sign. She'd be taking my scholarship slot. They had to promise her four years to get her to sign and so my chance was gone. I was devastated." The woman stopped speaking and swallowed hard, composing herself.

"And here's the thing. When this *prodigy* showed up, she had the worst work ethic I'd ever seen. She missed practice after practice, always with some excuse about her knees or hips hurting. You know?" She paused and looked around the room. "We're runners. Our knees and hips are going to hurt sometimes, that's part of it." Everyone nodded again.

"In fact, this prodigy only ran in three events that year, and I crushed her time in all three of them. But you know what? God was faithful. Word of my success reached the people at Samson Academy and they offered me a job, including a reverse scholarship that will help pay off my loans. I am currently training some of the greatest young runners in Nashville. In fact, I'm more than confident that several of my runners will make the Olympic team in a couple of years. So my prayer was answered, just not in the exact way I expected it to be. Don't ever give up, even when it seems like God has forgotten you. He's still got something in store." Kayla Ratcliff left the podium to great applause, waving at the group.

"Wow, wasn't she just amazing?" Erin shook her head slowly in thought. "What determination. What a great faith."

"Sure." Brandy got up quickly from her seat and hurried out of the room. She didn't want to think about this stuff anymore. Hopefully Janie was still somewhere to be found in the parking lot.

6

Sabrina took a seat at her usual table at Campus Eats, then opened her Communication Studies textbook to chapter 12. She began reading, but a general haze had descended across her brain and she couldn't quite seem to focus. This was the weirdest cold she'd ever had—sore throat, fever on and off, and a bit of a cough. No runny nose, no sinus congestion, but an overwhelming sense of exhaustion that she couldn't seem to shake.

For just a moment, she fantasized about going to Nana's, crawling under the covers, and taking a long nap. She could practically feel the warmth of the flannel sheets, smell the hint of lavender-scented fabric softener on her pillow as her head sank into its depths. Just a little rest, it sounded so wonderful.

No.

There was no time for indulgence right now. With two projects due and a test on Friday, she couldn't afford to slack off now. Not when the words *magna cum laude* were within her grasp.

She hunched over the book, leaned her left cheek on her hand, and tried again. *You must carefully decide the tone and style of your communication for each new project. These types of decisions . . .* It was no use. She couldn't focus. Perhaps a bit of caffeine would help. She pushed out of her seat, walked behind the counter, and began concocting what she hoped might get her through the afternoon. "Hey, Nicole, will you ring me up?"

"Sure thing." Nicole stood up, setting her romance novel aside, and sauntered over to the cash register. "What'd you make?"

"Skinny latte. With a couple of extra shots."

"Triple shot? Whoowee. I thought you were a little slow today, but it never entered my mind that the herbal tea girl would go to these kinds of extremes. Everything okay? You not sleeping?"

"I can't shake this cold."

"Well, it's in your own best interests not to give it to me. Unlike you, I'll call in sick. Unless you're keen on working my shifts and yours, you best be keeping your germs to yourself."

"I'll do my best." Sabrina went back to her table, dropped to her seat, and took a long deep swallow. Hopefully the caffeine would kick in soon.

"Hello there."

Sabrina almost spit out her coffee when she heard the voice, that warm, mellow voice, coming from just behind her. She looked over her shoulder. "Hi, Koen."

He stood there, in all his perfection, just looking at her. "We've got to stop meeting like this."

"You think?" *I sure don't.* Almost two weeks had passed since their last encounter and its disastrous end. Sabrina could only hope he would forget that part.

He slid the chair beside her away from the table. "May I?"

"Of course."

"So, you want to study together after psych tomorrow? You promised you'd help me, remember?"

Sabrina was more than certain she'd made no such promise, but if Koen Conner wanted to spend time with her, who was she to argue? "I work in here tomorrow from two to five. I could study with you after that, if that's not too late."

He leaned just a fraction closer. "I'm pretty sure I've never in my life thought five o'clock was too late for anything." He grinned. "Too early maybe, but never too late."

Was it her cold, or just Koen's normal effect that made her thoughts spin in so many directions, completely unable to find a coherent thought? Somehow she managed to say, "You say that to all your study partners." Could she be any more cliché and any less interesting? Somehow she doubted it. Lindy Stewart would have had a witty response, no doubt.

Trying to clear her thoughts, she looked away from him and out the window. A loose piece of paper blew across the school lawn and skidded off a trash can before landing beside a girl crossing the sidewalk. It took a split second before Sabrina realized who she'd just seen. "You gotta be kidding me." Sabrina looked again, but the girl was gone.

"No, I'm really not. I really want to study with you tomorrow." Koen's response recaptured her full attention.

"No, I wasn't talking about that. Of course we'll study together tomorrow."

"I must say, you had me worried there for a second." He grinned at her, but seemed uncertain.

"Sorry, just thought I saw someone. That girl from the police chase the other day, and it distracted me, that's all."

Koen turned to look out the window. "Oh, Gazelle Girl? It might've been her. I noticed her here earlier today. She was standing in the back of the parking lot when I pulled up. I watched her for a minute to make sure I felt safe to leave my car nearby. She sort of strikes me as the 'bust out the window to steal your stuff' type, you know what I mean?"

"You're a wise man."

"You know her?"

Sabrina tried hard not to let the sight of Brandy spoil this moment for her. "Bit of a complicated story, but yeah, it turns out our grandmothers know each other. I wonder what she's doing. She's not a student here."

"Funny thing is, the whole time I was watching her, she remained dead still and was just staring off in the same direction. I finally turned to see what she might be looking at, and . . . this is going to sound weird, I know . . . but you were walking from your car to the science building, and I could have sworn she was watching you." He shook his head and grinned at her. "Didn't we learn something like that in psychology? I know I watch you when I can, so therefore I feel like others would, too. Oh, *project*, that's it, isn't it? Projection?"

Sabrina twittered something that sounded more or less like a laugh, or so she hoped. "Something like that." She looked out the window again, and this time found Brandy sitting on a bench, looking directly at her. For a long moment they regarded each other, then Brandy stood up and strolled oh so casually in the general direction of the back parking lot. "That is so weird."

"It is a bit odd, I'll grant you that, projection or not."

Just then Lindy Stewart and friends breezed into Campus Eats. Sabrina grimaced. "Speaking of psychological behavior."

Koen glanced over his shoulder, then turned back. "Unfortunately, I think this is more than a case of projection. It's more of a fixation issue. She practically stalks me."

Sabrina couldn't help the jealous pang, and she hated herself for it. In an effort to pretend it wasn't there, she decided to confront the situation head on. "She is so pretty."

"Pretty's fine, but you talk about needy . . ." He let out a low whistle. "I personally like the independent and self-sufficient type. Some things just aren't worth the cost. Know what I mean?" He stood up. "Well, me and the boys are playing pick up b-ball in a few minutes, so I better get moving."

"Okay. See you tomorrow, then."

"Yep. Fourth floor of the library at five o'clock. Sound good?"

"The library?" Sabrina hated studying in the library. She liked the noise and activity of the snack shop.

His face went serious. "Is that not okay?"

"It's fine. Good, actually." No need to put a damper on things. "I'll make a set of note cards for us to study by."

"Note cards? Man, you are motivated. Just don't work too hard or I'm going to have to tutor you in how to loosen up a little."

"And I'm going to exert my best effort on bringing up your grade in psych to a respectable level. Looks like we are on opposing sides of this situation."

"Let's just consider this a challenge. At the end of the semester, we'll evaluate who made the most progress. May the best man, or woman, win."

"You got it." Sabrina watched him sling his backpack over his shoulder as he sauntered easily from the campus snack shop, waving at Lindy and her group as he walked past. She hoped she felt better tomorrow. Tomorrow . . . with Koen. She sighed with happiness at the thought, then opened her laptop, determined to finish her communications reading.

She made it through approximately three pages before she had to stand up and stretch in an effort to keep her mind moving. Her muscles ached, as did her throat. She had become familiar with the symptoms and knew she was running a fever again. Well, it didn't matter. She had work to do and she had to get it done. There was no place for slacking off now. She looked at the window, wondering about Brandy's presence and what she might be up to.

Koen's suggestion that Brandy was watching her, or perhaps it was just her bad cold, caused a chill to run up Sabrina's spine. She vowed to keep a close watch for the next few days. If Brandy was following her, she was going to find out why.

7

The silence roared so loud that Sabrina pressed her hands over her ears in an effort to shut it out. She looked around at all the heads bowed over books. How could people stand to study like this? She much preferred the lights and noise of Campus Eats, or a coffee shop, or at least an outside bench. But this . . . the weight of the quietness was oppressive.

Koen approached the table and mouthed the word *hi* before taking the seat beside her. In one swift movement, he deposited his backpack on the floor and pulled his seat just a fraction closer to her. He opened his Psych 365 book and began settling in. Oh yes. Perhaps silence wasn't such a bad thing, if studying in the quiet of the library meant Koen was near. Still, it baffled her why he preferred to work there.

He put his arm around the back of her chair, leaned close to her ear, and whispered, "So, before we get started studying, there's something we need to talk about."

Sabrina turned slightly toward him, afraid that if she moved too much he would back away and break the spell. She noticed a loose thread at the shoulder seam of his dark green T-shirt. "Really? What?"

"Do you know what today is?"

She leaned back just enough so that she could look him in the eye. "Thursday."

"Not the day, the date."

She didn't know the answer for sure, so she reached down and pressed the button on her phone. "February 14."

He smiled and nodded. "Exactly. I know that a couple of weeks ago when I asked you out, you shot me down in flames. But since today is Valentine's Day—" he reached into his backpack and pulled out a red heart-shaped lollipop—"I'm hoping you'll show a guy some pity and reconsider."

Sabrina felt her face grow warm as she reached out and took the candy, their fingers just brushing. She couldn't contain the smile which undoubtedly looked beyond goofy.

"I'm sitting here asking myself what I was thinking. I barely survived the last blow." He unleashed the full force of his one-dimpled grin. "Just a glutton for punishment, I guess. Or," he said, leaning just a little closer, "maybe you make me want to live a little dangerously."

Sabrina's mouth had gone so dry she wasn't certain she could speak. "I, well . . ." Her mind remained fuzzy, in spite of the rush his closeness produced. She took a sip from the water bottle in front of her, frantically searching for the correct response. She whispered, "You never said anything about going out. You said going over to Jared's house with a bunch of people to watch the basketball game."

"So, you didn't realize at the time that I was asking you on a date?"

"Shh!" The girl sitting in the study carrel closest to their table glared in their direction.

"I guess not." She kept her voice as low as possible. She smiled at him, hoping that there weren't bags under her eyes caused by her marathon cold.

"Maybe that's the problem I get from attempting to mix with the highly driven type. Since you actually have something else on your mind besides having fun, you don't see what would be obvious to most of my friends."

"I'm not sure if you just called me dumb or boring. But either way, it didn't sound good." Sabrina whispered as quietly as she could.

He shook his head and smiled. "No. I told you, that's what I like about you. I'm sick of needy girls. Being around you is like a breath of fresh air—a woman of independence. Still, some things are gonna take a little effort in communication on my part, I see that now. How about I make it more clear then?" He took her left hand between both of his. "Sabrina Rice, would you do me the honor of accompanying me on a date this Saturday evening?"

"Shh!" The girl in the carrel was glaring again, but this time, she wasn't alone. There were several faces turned in their general direction.

Sabrina's cheeks burned with embarrassment, or excitement, or some combination of the two. She turned her attention back toward Koen and gave a few rapid nods.

Koen pumped his fist in victory, then wiped his brow, feigning relief. There was just no end to his cuteness. He opened his mouth as if to say something, but then glanced toward the study carrels, closed his mouth, and pulled out a notebook. He began writing in large, rapid strokes, then handed the paper to Sabrina.

I saw Gazelle Girl standing near your car when I walked up. Is she following you?

Sabrina looked up at him, trying to gauge whether or not he was joking. He seemed perfectly serious. She mouthed the words

Be right back and hurried down the stairs to the ground floor and the front door. She got her answer before she reached the door. She could see Brandy walking down the sidewalk, looking back and forth as if searching for someone. Time to stop this once and for all. Sabrina pushed through the door. "Hey!"

Brandy looked up, then turned and ran in the opposite direction. *Enough of this.* Sabrina was going to get answers about what was going on and she was going to get them now. She sprinted toward the girl, heedless of the fact that her ballet flats were hardly meant for running.

She pushed her legs to move faster and faster, painfully aware of how foreign that feeling had become. Her muscles no longer responded the way they used to, no matter what her mind and will told them to do. When she got to the very end of the middle sidewalk of campus, she looked in every direction but no longer saw any sign of the girl's distinctive white and black hair. Her side ached and her lungs burned, forcing her to stop. Wow, when did this become so hard?

Slowly, she pivoted and turned back toward the library, trying in vain to ignore how much her body was failing her. She needed to refocus and quickly. She did not have time for self-pity. She would do what she always did: push these thoughts to the back of her mind until she'd pushed so hard they disappeared altogether. It was the only way to keep sane.

By the time she made it back to the library, her knees were already telling her what a mistake this whole thing had been. When she reached the bottom of the stairs, she stood and debated. One part of her insisted that she wasn't an invalid, that she should take the stairs as always. The other part reasoned that her knees were hurting now, and would be far worse by the time she reached the fourth floor. And the thought of facing Koen while trying to hold back the pain tipped the scales. She would take the elevator.

Koen was waiting for her when she reached the fourth floor. "Wow, that was some display out there." He motioned with his thumb toward the floor-to-ceiling window, from which he'd obviously seen the whole thing. In spite of the fact that he'd whispered the words, several more *shh*'s sounded through the room.

They walked back to the table and he pulled out Sabrina's chair for her, then leaned down. "Did you catch her?"

Sabrina shook her head, then made a point of reaching for her psychology text. They were there to study together. She'd pulled out her note cards and highlighter, prepared to get to work, when Koen put another piece of paper on top of her book.

Want to go for a run together sometime? I didn't know you were a runner until I saw you flying just now.

Sabrina took a deep breath and closed her eyes for just a moment, fighting through the barrage of unwanted answers that came to her mind. Finally, she picked up her pen and wrote:

I'm not a runner.

You sure looked like it to me.

Wrong. Now, what about our psych test?

Koen stared at her for a moment, but she didn't blink. She wasn't going to explain, not after hearing him say how tired he was of needy girls. No way would she let on just how messed up she really was. Better to be . . . mysterious.

He waited another moment and looked like he might press the matter. But he didn't. He seemed to decide against it and turned to his book. Still, every now and then Sabrina would catch him looking at her, a mixture of doubt and question in his eyes.

8

The courthouse was only two stories tall, but from the outside it seemed much larger. It loomed creepy and gloomy, the large dark wood doors like a mouth ready to swallow the underdogs, the unlucky, the unfortunate. Perhaps in time, after being chewed to bits, the poor suckers would be spit back out. As Brandy walked up the set of concrete steps, she realized that even though it was Friday and she was missing school, she wasn't feeling lucky at all.

Her hands were doing that weird shaking thing, so she put them in her front pockets before Grandma could notice. She was already plenty whacked out about today as it was, no need to make it worse.

"Now remember, every time the judge speaks to you, you answer, 'No, sir' or 'Yes, sir,' stand up straight, and look him in the eye. And whatever you do, watch your language."

"No prob. Got it handled." Brandy tossed her head in that way she always did when she wanted to look cool. If there was one thing she'd learned in the last few years, it was that appearing cool, acting like you couldn't care less, mattered more than how you actually felt. Cops, weed dealers, teachers—nobody needed to know if you were nervous.

"Brandy, I'm not joking. This is serious."

Brandy wished she were not so completely aware of that. Just last year she'd seen Lacey return from a six-month stay in juvie with her left eye set at a weird angle at the end of a long scar. Not only that, she also seemed to have gone completely off the deep end. Who knew what happened to her in that place. "Relax, Grandma. I promise I'll be on my best behavior."

She pulled open a door, feeling the rush of warm air flowing out into the cold day. "After you, Grandma." For all she knew, the judge might be nearby right now, watching. Being seen as being polite to her grandmother could not be a bad thing at this point. And the closer she got to the very real possibility of being sent away, the more she determined to do anything she could to prevent that, even if it was most likely too little too late.

Maybe it was just the heat, but as they walked further inside, the air grew heavier and heavier, thick with oppression. Several benches lined the lobby area. "Let's sit for a minute," she said, plopping down on the closest one without waiting for a response from her grandmother.

"Are you all right?"

"Oh sure, sure, it's just . . . aren't we supposed to meet Mrs. Maloney out here?" Brandy pretended to yawn, allowing her the chance to take the deep breath she desperately needed.

"No, I'm pretty sure she said she'd meet us in the courtroom." Grandma studied her hard. Was it because she looked as though she were going to croak, or had calling her lawyer Mrs. Maloney instead of Karyn been too much of a giveaway that she was freaked out?

"Oh, okay then. Better get moving." Brandy made it to her feet and somehow managed to move forward on numb legs.

Why hadn't she tried a little harder this time? They promised they wouldn't be so lenient and yet she'd blown it again. Stupid. Stupid. Stupid. She wanted to sit down in the middle of the floor, flail around, and cry. About everything. But tears had never saved her in the past. Now wasn't the time to start.

Karyn Maloney was waiting just outside the chamber doors. She wore her typical black suit and black shoes, and carried a black lawyerly looking briefcase. Her color choice seemed especially appropriate today. "Oh good, you're here. Okay, Brandy, you remember everything we've talked about, right?"

"Yes, ma'am."

Karyn lifted a gray eyebrow. "Wow, I guess you do. Good job. Now all we can do is hope the judge is in a good mood today."

"What are the chances of that, do you think?" Grandma sounded almost hopeful.

The door swung open and two women emerged, one practically supporting the other, who was crying hysterically. "My baby, my poor baby." She wailed and cried and repeated the same phrase all the way over to the stairs. Any other day, Brandy would have laughed. Today, it didn't seem that funny.

Karyn turned, looked at Grandma, and said, "Apparently not as good as I had hoped."

A glossy full-page magazine ad showed a young girl with perfectly white teeth holding up a tube of toothpaste, the words *Thank you, Mom* floating beside her in a cartoon bubble. "Too cheesy." Sabrina turned to the next page and the next. Finally, she flipped the magazine shut and reached for the next one on the stack. The floor just outside her room creaked, so she looked up. "Hi, Nana. Come on in."

"Doesn't that hurt your back?" Nana stood at the doorway, simply staring at Sabrina.

"You'd be surprised—it's really more comfortable this way." Sabrina lay on her bed, stomach down, but with her head and shoulders sticking off the edge. She kept the magazines on the floor and used one arm to brace herself and the other to turn pages.

Nana shook her head. "I don't know about you sometimes, girl."

"Don't knock it until you try it. I believe I learned that particular saying from you."

"Well, I guess you're right about that." Nana came into the room and sat down at the desk chair in the corner of the room. "I just got a call from Maudie Jenkins. She asked if she and Brandy could come over for a minute. She said they have something they need to talk to us about."

Sabrina looked at her pile of magazines and then back at her grandmother. "Do they really need to talk to me, or is it just you? I have a paper due on effective print advertising and I can't find one I want to use. And I've been through several forests' worth of magazines."

"She specifically asked if you would be here. Do you mind?"

In fact, she really did mind. She didn't care one little bit for Brandy, especially now that she seemed to be stalking her like some weirdo. Sabrina looked at the concern on her dear sweet grandmother's face and knew that she would say nothing of the kind. Who knew? Maybe Brandy was coming to apologize? *Right.* "Sure. I'll come down when I hear them at the door."

Dingdong.

"I'd say there's your cue, then." Nana grinned and stood up. Her speed up and down the stairs had decreased over the last few years, so Sabrina knew she should go on ahead.

"I'll go let them in," she sighed and made for the stairs.

"Thanks, dear."

Sabrina hurried down the stairs and opened the door to find Maudie dressed in a dark green suit and string of pearls, with even a touch of makeup on. Brandy had on an oversized white shirt and dark jeans, which looked positively formal compared to her usual bleach-spotted jeans and ripped wide-neck T-shirts. Her eyes were circled in the usual black eyeliner. Sabrina motioned into the house. "Please, come in. Would you like some water or tea or anything?"

Maudie shook her head as she walked past. "No need to go to the trouble. We're not going to stay but for just a minute. There's something we need to talk about right away."

Brandy didn't even look at Sabrina as she walked past. She followed her grandmother into the living room and took the farthest seat without saying anything. Maudie went over and perched on a seat near her granddaughter.

"My, my, don't the two of you look nice." Nana made her way into the room. "You must have come straight over from your court date. How did it go?" Her voice was soft with worry.

"Well, that's what we came over to talk to you about. First off, Sabrina, I want to thank you for talking to that coach for Brandy." Maudie nodded in her direction.

"You're welcome." Sabrina looked toward Brandy, who sat with her arms folded across her chest and stared out the window at the far side of the room.

"So, was that a help, then?" Nana asked as she sank into her usual chair.

"Yes . . . and no. The judge said that he didn't feel two practices a week were enough of a commitment. He felt that it would be too easy for Brandy to just go through the motions long enough to get herself out of trouble."

"I see." Nana put her left hand up to her cheek. "What's going to happen, then?" She rocked back and forth in her seat, deep in thought and worry.

"Well, to make a long story short, they put in a call to that coach to see if he would be willing to train her on some other days, as well. He said he couldn't because of other obligations."

"Oh no." Nana shook her head, still rocking.

"They talked about it for a while, and then the coach is actually the one who came up with another idea. He said that Sabrina would be the perfect person to do it."

"*Me?*" Sabrina shouted the word before she could think to do otherwise. She took a moment to focus on speaking calmly before continuing. "I'm not a coach. I have no idea why he would have suggested that. Is that even legal?"

"Please, Sabrina. You are our only hope. If you agree to train her three days a week, and fill out some sort of schedule stating that she did the work each week, then the judge will okay it."

"But—"

Maudie waved her hand. "He's one of those judges that likes to pride himself on doing things outside the box, throwing darts in a new direction and seeing if it hits the board, he calls it."

Which was all well and good until one of those darts collided into Sabrina. "Listen, I'd love to help, but I'm in school full time, I've got a job, and senior projects are coming out of my ears. I just don't know when I would have time to do it."

Brandy had remained motionless through the entire conversation, her face still turned toward the window. Something about her defiance, her arrogance, caused Sabrina to want to goad her just a little. "I mean, the only time I could possibly do it would be five in the morning on Wednesdays and Fridays—" she totally keyed in on Brandy now, ready for any reaction this last would cause—"and Saturdays. That's the only time I've got."

Brandy's left shoulder flinched just the slightest, and Sabrina counted it a victory. Of course Brandy would never consider such an early hour. Especially on the weekends.

"Oh, would you, Sabrina? That will be perfect." The relief in Maudie's voice was clear. "Right, Brandy?"

Sabrina gulped. There was no way the girl would go for it.

Brandy still didn't turn. She shrugged slightly. "Whatever."

"Oh wonderful, just wonderful. She can start tomorrow. Thank you so much, Sabrina."

What? They were actually going to take her up on this? Sabrina hadn't counted on that. "Uh . . . you're welcome." But really, how long could it last? She knew the answer. Not long. Probably not even through tomorrow.

Maudie stood up. "I'm going home right now to call them and let them know." She reached inside her purse. "This is the contact information for Mrs. Lauderdale. She's going to be the one monitoring your paper work, to make certain we are upholding our end of the deal. Where should Brandy meet you in the morning, Sabrina?"

More paper work? More of Brandy? Sabrina wanted to scream, *No! I can't do this.* Instead she said, "Right here, I guess. The sidewalk in front of our house."

"Thank you again so much. So very much." Maudie shuffled from the room and Brandy followed her, never once making eye contact or bothering to speak.

If Brandy did show up in the morning, Sabrina would work some of the swagger out of her. If she didn't, well, then Sabrina could forget about the whole thing with a clear conscience and watch Brandy get what was coming to her. If nothing else, this would at least be interesting.

9

*T*he gun fired and Sabrina surged forward, pushing hard so that she would be at the front of the pack. She couldn't afford to take the chance of getting trapped behind a slower runner.

She drove onward with all the strength she possessed, not daring to take her focus off the path ahead of her for even a split second. She wouldn't waste the tiniest amount of energy doing anything but powering forward, always forward.

The opening section of the course narrowed from the large grassy field onto a wide dirt pathway between the trees. After covering at least a couple of miles, she finally dared a glance to her right. She saw nothing. Then to her left. Again, nothing. Wherever the other runners were, they were at least far enough back that she couldn't see them without turning her head completely to the side. This knowledge increased her desire to move faster. Someone might be outpacing her at this very moment, moving up into her blind spot and hiding there until it was too late.

Her leg muscles burned from the lactic acid, but she had trained *herself to ignore that pain. All that mattered now was the rhythm of her feet meeting the earth, the feel of the wind in her face, the steady, deep pace of her breathing, and the impending threat of whoever might be running behind her. She ran faster and faster, out through the other side of the wooded area, along the curving stretch of land that led around the back of the course. It was here, right now, in these moments that she felt the most alive. As if nothing she had done until this point mattered, and yet everything she had done to get ready for this point mattered in the utmost.*

She rounded the last corner to come back to face the grassy field where she'd started. The runners' chute was before her, the colored flags beckoning, begging her to hurry. She forced her legs to give more than they'd ever given before and dove across the finish line to screaming and cheers. The next thing she knew, she was lying on the ground, exhausted, her mother and coach kneeling beside her, laughing and crying and shouting all at the same time. "You broke the women's record for this course by more than twenty-five seconds. You were absolutely amazing. Flawless," her coach was saying.

"Darling, I am so proud of you. So very proud." Mom's voice was quieter, yet bursting with the enthusiasm that only Mom could have. "You are amazing."

Then the sound all dissolved into silence and a jolt of pain shot through her left knee, then her right. It lingered and built steadily and then her shoulders and elbows joined in until it became so unbearable that Sabrina curled into a ball and cried with the intensity of it. The tears streamed down her face and soaked into her hair, and still the pain didn't relent.

Sabrina awoke with a start. Her pillowcase was wet, as were her face and the fringes of her hair. She sat up and shook her head, trying to clear out the last of the memory. The triumph had felt so real, just as real as when she'd actually experienced it—right up until the pain. That part of the dream her subconscious must have tacked on just to remind her that those glory days were over. Why couldn't it just shut down the whole thing? Strange, she hadn't dreamed about her "before" life in a long time.

She reached behind her and flipped her pillow over to the dry side, then lay back down. She couldn't linger on the pain—that path led to dark places—nor could she skip over it to her old life. Forgetting one meant forgetting both. None of those memories were to be entertained or encouraged, so she closed her eyes and searched for something else to grab her attention . . . school . . . the brochure she was designing for her upcoming interview. Now, which font should she use for the lettering?

"It's Saturday morning. What was I thinking when I agreed to this?" Brandy screamed the words up into a still-dark sky, knowing that at this ungodly hour there was no one to hear her but the fading stars. Everything inside her told her to turn around and go back to bed, but the threat of a quick trip to juvie was enough to keep her going. Not that she was afraid, but why risk it if she could game the system to get out of it? She'd scammed that judge. Not to mention, she was going to show that snotty Sabrina that she was wrong about her, just like all the rest of them. She rounded the corner to Sabrina's street and saw her sitting on the retaining wall, eating an apple and laughing. "What?"

"In answer to your question, you were thinking how much you're going to enjoy getting faster and stronger, and you were thinking how grateful that you are that you are going to be allowed to stay with your grandmother, and you were thinking that I am a wonderfully nice person to be out here doing this for you."

"Uh, sure that's what I was thinking, and how did you hear me?"

"I think most of the town heard you." Sabrina took another bite of apple, but because she was still laughing, she choked and began to cough.

Good. Served her right.

"Okay, I'm assuming you're mostly warmed up after walking over here, but do a few stretches and we'll get started."

Brandy hated the whole stretching thing. It seemed so pointless. Still, she lifted her right foot behind her, grabbed it with her left hand, and pulled. "So, are you a runner?"

"Nope. Now change legs."

Brandy switched legs. "Then how is it everyone thinks you're qualified to coach me?"

"It doesn't really matter, does it? Fact is, I'm saving your neck because they think so. As far as I'm concerned, that's all that counts. Lift your toes and stretch out your shins."

Brandy put in enough effort to make her halfhearted stretching look believable. "Okay, let's get started. Where am I running to?"

"First thing I want you to do is run as fast as you can to the stop sign. As soon as you touch it, I'll stop the clock." Sabrina held up the stopwatch in her hand.

"Why such a short distance? I'm supposed to be training for cross-country, right? Don't you want me to go around the block or something?"

Sabrina looked at her. "Are you going to do what I ask, or would you rather coach yourself?"

I'd rather go back to bed. "I was just asking a question." What was it with authority figures that they all got so completely whacked out on power? "Where do you want me to start?"

Sabrina pointed at a crack on the sidewalk illuminated by the streetlight just overhead. "Right there."

Brandy set up and waited until Sabrina said go, then ran for the stop sign with all that was inside her. No one could top her when she was running at her fastest—she loved the feel of this kind of speed. She reached up and slapped the sign as she passed by, then turned to see Sabrina's response. It was obvious from the look on her face that she was surprised by the time. Ha. Brandy had showed her.

"Okay, now jog back to the start and do it again."

This was pointless. Running distance had nothing to do with short-distance sprints. This girl was obviously just trying to push her buttons though, and Brandy wouldn't give her the satisfaction of knowing she'd gotten to her. She jogged back to the starting line.

"I want you to do that again, but it's important that you don't get a slower time than your first sprint."

"Not a problem." Brandy managed to say the words with more confidence than she felt. If she'd known this was how it was going to work, she would have given herself a bit of slack to work with.

"Go."

Brandy ran with all she had inside her and leapt forward and smacked the sign. She knew she'd gone plenty fast.

"You lost one tenth of a second. Do it again."

Brandy did but her legs hurt more now, her breathing was less controlled.

"Another tenth. Again."

An hour later, Brandy was dripping with sweat and could hardly breathe. Sabrina finally said, "Alrighty, I think that's enough sprinting for the day. On Wednesday we'll concentrate on some distance work."

"Great. Sounds great." Brandy picked up her water bottle, downed about half of it, then stumbled toward home. "If I survive that long," she mumbled under her breath.

"That's my goal," Sabrina called out. "Either bring you to your full potential or kill you in the process."

Brandy hadn't intended for that to be overheard. She stopped and turned. "Sounds to me like you don't much care which way it goes."

"Well, if you keel over, I can go back to sleeping in on Saturday, so I guess both sides have their advantages." Sabrina cocked one eyebrow in that "I'm better than you" kind of way that prissy girls liked to do. Brandy's hands balled into fists out of instinct, but before she made a move, Sabrina burst out laughing. "Oh, Brandy, you should see your face. Relax, will you. If we're going to have to do this thing three times a week, you're going to have to lighten up a little."

Brandy stared at her, trying to decide whether she still wanted to hit her. But little by little, as she watched Sabrina laugh, her anger faded until she sort of grinned, too. "Uh . . . thanks for the support?"

"You are more than welcome. Now get home and start plowing through your backlogged schoolwork. I don't want any calls from Coach Thompson complaining that you're not doing your part."

"Is cross-country a sport, or is it house arrest?"

"The way I see it, if you're really serious about it, there's not a lot of difference. Now get moving."

Brandy pivoted on her left foot, and just to show Sabrina that she hadn't beaten her, she began to run toward home. It took everything she had left to make it around the corner before she slowed to a walk, but she'd never been one to admit defeat. No reason to start now.

10

Sabrina looked into the mirror for the dozenth time. Unfortunately, nothing had changed. Not only was she tired from getting up that morning to coach Brandy, but her hair was a complete wreck and her jeans were too tight. She turned sideways to look in the mirror at the stomach pooch she had developed recently. In the three years since she'd stopped running, she had gained weight, but this was different. It didn't make sense—she hadn't been eating more than usual. Maybe it was just the last vestige of her former self slipping away. No more washboard abs, just her metabolism slowing from a sprint to a crawl.

Great. Just great.

She walked down the stairs, wishing she'd thought up an excuse not to go tonight. No, that wasn't true. She wanted to go out with Koen more than anything, it was just that the whole thing was so out of her control—and that drove her crazy. Running had been in her control. Her grades were under her control. The upcoming job interview was under her control to at least some degree. But whether or not Koen liked her, or was bored out of his mind tonight, well, she didn't know what to do to control that.

"Don't you look nice." Nana was sitting in the living room, knitting a pink blanket for the neighbor's new daughter. "What's this young man like?"

Sabrina sighed and sat down on the ottoman at her grandmother's feet. "Perfect. Amazing. And way out of my league."

"Hmm, somehow I doubt that. You're in a league all by yourself."

"Spoken like a true grandmother." Sabrina smiled at her, thankful for the unconditional love shown by both her grandmother and her mother. They were the two people she could always count on for support.

Dingdong.

Sabrina felt the doorbell all the way down into her stomach. She stood up and started for the door, her legs a bit wobbly. *This is stupid. You see the guy almost every day. You studied with him just two nights ago. Relax, you freak!* Sabrina pulled open the door, hoping her face didn't reveal the level of sudden panic she felt.

And there he stood, smiling at her. The dark blue shirt he was wearing made his eyes look all that much brighter, his white-blond hair that much lighter. His grin was just a trifle lopsided, causing his dimple to stand out. He looked even better than his usual level of perfection. "Hey." He just looked at her and waited for a response.

"Uh, hey. Come on in, I'll just get my jacket." She walked into the living room and picked up her jacket from the chair where she'd laid it. "Nana, this is Koen Conner. Koen, this is my grandmother."

Nana stood to her feet and stuck out her hand toward him. "Louise Springer, nice to meet you."

"It's nice to meet you, Mrs. Springer."

He turned his charming smile on Nana, who nodded her approval. "You two have a nice time this evening."

"Oh, I'm sure we will." He turned toward Sabrina. "You ready?"

Nana, behind him now, widened her eyes and gave Sabrina the OK signal with her fingers. Koen must have caught the general direction of Sabrina's smile because he turned around to see what she was looking at. Thankfully, Nana pulled her hand down just in time and sat back in her seat, looking every bit the innocent grandmother.

They walked out the door and down the sidewalk toward Koen's beat-up white pickup truck. He held the passenger side door open for Sabrina. "Ma'am." Oh, he was adorable.

A few minutes later, they pulled up in front of Jerry's Lakeside Grill. It was a local favorite, with casual American fare, cozy fireplaces situated throughout the dining room, and one entire wall of windows providing amazing views of the lake. Even now, in mid-February, with the surrounding trees bare of leaves, the setting was beautiful.

Koen walked up to the hostess. "Reservation for Conner."

The hostess looked down her list. "Ah yes. Let me go make certain your table is ready."

"Sabrina? So nice to see you again so soon."

Sabrina turned to find Coach Thompson and his wife standing just behind them. "Nice to see you, too." She quickly introduced Koen to everyone.

"I have to say, Brandy has proven to be an even better runner than I imagined her to be. I'm glad you talked me into giving her a shot. I just hope she can hold up her end of the bargain."

"So do I." Sabrina started to tell him about that morning's workout and the bursts of speed she'd seen displayed over and over again, but Koen's presence made her think better of it. She didn't want to try to explain any of this to him. "Maybe she'll surprise all of us."

"Well, she'll have you to thank if she's able to pull it off."

Koen had stood quietly listening to the entire conversation, his eyes narrowed in concentration. He looked at Coach Thompson. "How is it that you and Sabrina came to know each other?"

"I'm the cross-country coach at the local high school." He added no more, clearly expecting that this tidbit would be information enough for Koen to understand the connection.

"Okay, so how does that—"

"Right this way." Sabrina had never been more happy to see the hostess approach with a couple of menus in her hands.

Whew.

The hostess led them to a table by the window. "Ronie's your waitress, she'll be right with you." She put two menus on the table. "Enjoy."

"So, I'm confused. Tell me again how it is you know Coach Thompson. I get that he's the high school cross-country coach, but you didn't go to high school here, right? What's that got to do with you?"

"No, I didn't go to school here." Sabrina was frantically scrambling for an explanation that fell shy of lying but didn't come near the full truth. "I . . . uh . . . well, you remember that girl we saw running from campus security that day? Gazelle Girl?"

"Yeah." His eyes were squinted in concentration.

"Well, I told Coach Thompson about her and he decided to give her a chance. On next fall's cross-country team."

"O-kaaaay . . . but that begs some more questions, like how do you know him in the first place? And why would he take your advice about something like that?"

This was not going the way Sabrina wanted this night to go.

Not at all. And there was no way she was going to spill everything right now, right here. "It's a long story."

"I've got time."

"Hello, my name's Ronie and I'll be your waitress this evening. Can I start you off with something to drink? An appetizer maybe?"

Once again, Sabrina felt immense gratitude for the interruption. This was bound to be her last reprieve, she knew that. She'd have to come up with a new subject and take the offensive as soon as the waitress left the table. "Water for me, please."

"Coke, please."

As soon as Ronie turned to leave, Sabrina said, "So, let's talk about you. I know you grew up on a farm. What does your family raise?"

"If I didn't know better, I'd think you were deliberately changing the subject."

"Good thing you know better. Now, let's see, is it soybeans?"

He leaned forward, putting his chin in his hand. "You are a mysterious woman, that's what you are. I'm thinking it's going to take a little bit of digging to get to the bottom of your story."

"Believe me, it's not particularly interesting."

He reached over with his free hand and put it on top of hers. "I'll be the judge of that. It may take me a little time, but I think you're stuck with me for a bit while I get it all figured out."

Ah, and there was the best reason of all not to tell him anything. Sabrina couldn't help but smile.

11

Brandy's timing couldn't have been better. She'd rounded the street corner just as Sabrina was stepping out of a lame beater pickup and walked to the front door with the driver, who left soon after. Brandy assumed it was a date, but it was too dark to say for sure. After Sabrina went inside, Brandy crept closer to the house, staying hidden in the shadows. She wasn't totally sure why she was there. Just something about this girl seemed off.

When the coast seemed clear, she crept up to the house, careful to open the gate slowly. Squeaking hinges and stealth never went well together. Any normal person would have just picked up the phone, or rung the bell, or would have asked the question during training that morning. Normal probably wouldn't get answers though, so Brandy opted for a different plan.

She came around into the dark backyard and looked through the windows. Brandy didn't know what kind of activity she was watching for, just something that would tell her what was the deal with Sabrina. A sign of some sort. A flash of movement near the back door drew her attention.

Sabrina appeared in the kitchen. She'd changed into pajamas and pulled her hair back in a messy bun. Brandy watched as she filled a glass of water from the faucet and finished the whole thing in three straight gulps. She rubbed the back of her neck, then refilled the glass and reached down into a drawer and started fishing around for something.

For a second, Brandy thought about leaving. This was just a college girl getting ready for bed, but then she saw what Sabrina had pulled from the drawer. A pill bottle. She pried it open, shook two into her palm, popped them into her mouth, and followed them with a gulp of water. She repeated this process twice more.

Pills? Could be anything. Brandy moved even closer, as if somehow she might discover the truth about Sabrina in the identity of those pills.

She was only a yard away from the house. Dark though it was outside, a direct look out of the window carried the chance that she would be seen. She made sure to stay out of the light that spilled from the inside.

Once again, Sabrina reached down for something on the counter. Brandy couldn't help herself and moved closer.

This time, Sabrina came up holding a half-full syringe. She held it up to the overhead light, flicked it with her fingers a few times to dislodge air bubbles, then bent over, presumably to inject it into her leg.

So it was drugs! So much for the goody-two-shoes her grandmother thought this girl was. So much for what Coach Thompson thought about her. It was midnight and the girl was shooting up. Brandy stood for a moment, letting every bit of the hate she felt in that moment transfer from her being toward that window. She wondered if the glass wouldn't crack from the force of it.

Just then Sabrina stood back up and looked at the window. Brandy took a step back, but it was too late. Sabrina jumped toward the door, and Brandy ran for all she was worth.

Sabrina pushed out the door, ran through the backyard, and out through the still-open gate. By the time she reached the end of the driveway she had no idea which direction Brandy might have run. Without pausing to think about it, she decided she'd take the fifty-fifty odds, turned right, and continued running. By the time she got to the end of the block, she'd seen no sign of Brandy, and by then it didn't matter. She couldn't have continued under any circumstances.

She turned and started walking back toward the house. With each step, barbs of pain shot through her right knee. Why had she run after that girl again? Any sane person would have learned a lesson the first time. She reached down and rubbed her knee. It was still extra puffy and this little escapade was sure to increase that. She limped back toward the house, vowing not to do this again.

Wednesday morning, if Brandy bothered to show up, Sabrina was going to lay down some ground rules. The first one would be something like "Absolutely no stalking." What did that girl want, anyway? It was creepy, that's what it was.

"You're limping." The voice came from behind her.

Sabrina whirled around and saw Brandy sitting on Nana's retaining wall in the shadows. She had her legs crossed and was leaning back on the well-manicured lawn.

"Why are you stalking me?"

Brandy shrugged and jumped down. "I'm just trying to figure some things out."

"Like what? It might be easier for both of us if you just asked me."

"Yeah, well, asking someone is not always the way to get a truthful answer, that much I know for sure."

"And lurking outside people's windows works better for you?" Sabrina sat on the steps to her grandmother's porch and rubbed her knee.

"How long you been using?"

Sabrina looked up. "Huh?"

"You heard me. How long have you been using?"

"Using what?"

"Oh come on, I saw you. You took a bunch of pills and then you injected yourself with something. Don't tell me you don't know what I mean."

"I know what you mean, you just don't know what you saw."

"Pssh. I knew I was wasting my time trying to get straight answers out of you." Brandy turned and started back toward the street, shaking her head and muttering something as she went.

"Brandy, wait. Come back and I'll tell you."

"Right." She didn't bother to turn, or even stop walking.

"Keep going if you want, but I'm telling you this is your one and only chance. Walk away now and you'll never get the answer to any of it."

She stopped, turned, and walked back in a slow, jaunty strut. "All right then, let's have it."

"You might want to sit down for this. It's kind of a long story." Sabrina scooted over to make room on the steps.

Brandy didn't move. "I'm fine right here."

"Suit yourself." Sabrina wondered where to begin the story. Brandy wouldn't care about what came before, about all the years of hard work and sacrifice for the dream. "I was a runner for a long time. Pretty good at it in high school."

"How good?"

"Good enough that I got a scholarship for track." There was so much more that Sabrina could tell her about, state championships, record times, multiple scholarship offers, but there was no reason to give those kinds of details, and it would sound like bragging if she did.

"Where to?"

"The University of Tennessee."

"Weird."

"What's weird about that?"

Brandy shook her head. "Never mind. Keep going."

"The thing was, a scholarship to me was just like a paving stone on the path to the place I really wanted to go, which was the Olympics. For as long as I can remember I've wanted to run the Olympic marathon someday. Since they don't even allow teenagers in most marathons, and it's generally considered a bad idea for younger people to run that far, I started cross-country in high school. Again, just another interlocking stone."

"So, why aren't you still at Tennessee?"

Sabrina's mind began to travel down a path she didn't want it to follow. The roaring of the Tennessee River running past the campus after a big rain, the musty smell of her dorm room, the cookouts in the quad. "I . . . uh . . . well." She blinked back the memories, wanting to stop them all. "During the summer before I started, I upped my training. I wanted to prove to everyone that I had earned my spot on the team. I wanted to be the fastest freshman runner in UT history. So I pushed myself. Hard. Really hard. Close to the end of the summer, I was actually gaining time instead of losing it because my knees hurt so bad. My mother took me to the sports medicine doctor and he told me I needed to rest for a couple of weeks. Needless to say, that's the last thing I wanted to do right before school started, but at this point, the pain was bad enough that I didn't have much choice."

Sabrina remembered sitting in her bed, ice packs on both knees, reading books on running, and most of all, reading biographies on her hero, Eric Liddell. God had called him to run. He'd won the Olympic gold medal and then gone off to China to be a missionary. A path almost identical to Sabrina's own plan. She wouldn't tell Brandy that part of the story.

"When I arrived on campus, I was still in pain—in fact, it had gotten worse, not better—and I hadn't trained in two weeks. My times kept lengthening and the pain . . ." She swallowed back the memory. "They packed me in ice, gave me lots of anti-inflammatories. I tried to push through it because that's what you do with pain. You push through. But the first few meets of the season, my times were worse than any of my times had been my junior or senior year in high school."

Brandy grew still during the telling, began nodding her head and staring off into space. "What'd your new teammates think about that?" She sort of whispered the question.

"Most of them were nice enough about it. But, I mean, all runners have aches and pains, so I don't think they really gave me much credit for truly trying. There were a few people . . . let's just say, they delighted in letting me know that I was a failure." Sabrina put her hand to her forehead, trying to stop the flashes of her life that kept appearing in her mind.

"So what happened? You turned to pain-killers and got addicted and that's why you left?"

Sabrina shook her head. "I don't use drugs in the way that you think of using drugs."

"Don't give me that. I saw you."

"I . . . the doctors had a hard time reaching a definitive diagnosis about me for a long time. My blood work never really showed anything conclusive, and I didn't have a lot of swelling in my joints. Everyone had come to believe it was just overuse, or my whining, depending on your point of view. When I came home for Thanksgiving break, I mentioned to my mom that my shoulders and elbows were hurting, to the point that they sometimes woke me up at night. She's actually the one who put all the pieces of the puzzle together. She got on the phone that morning to my doctor and arranged for me to see a rheumatologist."

"A what-a-whata?"

"It's a doctor that specializes in rheumatic diseases like lupus, and scleroderma, and. . . . rheumatoid arthritis. Long story short . . . after several months, lots of MRIs, X rays, blood tests, and every other imaginable test, they finally diagnosed me with probable rheumatoid arthritis."

"Arthritis. Grandma has that. You're just making this up."

Sabrina shook her head. "I'm not. It's a different type. They call it juvenile rheumatoid arthritis when a kid has it, and even really young kids do get it."

"And that's what you've got?"

She nodded. "I have dry arthritis, which is an unusual type. Unfortunately, it took long enough to diagnose that I have permanent damage to my knees and hips, so I'm not able to run because we don't want to damage what is left. You didn't see me taking drugs, you saw me taking medication. Lots of it. Anti-inflammatories to help with pain and inflammation, medicine to protect my stomach from the anti-inflammatories, a couple of different immune suppressants."

"Immune suppressants?"

"The kind of arthritis I have is when my body attacks my own joints like it would an invading virus or bacteria. They have to give me medication to stop that or my joints will be destroyed.

Unfortunately, it makes me prone to get sick easily. I've had a weird cold off and on for a month now."

"So you lost your scholarship because you couldn't run anymore?"

Sabrina almost said, *I lost everything because I couldn't run anymore,* but she managed to choke out a simple yes instead.

Brandy reached down and picked up a piece of gravel from the edge of the garden. She twirled it between her thumb and forefinger, staring at it as if hoping it contained the answer. Finally, she dropped it and looked up at Sabrina. "I guess I misjudged you."

Sabrina shrugged. "You're in good company."

"I've never heard my grandmother mention anything about it."

"I'm sure she doesn't know. It's just easier not to talk about it."

"Yeah." Brandy shook her head. "I know about that." She took in a deep breath, exhaled slowly. "Why did you ask Coach Thompson to give me a chance? Any fool could see that you don't like me."

"No, I don't." Sabrina pulled her knee into her chest and then straightened it back out. "Not yet at least. But I saw you running from campus security the day before our dinner. I saw how fast you could run, and that's a gift. I guess I don't want to waste it. That talent . . . it could take you anywhere you want to go, and you're on the verge of throwing it all away."

Brandy glared at her. "Yeah, well maybe a lot of people misjudge me, too. You included."

"You've got the next few weeks to prove that." Sabrina wondered if she would. Somehow, she rather doubted it.

12

The front yard looked bleak in the pale light of not quite morning. The trees, barren of leaves, stood alone and empty above the brown lawn of late winter. This time of year always felt heavy and depressing, especially in the early morning gloom.

In spite of her gloves, jacket, and knit cap, Sabrina shivered as she walked out into the cold. Brrr. This cold front that had moved in was really something.

She sat on the retaining wall, figuring she'd give Brandy ten minutes before she went back inside and dove back into bed.

"'Bout time you got out here, slacker."

Sabrina jumped at the sound of Brandy's voice. She turned to see her jogging in place beside the neighbor's shrubs. "Wow, you're looking motivated this morning."

"It was a choice of freezing to death out here waiting for my trainer to finally show up or keeping the blood flowing. I chose life."

Sabrina checked her iPhone. "It's three minutes until five. I'm not late, you're early."

Brandy shrugged but kept jogging. "Don't tell anyone. I wouldn't want word getting around."

"Your secret is safe with me." Sabrina opened a training app she'd spent the last few days honing. If she was actually going to coach this girl, she needed to follow some sort of plan. Something that would challenge her without being overwhelming. "Okay, this morning, your goal is to run for the entire session. You don't have to push yourself for speed, just keep a nice steady, comfortable pace. The only rule is that you are not allowed to stop and walk."

"You're not even timing me?"

"No. I want endurance, not speed."

"Pssh. Kid stuff."

"We'll see about that. Around the block, get started."

Brandy shook her head and took off at a snail's pace of a jog toward the first corner. It was almost as if she were jogging in slow motion, her movements were so slow and exaggerated. This continued for as long as Sabrina could stand it. "And if you're not back around here in five-minute intervals, we're going to switch back to sprints like the last time."

"Kid stuff." Brandy changed to a trotting pace and went around the corner.

When she came around after the first lap, Sabrina stood up. "You're doing egg-beater arms. Move them like pistons, always pushing forward, like this." She pumped her arms up in straight lines in front of her.

For the entirety of the hour, she came around at five-minute intervals, making a show of pumping her arms while tossing out comments like "Woo, I'm breaking the sound barrier now" and "Look at me, I can run as fast as a grandmother."

By the end of the workout, Sabrina had learned one thing about Brandy. She needed to be pushed. Hard. Anything less seemed to insult her.

Time to tinker with the plan.

13

"It's been two weeks now, and it seems to me that Brandy is putting forth more effort than I would have given her credit for." Almost home from church, Nana was looking out the passenger-side window toward Maudie Jenkins' house as she made the statement. "'Course, you're the one actually dealing with her. Is that what you think?"

Sabrina nodded and turned the corner. "I never expected her to make it through a single five a.m. workout, to be honest with you. Yet she's never been late even once."

"How is her speed? Is she really that good?"

"She's insanely fast in the sprints, absolutely amazing for brief spurts of time. Not a lot of endurance yet, and completely lacking in discipline, but she seems to enjoy distance running. If she keeps working at it, she'll be more than ready come this fall."

Sabrina's heart squeezed tight inside her chest as the unwanted refrain began to chant through her head again. *It's not fair. It's not fair. I worked hard, I did everything right, it's not— Stop!*

"It's funny, she's not self-motivated, per se, but if she thinks

I'm going easy on her she gets defensive and huffy. If I push too hard, she starts to find little ways to cheat. If we can find the right balance, and she sticks with it, I think she has the potential to be something special." The only way to get past this was to say things like this enough that they didn't hurt so much anymore.

"I'm glad to hear it. You'll do a good job with her, I know you will. This is going to change her life. *You* are changing that girl's life."

"I wouldn't go that far, Nana." Sabrina put the car in Park, with something that felt a lot like guilt suddenly weighing on her. "I'm not really doing much."

Nana climbed out but didn't miss a beat in the conversation. "You're giving her a goal, and someone who cares whether or not she reaches it. That's something that has been missing in her life up until now."

Regardless of whether she was changing Brandy's life, Brandy's presence was definitely changing Sabrina's. And not for the better. Her dreams had been full of running and failing and pain for the past couple of weeks. At times, Sabrina thought she was going to lose her mind.

"I'm heading over to campus as soon as I get changed. Do you need me to pick up anything while I'm out?" Sabrina held open the front door for Nana.

"No, can't think of anything. How long will you be, do you think?"

"All day. Until the snack bar closes down anyway. I've got a ton of work to do."

"Will that nice young man be there, too?"

The mention of Koen jolted her. "No. I don't think he gets back into town until late tonight, but I'm not sure." She'd seen little of him this week, and he'd offered some vague story about going out of town for a family event. Well, it wasn't like he owed her an account of his whereabouts, or what he did, or who he was with—especially with Lindy Stewart seeming to appear everywhere Sabrina had seen Koen this week.

"I worry about you sometimes. Seems like you study so much, I'm just afraid you're going to burn out."

"Well, just a few more months to go and that won't be a problem anymore. I've got to keep my focus set on the finish line up ahead and do whatever it takes to get there."

Nana shook her head. "I was saying just this thing to your mother this week. I've never known another person, of any age or persuasion, to have the kind of single-minded drive that you've always had."

"Daddy would say that's a good thing."

"And so would I . . . most of the time. It's just that sometimes I wish you'd put a few of your jelly beans in different jars."

"Hey, I'm plenty diversified. Working at the snack bar is a different jar than studying. And there's my newest jelly bean jar—the Coach Sabrina jar."

"That's not exactly the kind of thing I was talking about." Nana grinned and shook her head. "I just wish you'd slow down a little."

"I'll take it under consideration." Sabrina kissed her grandmother on the forehead, but they both knew that nothing was going to change. "I'm going up to put on something more comfy."

"Well, at least eat some lunch before you go. You'll sit in that snack shop and eat nothing but a granola bar all day." Nana was already unclasping her faux pearl necklace and making for her room. One trait the two of them had in common was a general discomfort with dress clothes. The first thing they both did upon arriving home from church was to change into something more comfortable, and then the day could proceed into whatever direction it was going to go.

"Don't have time. I'll take an apple along with my granola bar, if it'll make you feel better." Sabrina climbed the stairs to her room two at a time. There wasn't time to waste today.

She pulled on a T-shirt and jeans, hung up her church dress, and was in the process of pulling on her Uggs when she heard the doorbell sound. Likely one of the neighbors coming over to have a little Sunday-after-church visit, as they liked to call it. She'd have to make a quick escape or she'd end up caught in the middle of it. Sabrina was grabbing her purse and keys, prepared to make her getaway as soon as possible, when she heard Nana calling to her. She opened the door to the hallway and could see her grandmother waiting at the bottom of the steps looking up.

"Have you spoken with Brandy?" she called.

"Not since her workout yesterday. Why?"

"Maudie is here. She says Brandy disappeared yesterday after lunch and she hasn't seen or heard from her since."

"What about her cell phone?" Sabrina started down the stairs and saw Mrs. Jenkins sitting primly, nervously it seemed, in the living room.

"She's not answering." Mrs. Jenkins looked even more worn down than the last time Sabrina saw her. The dark circles under her eyes were puffy, the wrinkles on her face seemed to have deepened. "She's gone missing before, once, but by the next morning I could get her to answer her cell phone. This time, I don't know, something just feels wrong."

Sabrina thought about the morning workouts from this week. Brandy never said much, volunteered little in the way of personal information, and Sabrina didn't ask for any. They were there to work, nothing else. Still, she'd shown up every morning on time. Something did feel wrong about her disappearing without a word to anyone.

"Have you talked to any of her friends?"

"I don't know how to reach any of them. Once, when I told that Janie girl there would be no smoking at my house, she threw her cigarette down onto my kitchen floor and stubbed it out on my white linoleum. I asked her to please leave and haven't seen any of her friends since."

Sabrina pondered how to respond to this. Finally, she said, "Well, she's made all our runs this week. And one of the points of our deal was no drinking and no smoking. If she is committed enough to get up that early, even yesterday, I'm thinking she wouldn't go out and do something stupid quite so easily. Maybe the battery in her cell phone is dead, or maybe she fell asleep at a friend's house and just forgot to call you." Even as she made the excuses, Sabrina knew how hollow they sounded, because they felt hollow as she spoke them, too. "I can go drive around town, see if I see her car anywhere."

"Oh, Sabrina, would you do that for me? I don't drive anymore and I just feel so helpless." Mrs. Jenkins' eyes were full of tears. "I'm just too old to be what that girl needs, but there's not anybody else to help her. I don't know what to do."

What Sabrina wouldn't have given to get her hands on Brandy at this moment. The girl might have had a rough life, but to worry her grandmother who obviously cared about her, and to so selfishly take up everyone's time with searches and worry, well . . . Sabrina tried to ignore the tension in her shoulders, to control her anger and forget about her own stresses so that she could concentrate on the best course of action. "Do you have any idea where I should start?"

"I know her friend Janie lives over in the Creston Acres area, and they all like to hang out at that arcade over behind the old theater."

"All right." At least the initial search area was fairly small. Hopefully Mrs. Jenkins' guess would prove correct. She turned the knob to the front door. "Nana, I've got my phone with me. Call me if you hear anything while I'm out."

"Of course I will." Nana turned her attention to her friend. "Maudie, you just come in here and sit down. I'll fix you a glass of tea and we'll do us some praying for that young lady."

Mrs. Jenkins nodded. "Thank you, Louise. I just don't know what else to do with that girl."

Sabrina hurried out the door and into her car. "God, please help Brandy to be okay, and please help me to find her fast." She didn't pray the rest of the sentence aloud, but she knew that God understood her thoughts as well as she did, so He knew that her motive was far from selfless. *Help me find that troublemaking brat so I can get back to my work.*

Creston Acres was a subdivision full of small brick homes that had been built fifty or sixty years ago. At the time, it had likely been a place for folks starting on their American dream, full of big plans for the future. Now the houses just looked worn and tired. Multiple cars filled the driveways and spilled out along the curbs, giving the entire area a cluttered look and making searching for Brandy's car that much more difficult.

Sabrina slowly made her way down the first block, pausing any time she saw an older, larger black car. A group of young boys were playing basketball beneath a portable goal along the street. When they saw Sabrina's car coming, they continued their game, though a couple of them did glance her way occasionally, apparently to make sure she got the message that they had right-of-way here. Sabrina slowed her pace to avoid hitting one of the kids. Any other day, when she had less to worry about, she would have been furious, wondering what kind of parents would allow their kids to behave in such an unsafe manner. Today, she just shook her head and drove on.

She crept through block after block, looking for any sign of

Brandy or her car, and dodging countless neighborhood kids who were playing on the streets with abandon. At least three times she was forced to slam on the brakes, in spite of her slow speed, to avoid a kid running out from between cars to retrieve a ball, or to simply get to the other side of the street. By the time she'd finished the last block, Sabrina was no closer to finding Brandy, but her nerves were frayed from all the close calls.

Unable to bear the thought of returning to Nana's house without any information at all, she drove toward the theater and the arcade. What would she do when this turned up nothing?

Turning left at the town square, she saw the old theater. It was rarely used now, and then only for special public events. There was no sign of Brandy's car anywhere, so she drove down the side street that led to the old arcade. The parking lot was about half full, but Brandy's car was not among those parked there.

Thwarted, there was nothing to do but turn back and return home. Before she'd even put the car in Park, Nana and Mrs. Jenkins were out the front door and waiting. "Anything?"

Sabrina shook her head. "I didn't see any sign of her car anywhere." She looked from her grandmother to Mrs. Jenkins. "Should we call the police? Report her missing?"

"No, oh please, no." Mrs. Jenkins shook her head vehemently. "I promised them I would keep her out of trouble. If I call them now and tell them that I've lost her like this, they'll take her away for good. Please, could you drive through town one last time and look for her?"

"But I—" The argument died on Sabrina's lips. This poor woman had been through the loss of her son and was now doing her utmost to save her granddaughter from a terrible fate. Undeserving though Brandy might be, to take away Mrs. Jenkins' last hope was something that Sabrina didn't have in her to do. "I can drive through again if you'd like, but I don't think the odds are in our favor."

"Please, just please do this for me. If you don't find her, then I'll call the police, and then I'll finally have to face the fact that I just can't handle this, but please give me this one last chance."

"All right." Sabrina sat back down in her car. "I'll let you know if I find anything."

Sabrina pulled out of the driveway, battling so many emotions she didn't know what to feel. Pity for Mrs. Jenkins and her plight partnered with fear for Brandy's safety against a growing anger at Brandy for doing something stupid. Not to mention Sabrina's own increasing stress when she thought of the work that was not going to get done today.

Forty-five minutes later, Sabrina was still driving in circles in the areas Mrs. Jenkins had suggested when her cell phone chimed. "Hello."

"You can turn around, sweetheart. Brandy is home safe and sound."

Equal parts relief and frustration hit Sabrina at once. "Where has she been?" She turned right at the next intersection, preparing to head for Nana's house.

"I didn't get all the details before Maudie left, but I think the gist of it was that she was with friends, camping at some lake. She says there wasn't cell reception there, so she couldn't call."

Sabrina swallowed back any response. The battling for her emotions was over and now a simple fury took the clear and resounding lead. The girl was nothing but a selfish punk, and Sabrina was finished with her. Done with this whole thing. But not until she'd let her know, to her face, exactly how boneheaded this last maneuver had been.

Tomorrow. Today she'd already wasted enough time on the girl.

14

Brandy walked down the sidewalk of the college campus. On this Sunday evening it was mostly deserted, with just the occasional student passing between buildings. As she approached the student commons, she thought about turning around and going back to the house. Grandma had insisted that she come find Sabrina and apologize in person, but initially Brandy had balked. There was no need to do it right away. It'd be better to talk to Sabrina in a couple of days, after things had time to cool off.

But Grandma was all wigged out, and Brandy wasn't going to start acting like a coward now. Besides, grown-ups overreacted about these things so much. Sabrina was young enough that she likely had some idea what the reality was. She probably wouldn't even need an apology.

Brandy passed the windows where she knew the snack shop was, and she knew that Sabrina was probably inside there somewhere, studying, or whatever it was that she did over here so much. She started up the stairs toward the front door, but before she was halfway up, the door to the student commons flew open and Sabrina came out. Her arms were folded across her chest and her face was bright red. "What are you doing here?"

"I came to—" Brandy tilted her head to the side—"apologize, I guess."

"You guess? You've got some nerve."

"It was just a big misunderstanding. Like I told my grand-mother, we decided to go camp down at the lake. We'd already gotten there and unpacked before I realized there wasn't phone service. What was I supposed to do? It was an hour-long drive to get back there."

"A whole hour? Oh, that would be terrible. Do you have any idea how long I spent looking for you today because you couldn't be bothered to drive back close enough to town to make that call? It was a lot more than an hour, I'll tell you that much."

Brandy shrugged. She hadn't really counted on Sabrina being this angry. Annoyed, yes, but this was over the top. Did these people really expect her to check in every time she went some-where? Ridiculous. "Sorry. I didn't expect Grandma to get so hysterical about the whole thing. Who knew she was going to get you involved in it? It never occurred to me."

"It seems to me like there are a lot of things that have never oc-curred to you. You've got a grandmother who's doing everything in her power to keep you safe, to help you *stay out of* juvie right now, and you don't even respect her enough to make a stinking phone call and let her know where you are. No, I take that back. You should have made the call to ask her for permission before you went camping in the first place. She deserves respect. A simple phone call is not too much to ask of anyone."

"Okay, deep breath. You're getting a little worked up. It's not like I don't appreciate Grandma. I just *made a mistake.* I'm sure even you have made a few mistakes in your lifetime."

By now, Sabrina had angry tears in her eyes. "I just cannot bring myself to understand the kind of girl who would treat the woman who loves and takes care of you with so little regard."

"You have no idea what my life has been like."

"I know enough to think you would appreciate something good when you're living in the house with it."

Those words hit Brandy harder than she'd expected. For just a moment, she thought about all the nice things her grandmother had done for her over the years, all the times she'd gone out of her way to help her, and yet . . . She turned her attention to the sidewalk. "Maybe you're right."

"There isn't any maybe about it."

Brandy looked up, knowing what the answer was about to be, but needing to ask it anyway. "Does this mean you're not going to train me anymore?"

"We had a deal, which you broke."

"There wasn't anything in our deal about me checking in at home before going camping." She held up her hand to stop the argument she knew was coming. "Okay, I get it, that was wrong, but it wasn't part of the deal."

"Drinking and smoking *were* part of the deal, though. You going to tell me you spent the night camping at the lake with your friends and you didn't do either?"

Brandy lifted her head a bit higher, straightened her shoulders. "As a matter of fact, that's exactly what I'm going to tell you. I didn't touch anything all weekend long. My crew didn't like that so much—" she snorted a laugh, thinking about the look of horror on Janie's face—"but I told 'em I was taking a little break."

Sabrina scoffed. "Honestly? Why in the world should I believe *you*?"

Brandy knew the argument was lost. Right there. "There isn't a reason, okay? I get it. Nobody takes my word for anything, and

I guess I understand that. But it's the truth, whether or not you want to believe it." And there it was.

The sun was starting to sink in the sky behind the campus buildings, leaving long shadows and increasing darkness in its wake. Brandy turned toward her grandmother's house, shivering in the growing cold as she walked. High school cross-country had lasted less than three weeks. She supposed that was about two and a half weeks longer than most people expected.

Come to think of it, this was a relief. The pressure was off. No more early morning or late afternoon practices. No more conversations with people like Erin Methvin, who pretended to want to include her. Exactly. A relief. Who needed all that?

That's when the full implication hit her. She needed all that. She'd just blown her last chance to stay out of juvie. "Why are you so stupid?" The question to herself came out louder than she'd intended but there was no one around to hear.

A brown paper sack blew across the sidewalk and came to a stop at Brandy's feet. She drew her foot back and kicked it as hard as she could. It flew up into the air just as the wind came and pushed it right back down beside Brandy's foot.

"Be at my house tomorrow morning at five o'clock. Sharp." Sabrina called the words from somewhere down the street behind her.

"Tomorrow's Monday." Brandy shouted the words without turning.

"We're having an extra practice this week."

Brandy lifted her left hand in acknowledgment, but otherwise kept moving. Half a block later, she realized something. She was smiling.

15

Pace yourself. Running faster only when you're in front of me isn't teaching you anything except about how to fake it." Sabrina had to call the words out to Brandy as she ran by for another lap around the block.

Brandy had been a diligent worker both Monday and today without a single complaint about the early start time. Mrs. Jenkins had informed Nana that she was being shown an unprecedented level of respect and this had truly been a turnaround experience. Somehow Sabrina felt a little less optimistic, but that's what grandmothers were supposed to do, so more power to them. Neither Sabrina nor Brandy mentioned the weekend's debacle and the subsequent fallout. It had been relegated to exactly where Sabrina liked things that were unchangeable—in the past and forgotten.

Brandy disappeared around the corner and Sabrina looked down at the stopwatch, noting the time. She tried to picture Brandy, who just about now should be rounding the corner in front of the Benders' house. Their little dachshund was likely pacing around the tidy lawn, poking his long black nose through the slats of the freshly painted white picket fence. He'd yap a time or two each time she passed, then return to his pacing until the next round.

Sabrina could almost feel the ball of her foot absorbing the impact, the strain of her thigh muscles, the way her lungs needed just a bit more oxygen. The pure joy that could only be accomplished by the wind in your hair, entirely controlled by your own muscles, your own speed, your own willingness to override the body's urge to stop and to keep moving further, harder, faster, to the place where only champions would dare to push themselves. How long had it been since she'd felt that? Its absence burned inside her; at times like this the heat became almost unbearable.

Stop. Nothing good was to be gained by crying over what you couldn't have, no matter how hard you worked for it or how badly you wanted it. Or how much more you deserved it than the people who actually might achieve it. Brandy rounded the corner.

"What makes you think I'm slowing down when I'm out of your sight?" She called out the words between gasping breaths.

Sabrina held up the stopwatch. "The clock never lies."

"Great. Just great." Brandy huffed past, her face red from exertion.

"Slow your pace the entire round this time. It's time for a cool-down lap."

Brandy cast a backward glance over her shoulder, clearly surprised, but she did slow her pace a bit. Sabrina watched her take the corner, then looked toward the sky, toward God, whose voice she had misunderstood. Maybe she'd never even heard it at all. It wasn't that she'd lost her faith in God, it was more that she'd lost her faith in ever understanding Him.

Well, there was no reason to sit here and feel sorry for herself about the whole thing. The best she could do now was move forward with this new reality. Always push forward. It had worked in running, and it would work in life. Launching her career in the best possible way was the thing she needed to think about now. This was where she had some level of control.

She looked down at her communications book, thankful for the streetlight overhead, and began to review the chapter they'd just covered in class. That was one nice thing about the days she and Brandy worked distance rather than sprints: it gave her a chance to do some studying while Brandy was out of sight. Multitasking was a good thing. And with at least half of the current page highlighted in pink, it was obvious there was much she needed to remember.

A minute later, Brandy coasted to a stop in front of her, then paced back and forth, cooling down. "How come you cut this morning short?" Her eyes were bright in spite of the fact that she was breathing heavily.

"I didn't. We're done for the day."

"How come we're not going the full hour?"

"We did." Sabrina looked at her watch. "An hour and three minutes, to be exact."

"Really? It didn't feel that long today."

"You seem to enjoy the distance work better than the sprints."

"Yeah, I guess I do."

"I'm glad, because you're running in your first 5K this weekend."

"Huh?"

"You heard me. There's a 5K downtown on Saturday. I've already registered you. It'll be fun."

"Fun?" Brandy didn't look at all convinced. "Well, yeah, okay, I'll give it a go."

"Yes, you will. Then, three weeks after that I've got you signed up for another one, a bigger one. It's in Columbia, up near Nashville, very prestigious. This will be a nice warm-up."

Brandy puffed her cheeks full of air, then blew out. "Bigger one. Cool."

"You don't run from a challenge." Sabrina closed her book and jumped down from the retaining wall. "You're going to make a great distance runner if you stick with it. Maybe you can finish what I wasn't able to."

Brandy stopped her pacing and studied Sabrina for a moment, her nose ring shining in the glow of the streetlight. "I'd really like it if I could do that."

Sabrina's heart came up into her throat, and even after she watched Brandy jog back toward home, she still found it difficult to swallow. "Maybe I would, too." And maybe she truly would.

She went up the stairs to her room and picked up her phone to do a quick email check before taking a shower. The top email on the list was from Rita Leyva. *Oops. Guess I never emailed her back.* Sabrina clicked it open.

Dear Sabrina,

I haven't heard back from you, so I wanted to double-check and make certain you received my previous email re applying for a position with Bridges. I am very anxious to connect with you as soon as possible, as I am leaving for South Africa at the end of the week. I would love to speak with you before then when you have a few available minutes.

In Him,
Rita Leyva

Sabrina hadn't given the previous email another thought. She supposed she should call Rita back and at least thank her for the confidence, but she didn't have time to deal with it right now. She hurried into the shower to get ready for her eight o'clock class and the rest of the day.

Hours later and back at her desk after three classes and a four-hour shift at work, she decided it was best to go ahead and make the call. Best to get it over and done with, and in spite of the fact that she wasn't really interested in the offer, she didn't want to seem rude or ungrateful. She found Rita's number and called, already formulating her polite decline. But the conversation quickly veered out of her control. Rita Leyva proved to be a much more dynamic person than Sabrina had assumed and she was finding it hard to get her to take no for an answer. Her excitement bubbled over any obstacles, effectively drowning the subtle protests that Sabrina offered. Finally, Sabrina decided the only tactic that would work was the absolute blunt truth.

"Mrs. Leyva, I'll just be honest with you. Truth is, for most of my life—including that time when I spoke to that youth group and wrote that silly devotional—I was utterly convinced that God had called me to be a public speaker as a ministry. I believed it with every fiber of my being."

"That devotional was not silly. It was raw, but it was powerful. Just like your speaking. That's why I'm so convinced—"

"I was wrong."

The declaration hung in the air between them, leaving nothing but silence for the space of several heartbeats. "But you weren't."

"Don't you understand? I either didn't hear God after all, or I misunderstood Him so badly that I am obviously not the kind of person you need working in your mission organization. I thought God had called me to be a missionary via my platform as an Olympic medalist. Mrs. Leyva, there is no Olympic medal in my future. I am simply a person who thought she heard the voice of God when she did not."

"The talk that I heard didn't mention the medal. You simply

103

said you believed that God had called you into working on behalf of the poorest nations in the world, and that you believed that your running was the conduit that God was going to provide to get you where you needed to go. That you were going to trust Him with the process."

"Exactly. See what I mean? Running was the key that would open doors. Running was why people would want to hear what I had to say. I was mistaken."

"What if it was the key, though? Sabrina, running is what caused you to make that talk in the first place—it's what led me to finding you. God used your running to bring us together at the perfect time."

"I—" Sabrina opened her mouth to argue, but Rita Leyva was very persuasive in her way of twisting words around. Finally, Sabrina did manage to say, "You're pulling my words out of context."

"With all due respect, Sabrina, you might be pulling God's call out of context. I beg you, spend a little time praying about it. Spend a little time going back and looking at that little devotional you wrote. Promise me you'll do that before you give me a final answer."

As Sabrina was more than firmly convinced that Bridges had nothing to do with her future call, it was an easy promise to make. "All right, I promise."

"Great. Feel free to call me any time you have questions or concerns. Otherwise, I'll prayerfully await your decision."

"Thanks." Sabrina hung up the phone and went downstairs in search of something comforting.

She had her head stuck completely inside the cupboard when she heard Nana's laughter behind her. "Hungry?"

"Need chocolate." Sabrina turned to flash her grandmother a smile and then returned to her choices.

"That bad, huh?"

"You have no idea." She turned her attention to the back corner and finally found the Swiss cake rolls. She pulled out two packs and offered one to her grandmother. "Want one?"

"No, thanks." She tilted her head and looked from the chocolate snacks to Sabrina. "Why don't you tell me what's going on."

"It's complicated."

"So I'm gathering by your choice of after-dinner treat."

Sabrina peeled open the plastic wrapper. "I just got off a phone call. . . ." She relayed the conversation to Nana as best she could.

"Oh, I loved that little devotional. You made copies for all of us, remember? I still have it, not that I need it anymore. I've read it so many times I've practically memorized it."

"Well, that's embarrassing."

"Why on earth? That devotional was heartfelt. Remember what you said about God calling the children of Israel out of Egypt? I certainly do. They all thought that was the greatest thing ever. Freedom, their own land. He parted the Red Sea, led them across."

Sabrina rolled her eyes. The last thing she needed right now was a Sunday school lesson. "Yeah, and then they started whining and complaining and wanted to go back. Failure. End of story."

"Ahh, you've forgotten what you said. You reminded us that they went three days without water right after the Red Sea. Three days. No water. When you wrote that part of the story, you were so utterly convincing, my mouth felt dry. You talked about a life-threatening thirst, an agonizing pain kind of thirst.

"You said they thought they were being called out to this life of freedom, and all of the sudden they were facing the possibility of a miserable death. Never would it have occurred to them that they were going to encounter the Promised Land through difficult situations like that." Nana put her hand over her heart and smiled. "Beautiful thoughts, really." She reached over and squeezed Sabrina's hand. "Now that I think about it, it does remind me of you, just a little bit. Maybe Mrs. Leyva is right."

"What do you mean?"

"You thought you were going to serve God by Olympic glory. Well, maybe the truth is you are going to serve God because of your running, but through a much more difficult scenario than you'd expected—one involving pain and suffering and loss. Perhaps you didn't misunderstand God's call, perhaps you took some of the details in the middle for granted."

The words hit Sabrina hard, much harder than she would have ever believed possible. She'd spent years of her life pouring all of her energy into something, believing with all her heart that God had called her there, only to have her own body betray her and make it impossible to continue. It wasn't meant to be. It wasn't. "You're wrong."

"Am I?" Nana let the question hang for just a minute. "Sabrina, you know I love you with all my heart. I'd give anything to take away your pain, and that's the truth of it. I will always be proud of you no matter what you do or decide. But I think you should spend some time remembering your own words and praying about whether or not you might have turned back toward Egypt."

The chocolate cake and cream filling stuck to the roof of Sabrina's mouth. She gulped water so hard her eyes watered, then waited through a deep breath before trusting herself to speak. "It's a nice thought, Nana, but you're wrong."

"Maybe so. That's between you and God. I'm just telling you it's something to pray about."

Somehow Sabrina managed to climb the stairs to her room before the entire weight of all she'd hoped and all she'd lost crashed down on her in one giant hammer stroke. She fell across the bed, one question repeating through her mind. It was the same question she'd asked a million times before with no answer.

Why?

After a few minutes though, a second question began to insert itself into her thoughts. One that she had never experienced before and one she didn't want to hear now. Still, she couldn't quite shut it out, even though she knew it couldn't be true.

Have I turned back toward Egypt?

16

"Tell me again why I'm doing this?" Brandy looked down at the rectangle of paper pinned to her stomach, the number 154 in large block numerals across the middle of it.

"I told you, it will be good practice. There's absolutely no pressure to perform today. All we need for you to do is go out there, get the feel of the distance, get the feel of running in a group of people, learn how to pace yourself in spite of what the people around you might be doing. This is the perfect venue for you right now."

"I guess." Brandy looked toward the banner strung across the road, declaring *Start* on one side and *Finish* on the other. A group of people were standing near it, talking and stretching. They were all older than she was, and several of the women were overweight. A couple of them were downright heavy. Unlike the fast group at school, these were people she could beat without even breaking a sweat. "Yeah, maybe this won't be so bad."

"At least you get a T-shirt out of it, right?" Sabrina held up the green shirt. It had the words *Shamrock Shuffle 5K* printed across it, with a lucky clover forming the O in *Shamrock*. "Kind of a cute one, I think."

Brandy looked at it, wondering what Janie and the rest of the crew would say if they saw her wearing it. It wouldn't be warm and fuzzy, she knew that much. Still, Sabrina was looking at her like she expected her to say something, so she said, "Cute," then bent over and pretended to check her laces.

"Brandy! Brandy, hi," someone called. "I didn't know you were going to be here. Do you want to go warm up together?"

Brandy straightened up to find Erin Methvin's smiling face directly in front of her. "I'm so glad to see you here. Several other members of the team are here, too." She scanned the crowd. "Emmy, Janice, and Robert for sure, and I think a few others may be coming. Have you seen anybody else?"

You've got to be kidding me. "No, I haven't seen anyone." *Why? Why do Erin and the other kids have to be here?* Brandy turned toward Sabrina and introduced her to Erin, while silently trying to figure out an excuse to get herself out of there.

"Nice to meet you, Sabrina. Are you running today?" Erin asked.

This was going to be disastrous. Sabrina was going to tell Erin that she was Brandy's own personal coach, and it was going to be that much more embarrassing when she lost. Why had she let Sabrina talk her into doing this? Shouldn't she have known that something like this would happen?

"No, I'm not running, I'm just here to . . ." Sabrina cut a quick glance toward Brandy, "watch the event for a psychology paper I'm writing."

"A psychology paper on a 5K? Really? Now, that's a paper I could get into writing." Erin smiled. "What's your angle?"

"The mentality of runners, hard work, dedication, and I'm thinking of adding runner's high."

"Oh cool, I definitely think you should." Erin nodded, her ponytail bouncing with the motion. "I love it when that happens."

Runner's high? That was a new one, but Brandy made a mental note to find out about it later. She certainly wouldn't make herself sound stupid by asking in front of Erin.

"Good luck with your paper. So, Brandy, shall we go warm up?"

Sabrina blinked her acknowledgment toward Brandy, then smiled at Erin. "You two have a good race, and maybe I'll talk to you at the finish. Okay?"

"Uh, sure." Brandy followed Erin, chancing a backward glance when she thought it was safe to do so.

Sabrina nodded once and gave her a barely noticeable thumbs-up, then turned and walked toward the starting line.

"Is this your first 5K?" Erin bent down, touching her nose to her right knee.

Brandy bent over trying to copy the move, but flexibility had never been her strength. She turned it into a right-sided toe touch and made like that's what she'd intended to do all along. Well, she wasn't going to let Erin get the best of her. "Nah. I've run lots of them. How 'bout you?"

Erin didn't release her stretch but she did turn her head in Brandy's direction. "Me too. Funny we've never bumped into each other before now."

"I just moved to town a few months ago."

"Oh, right. That must be it." Erin moved her stretch to the middle, then shifted so that her nose was pressing against her left knee. "Did you set a goal time? I'm aiming for 18:40."

"Um, uh . . ." Brandy started to tell the truth, that her goal was simply to finish somewhere in the top third, but she didn't really care if she met that. But Erin's declaration, her confidence, and the fact that she obviously expected Brandy to finish far behind her, grated on her. "Eighteen minutes."

"Eighteen minutes flat?" Erin's eyes opened wide. "My best ever was 18:45."

Brandy shrugged. She regretted her quick answer but certainly wasn't going to eat it now, not in front of Erin. "I've done it before."

"Really? Wow, that's amazing. Maybe if we run together it'll make for good pacing for both of us." There was absolutely no guile in her words. Erin was so naïve and perky, it would never enter her mind that she'd just been told a bald-faced lie. Worse than that, it was a lie that Brandy was going to have to live up to.

"Oh hi, there you are." A group of six or seven more kids from the track team walked up. The three girls all hugged Erin, the boys exchanged high fives and fist bumps, and they all looked sort of nervously at Brandy. She did the single head nod, which none of them seemed to know what to do with, so they did what the popular kids always did. They turned away from her. They chattered amongst themselves about the race, their weekend plans, and the upcoming track meet against Franklin School.

"Runners, please approach the start." A middle-aged man wearing a Shamrock Shuffle T-shirt over his pudgy midsection stood on a chair and spoke through a megaphone. "We'll be starting in just a couple of minutes. The course will start here down Main Street, turn right just past the courthouse, then continue on down Breckenridge until you loop back around to Main. For you speedsters, remember the outgoing runners get the sidewalk. You'll be on the street inside the cones. There's plenty of people in orange vests directing traffic so I don't foresee any problems. Do we have any questions?"

No one said anything, but the group as a whole crowded toward the start line. Brandy and Erin lined up behind a couple of men who looked to be in their early thirties, whose running shorts—even in this cold weather—revealed legs that had put in a lot of miles running. "These guys'll move forward quickly and then we'll have open pavement ahead of us," Erin said. "We can set our own pace without having to try to pass anyone in the process." She reached up and flipped her ponytail. "All we've got to do is avoid being passed."

"Not a problem." Right.

The horn sounded and the pack took off like a herd of animals. Brandy knew about herds: the weakest, the ones who weren't smart enough or fast enough, were the first to get eaten by the predators. She formed a mental picture of the police chasing her down the street and pushed herself to move faster. In a matter of a couple of minutes, she'd left most of the pack, including Erin and the rest of the team, somewhere behind her. That would show them a thing or two.

The course was on a slight uphill, and Brandy's legs were beginning to burn, but she continued to imagine the pursuing cops behind her and pushed forward in spite of the pain. By the time she turned onto Breckenridge, her leg muscles were screaming. This she could have endured if she hadn't been so surprised by what she saw at the turn. The next quarter mile was up a hill, a steep hill. How was she supposed to manage that with her legs already about to lock up?

She slowed her pace a little and tried to look around and focus on the little cafés and shops lining the road in the historic downtown neighborhood. The brick storefronts were weathered but comfy looking, with large windows filled with children's clothes and furniture. Those little tables at the cafés looked so inviting right now.

The road grew steeper and steeper, and her pace grew slower and slower. She wanted to stop and walk so badly she almost allowed herself to cave in to it, but the knowledge that Erin was somewhere behind her kept her going. She didn't want to look like a complete fool. Her quad muscles felt as though they might simply lock up at any moment. *The police are chasing you—you've got to get away.*

The thought wasn't as helpful as it was in the real situation. Usually, this far into running, she'd left the cops so far behind there wasn't a reason to even be jogging anymore. She was almost to the top of the hill when her legs betrayed her and simply stopped running. Before she'd made anything close to a conscious decision to do so, she was walking.

Just for a few seconds. Just until the top of the hill. She was struggling hard to pull in deep breaths, trying to make her body ready to move forward.

"Brandy, you okay?" Erin's voice was coming up rapidly behind her.

Brandy didn't bother to turn, she knew wouldn't need to. Sure enough, in a matter of seconds, the swinging ponytail was right beside her. Erin slowed to Brandy's speed but kept her feet moving in a jogging motion. "You get a leg cramp?" Her voice was full of concern.

"Uh, yeah. Leg cramp. I think I'm good now, though." Brandy forced herself back to a jog, faking a slight limp for the first few steps. At least they were at the top of the hill now. Uphill or not, her body was still in full revolt. This was where mind over matter would come into play. This was something that Brandy excelled at, so she determined she would keep up with Erin no matter how bad it hurt.

"I'm so glad you're able to keep going." Erin's voice was breathy, but not the all-out puff fest that Brandy's was.

"Me too." Right.

When they rounded the curve and returned to Main Street, there were still quite a few people heading in the other direction, still in the first third of the race. There was a duo of women running together, each easily fifty pounds overweight, faces already bright red with exertion, but they still kept jogging forward at a barely moving pace. "Good job." Erin clapped her hands, offering applause and encouragement, at which the women smiled.

The line of people coming toward them thinned down, comprised almost entirely of walkers. Several were pushing strollers or holding the hands of skipping toddlers. But then Brandy noticed a man running back this way. He looked to be about thirty, in absolutely prime condition, running at a rapid rate. Not long after him came another man, then another, all very similar in appearance and speed. "Show-offs," Erin mumbled.

"Who are they?"

"Some of the faster runners will run the course twice." She shook her head, then looked down at the athletic watch on her wrist. "Let's push for the end."

Brandy gestured forward with her left hand. "My leg is starting to cramp again. You go ahead."

"See you at the finish." Erin sprinted away, her ponytail swinging in time with her long strides. Brandy resisted the urge to return to a walk. She watched Erin pull away and somewhere deep inside her she vowed that she would keep pace as best she could. She kept her eyes focused on Erin, desperately wishing she hadn't pushed so hard at the beginning, because she had nothing left to dig into now. Somehow, she gutted it out until the finish line, crossing with a time of 20:11. She managed to resist the urge to fall to the ground once she crossed the line. Instead she bent forward, gasping for air.

A hand holding a water bottle suddenly appeared in her line of vision. Brandy looked up to see Sabrina standing over her. "So much for that, huh?"

She took another deep breath, then managed to stand up straight and take a long draw of water.

"Part of today's goals was to learn about pacing. I think that's a lesson you learned the hard way, one you won't soon forget."

"You can say that again." Brandy shook her head.

"Oh, there you are. Great job today, especially with a cramp and all." Erin looked at Sabrina then. "She had a leg cramp in the middle of the race and had to walk it off. I think it was amazing that she came back to finish so strong."

"Hmmph." It was as much as Brandy could manage.

"I went over to the timekeepers table. We finished first and second in our age group. You've got to like that, right?" Erin bounced as she said it.

"Good for you." Sabrina seemed sad when she looked at her. "What was your time?"

Erin bounced as she said 18:22.

"That's a good time. Really good."

"Thanks. It's a personal best for me. Hopefully the coaches at Scofield U will like it, too."

"Have they made a scholarship offer?"

Erin crossed her fingers and placed them over her heart. "I sure hope so. At first they were saying I could run for them as a walk-on, but a few months ago they started talking potential scholarship. I could really use that, you know?"

Everything about Erin was so perky, and happy, and perfect. Brandy hated her, or she wanted to, but couldn't quite bring herself to it. "I've got to go. I promised my grandmother I'd be home in time to help her with some chores." Brandy started walking toward the parking lot without ever looking back to see if Sabrina was following.

She would. First, though, she'd make some polite conversation and a plausible excuse to get out of there without seeming rude to Erin.

The pounding of footsteps coming from behind proved her point. "Leg cramp, huh?" Sabrina was smiling.

"What was I supposed to say? 'I ran too fast because you were so excited about your stinking goal time, and it made me mad enough to mouth off?'"

"Mouth off, huh? What did you say?"

"I told her my goal time was eighteen minutes flat."

Sabrina laughed. "I've got to admire your spunk." She looked back toward the race course. "I like her. She a friend of yours?"

"Right. As if I have anything at all in common with a girl like that. She's such a do-gooder. She was looking at the fatties still coming from the start gate on our return, clapping and saying, 'Good job.'"

Sabrina burst out laughing. She laughed and laughed, well past the point where it made any kind of sense.

"What's so funny?"

"That reminds me of my very first 5K. I was, I don't know, twelve, I guess. My mother and I officially ran it together, but of course I dumped her somewhere around the starting line and ran for glory. Sort of like you today, I took off too fast and it cost me further down the road. But the leaders of the race were coming back around and they saw this spunky little twelve-year-old girl chugging along, and several of them said, 'Good job,' or something along those lines to me. It made me feel good and gave me the motivation to keep pushing.

"I was somewhere in the middle of the pack, so when I made the turn and started toward the finish line, I tried encouraging the people coming the other way. I said, 'Good job,' to this middle-aged man, and he snarled at me and said something to the effect of 'humph.' It really hurt my feelings at the time. I just couldn't understand why an overweight middle-aged man wouldn't be delighted to hear encouragement from a skinny, athletic preteen girl. Looking back on it now, it just really strikes me as hilarious."

Brandy shook her head. "You've got a weird sense of humor."

"I guess so."

They continued walking toward the parking lot. Brandy had pulled up here with such high hopes, visions of glory in her head. Now she was leaving in total defeat. As someone who had even walked part of the race. "Maybe this running thing just isn't for me."

"Brandy, you have a natural gift for running. I've seen it, and so has Coach Thompson. The decision is up to you now, whether you're willing to do the work to make something really special out of that gift, or whether you want to quit because it's hard. Everyone who wants to be great at something has to work at it. Hard. Success doesn't come overnight, either. You've got to make up your mind you're going to stay the course, no matter how steep it might seem sometimes."

"I blew it. Big time."

"Some lessons, like pacing, you've got to learn the hard way. But you still finished second in your age group—behind a girl who's likely been running four years of high school track, a girl with a potential scholarship. That's an all right place to start."

"Yes, but she's a two miler, not a distance runner. This isn't even her thing. Besides, you said that big race in Columbia in a few weeks will have five times as many people as this—I bet a lot of them are distance runners."

"That's right. And there will definitely be scholarship-level distance runners there, maybe even some Olympic hopefuls. What you've got to concentrate on is you. Whether you eventually come to beat those other runners or not, you've got to learn to give it your best, let everyone else do her own best, and know that in the end, your absolute best is your absolute best. Win or lose."

"Yeah." By now, Brandy had reached her car. She looked at Sabrina, so many arguments coming to her mind, so many things she'd like to tell her. What came out was "See you at five o'clock on Monday."

"Monday?" Sabrina tilted her head to the side and grinned.

"I'm thinking I could use an extra practice."

Sabrina just looked at her, and for a minute, Brandy thought she was going to refuse. "Now that you mention it, an extra practice would be a good thing."

17

What did you do today?" Koen leaned his chin in one hand and looked at her, waiting for the answer.

"Me? Not much. The usual, you know, study, help Nana around the house." Something about the nonchalant way he asked the question caused Sabrina to be uneasy, which was silly. "How about you?"

"Not much. The usual, you know, played some b-ball with the boys, avoided studying or doing anything around the apartment." He played with her hand across the table. "So, is that all, then? You didn't do anything else?"

Whatever uneasiness Sabrina had felt before went into an all-out alarm with the repetition of the question. She shrugged, focusing her attention on their interlocked hands rather than on his soul-piercing eyes. "Mostly."

"Mostly." He repeated the word quietly. "I see."

"You see what?" This time she did look up at him.

"I heard a rumor you might have been spotted at the St. Patrick's race this morning."

121

"Who told you that?" Even as Sabrina asked the question, she already knew the answer. She'd seen several people from school there that she recognized. There was one who stood out from the rest, however—Lindy Stewart.

"Did I hear wrong?" He wasn't being accusing or combative, but he was clearly on a mission to find out the truth. Sabrina supposed there wasn't any reason to try to hide it.

"No, you didn't hear wrong. I was there."

"So what is the deal then with you and running? I saw you run after Gazelle Girl a few weeks ago, so I know you're fast. You told me you don't ever run, but then you go to a 5K. Do you run or don't you?" Again, just making conversation. He had no idea how close he was getting to a truth she didn't want to get into.

"I don't." She looked out the window of the pizzeria toward the street. "I just went to watch."

"Because?"

Why couldn't he just let this go? When she told him the truth, he would see that she wasn't so independent and strong, and any advantage she had over the athletic Lindy Stewart would vanish. She'd lost enough from her disease. She wasn't going to let it ruin any chance she had with Koen, too. She pulled her hand away from his. "Because I like to watch people run, okay? Is there something wrong with that?"

His head snapped back as if she'd struck him. "No. Wow, okay, so in my effort to learn more about you through casual conversation, I guess what I've learned is that you don't like a lot of questions. I'll be sure to put that one down for future reference. Maybe that's the downside of your independent streak, hmm?" He never took the full force of his gaze away from her face.

"Look, I'm sorry. I . . ." Sabrina rubbed her forehead, trying to find the right words. "I used to run, a long time ago. I don't anymore, and I don't really like to talk about it."

"O-kay." He leaned back against the red plastic cushion of the Pizza Palace booth. "New subject." He sat quietly, likely wondering if there were other subjects that might bring on a similar reaction and afraid to say anything, just in case.

Could this be any worse? It was the first time they'd spent an evening together in a while, and this was certainly not the way Sabrina wanted it to go. She frantically searched for something that might return some sense of normalcy to the evening. "How did you do on the psych quiz yesterday?" It wasn't perfect, but it was all she could come up with.

"Okay, I think."

"Haven't you looked at your grade? She posted them last night."

"Nah. There's nothing I can think of that I'd rather do *less* on a Friday night than to check my grades online."

Sabrina laughed, and then they fell into another awkward silence. The waitress refilled their sodas, asked if they needed anything else, then cleared the plates. Plastic plates clinked against metal forks, providing the only sound. In the booth behind them, a man let out a bellowing laugh, rocking back against his seat hard enough that Sabrina's seat shook with the force.

"You ready to go?" Koen stood and offered his hand, which Sabrina took, hoping to restore something of their former magic.

When they got almost to his truck, she stopped and turned. "Listen, I was at the race this morning watching, like I said. I'm sort of coaching Brandy—Gazelle Girl, as you call her—and this was her first 5K. That's why I was there. I . . . well, I'm sorry I was so snippy with my answer."

"Coaching her?" The surprise in his voice was quickly squelched by the pained look on his face. "Oh, sorry. Forgot, I'm not supposed to ask questions about that. Do you want to drive over to Jared's? He's having a bunch of people over—he told me we should drop by."

"I . . . uh . . . sure, I guess so."

He opened the door and held it while she climbed in, his piercing eyes seemingly searching her face for clues. Still, he didn't ask, he simply shut the door and walked about to the driver's side.

She knew she should say something, tell him about what happened, but somehow she just couldn't bring herself to do it. She didn't want his pity, couldn't stand the thought of it. So she would keep her silence and hopefully he would be all right with that. Only time would tell.

18

*S*he was running, leading the pack, but the sound of feet pounding against pavement came from close behind. She pushed harder to keep her lead. The finish line was just ahead, less than ten paces away. Her foot caught on something and she flew forward, her entire body launched into an uncontrollable free fall. The asphalt loomed closer and closer, but there was nothing she could do to stop it. Her face crashed hard, followed by the rest of her body. She could still hear the approaching runner behind her and knew that she needed to get up quickly, but before she could, she was slammed down again, the entire weight of her competitor's shoe landing between her shoulder blades. The other runner never slowed, never gave any indication of remorse for running across Sabrina's back on the way to victory. Sabrina looked up at the finish line to see who could have done such a thing. She couldn't believe who she saw there.

Brandy.

Brandy jumped up and down in victory, her fists pumping the air. "Yes! Yes! Yes!"

Koen was standing by, watching the entire scene, shaking his head in disgust at Sabrina's failure. He turned, put his arm around Lindy Stewart, and walked away.

Sabrina woke up drenched with sweat, her pillow soaked with tears. Again. The bedside clock said three a.m., but to fall back asleep meant the potential for another dream. She pulled out a book and tried to study, but found it impossible to concentrate. How much more of this could she take before she fell apart? Something told her she was about to find out.

For whatever reason—perhaps Rita Leyva's repeated contact— she started thinking about the position at Bridges. That was totally not the way she had her life planned, but something about Rita's mission had struck a nerve deep inside her. She thought about returning to Egypt, the children of Israel, all of it.

Since she couldn't sleep anyway, she got up and went to the box in the very top of her closet. She hadn't opened it in several years, but still she kept it nearby. She pulled it down, opened the top, and dug through the old journals until she found the one that she knew contained her thoughts about the Exodus, the ones she'd used to create that embarrassment of a devotional she'd been so proud of when she was seventeen. She flipped through mindlessly, finally stopping on a page to read that day's entry.

Oct. 17— The children of Israel have crossed the Red Sea, the Egyptian soldiers who pursued them have all drowned, and now they're moving out toward their destination. But three days later, they haven't come across any water. So they grumbled against Moses.

My thoughts—THREE DAYS WITH NO WATER? Even if they had a supply when they started, I'm assuming they've still gone a significant time without anything to drink. Wow. Talk about a painful, aching thirst. I'd always thought they were whiners, never really occurred to me until now that they had significant pain. Need to spend some time thinking about what they should have done in this situation. Obviously grumbling against Moses wasn't the correct response, but when you're that thirsty, what are you supposed to do?

The answer must begin with looking back at all God had already done for them and giving thanks, then continuing to move forward in faith.

Sabrina couldn't read any more. Everything inside her felt raw and tender, and reading this, remembering the serenity she'd once felt and the deep faith she'd once had, well, it wasn't helping anything. Those words had been written by a naïve teenager who had thought life would always work out the way she'd planned. For whatever reason, she didn't return the journal to its box. She put it in a drawer at her bedside table, fully intending never to look at it again.

Six hours later, Sabrina was about to be late for her first class. Worse, every parking space looked filled, as was every available open space of curb. Dozens of students were hurrying toward brick buildings, looking at their watches and moving a little faster.

Sabrina's neck and shoulders ached from the tension across them as she turned the corner down the very last aisle of the lot, hoping for the miracle of an empty space. She drove the length of it as quickly as she dared, already knowing that it was useless. She'd have to go find a parking spot on the street somewhere.

She hated being late. Despised it. Enough so that she was never late. Never. Ever. Until this morning.

Things needed to change. She couldn't keep doing what she

was doing right now. She'd hardly slept the last two nights, and when she did fall asleep she had the same disturbing dreams over and over and over. It wasn't real, but it *felt* real.

A girl emerged from between two parked SUVs and was suddenly in the road ahead of Sabrina, although she was too busy texting to notice. Sabrina slammed on her brakes, causing her tires to let out a brief squeal. The girl looked up. "Watch it. You need to slow down." She cast a fearsome scowl in Sabrina's direction, then started in the general direction of the science building, texting as she went.

I can't continue like this.

Sabrina exited the parking lot and had to drive for over a block before she found a spot she could pull into. She was definitely going to be late for class. She locked her car, slung her backpack over her shoulder, and started toward the communications building. She was almost there when her cell phone vibrated in her pocket.

Normally she would have ignored the call at a time like this, but for some reason—reflex perhaps—she pulled it out and looked at the caller ID. It was a number she didn't recognize, but the area code was from Georgia. Out of curiosity, she pushed the button. "Hello."

"Is this Sabrina Rice?"

"Yes."

"Hello, my name is Kim Gilbert with the Grace Rose PR firm in Atlanta."

Sabrina's feet planted firmly on the sidewalk. "Oh, hello." What else was she supposed to say? She was sure there was something, but she couldn't think of it at the moment.

"We were wondering if it would be possible to move your interview up. We've got you scheduled to be here on the twenty-ninth, but one of our partners has had a schedule change, and we'd really like you to come next Monday, a week from today, if you are available."

"Next Monday?" Sabrina thought of all the things she had hoped to do to be fully prepared for this interview. It was going to be a challenge to do all that now, but it wasn't like she was going to tell them she couldn't handle this. "Sure. Of course, that sounds great."

"Terrific. We'll see you here Monday at eight a.m. We look forward to meeting you." And just that fast, she was off the line and Sabrina was left wondering how she could manage to have everything ready on time. Somehow, she would find a way.

Little goals were the things that usually kept Brandy moving forward. "I'll run as hard as I can to that mailbox" or "I'll go for an extra minute after I want to stop" or "I'll beat the neighbor's car around the corner." Today she had one goal, one large goal only, and that was to get a positive response from Sabrina. That girl had more or less checked out Monday and today was no different. She seemed hardly even aware that Brandy was present, much less running circles around her.

Brandy had been training extra hard with not a single comment from Sabrina, good or bad. Today, for the two-mile timed run, she planned to smash her previous best time, thereby forcing Sabrina to say something. She used the very last ounce of energy to lean hard toward the crack in the sidewalk that served as the imaginary finish line. She blasted across it, then looked toward Sabrina, ready to hear the exclamation.

Sabrina was sitting on the retaining wall with her laptop open, looking at the screen and shaking her head. This had been her common position all week long.

Brandy ran up directly in front of her. "Well?"

Sabrina looked up. "What? Oh, sorry." She looked down at the stopwatch then.

Okay, this time would be several seconds late, but in spite of that, Brandy was more than confident she'd still achieved her goal. She couldn't wait to see the look of surprise on Sabrina's face. Yes, there it was, a double blink as she looked at the stopwatch. "Oh no."

This was not exactly the reaction Brandy had expected. "What?"

"I must have forgotten to push the button when you started. I totally missed the time on this one."

"You are kidding me." Every muscle in Brandy's legs screamed in protest and her lungs burned out their own complaint. To have worked so hard for nothing. Well, not nothing perhaps, but her strongest piece of ammunition for what she planned to ask next had just been taken away from her.

"Sorry." Sabrina sounded more annoyed than sorry.

"That would have been my best time, I'm sure of it."

"Really? Well, good for you. Next Wednesday we'll do another timed run and you can prove it. In the meantime, I'll see you Friday and then you've got a long weekend to work out without me. I won't be back from Atlanta until Monday night, so you'll be free of me until Wednesday."

Sabrina was pulling away from her, just like everyone did. This time though, Brandy was determined that she was going to hold on. She wasn't going to let someone else do this to her—not without a fight, anyway. "Which reminds me, I've got a better plan."

"A better plan than what?"

"You're going to Atlanta Saturday, right?"

"Yep, I'm leaving early. That's why there's not a Saturday run this week."

"Right. But I'm thinking maybe there should be one."

"Good for you. You can certainly train without me here. In fact, you should."

"Well, here's the thing. I went online last night and started looking around. There's a 5K in Atlanta on Sunday morning. I could go with you and run in it."

Sabrina was shaking her head in a big sweeping no. "Brandy, I'm not going to Atlanta to relax. In fact, I'm going on Saturday so that I can have a day to prepare for my interview, plus drive around the area so I'll be able to get to the right building on time without getting lost. I need some serious focus time."

"But this would give me a chance to run with other people where I'm not trying to show the kids at my school how fast I can start or any of that. It would just be me as a runner against other runners that I've never seen before. How about if I come down with you on Saturday, then on Sunday after the race I'll catch the bus home? It would be terrific practice for the upcoming Columbia run—it would give me an edge."

Sabrina leaned forward, rubbing her forehead with the heel of her hand, still shaking her head no. "Brandy, I can't."

"I've done everything you've asked me to do. I've given up everything that I was so that I could do this, so that I could finally become someone that people might notice again. How can you just throw me over just because you've got a stinking job interview? You're just like everyone else." Brandy jerked up her water bottle from beside Sabrina on the wall. "Thanks for all your *help*. No need to inconvenience yourself by working with me Friday, I know you've got lots more important things to be doing." She turned toward her grandmother's house and began to run for all she was worth—which apparently was not all that much.

19

The file stared back from Sabrina's computer screen, unpolished and unprofessional. The color scheme seemed all wrong now. So she went about painstakingly changing the background from green to pale blue. Then the font seemed flat and boring. Or did it?

Exhausted, Sabrina folded her arms on the table in front of her, leaned her head in the crook of her elbow, and closed her eyes. If she cleared her mind of everything for just a minute, maybe then it would all come together. All she needed was a quick break and the right answer would come to her.

But it didn't.

When she closed her eyes, the only thing she saw was Brandy's face from that morning, unmistakable pain in her eyes. All day long that same vision had been in her mind, just beneath the surface of anything else she tried to concentrate on. *Sabrina, you've done all you could be expected to do for her. She's not your problem.* Somehow no matter how long she told herself that, she could never quite make herself believe it.

The chair beside her squeaked across the floor. "You're looking like you could use a friend right about now." By the time she looked up and realized what she was seeing, Koen had already taken the seat beside her, right elbow on table, leaning his right cheek against his hand. "You okay?"

"I'm fine. Just a little overwhelmed."

"I'm thinking perhaps a nice dinner of oh . . . say . . . pizza and a salad, followed by a trip downtown to see whichever band it is that's playing on the square tonight for Wednesday Night Lights ought to cheer you right up. What do you say, you game?"

Being this near to him, the desire to ignore all of the things on her to-do list and simply go enjoy herself for a while was almost overpowering. Almost, but not quite. "I can't."

He reached over and touched her cheek. "Sabrina, you look totally stressed and I don't like seeing you this way. Just for an hour? A little time-out?" His voice, his face, everything about him was so appealing, it took everything she had this time.

"I really can't."

"I see. I'm only now beginning to realize how big of a challenge I accepted when I vowed to help you loosen up a bit. I'm thinking I may need some extra time to work on this. What do you say we spend the entire day Saturday together? We could drive up to Nashville for the day?"

"I can't, and that's one of the reasons I'm so overwhelmed. They moved my Grace Rose PR interview to this coming Monday. I'm leaving early Saturday to go to Atlanta and get ready."

"And when will you be back?"

"Monday evening some time."

"I don't think I want to go that long before I see you again. Are you sure you don't want to grab a quick pizza right now? I promise I'll have you back and studying within the hour."

"I wish I could, really I . . ." A stirring of movement at the counter drew Sabrina's attention. Lindy Stewart and a group of her friends were all standing at the counter, laughing and talking as if they had no cares in the world as they ordered their usual round of chai lattes. One friend in particular had her eyes fixed on Koen, obviously watching and waiting. "I really shouldn't, I mean I . . ." Wouldn't just a little reprieve from all the stress be a good thing? After all, everyone needed to eat. Sabrina looked at her watch, then back at Koen, feeling better already. "Gotta eat sometime. Dinner sounds like a nice idea."

"Exactly what I was saying." He stood up and offered his hand, which she was more than happy to accept. She couldn't bring herself to look at the group at the counter as she passed by, but she hoped Lindy Stewart would see them and decide to turn her attention elsewhere.

Fifteen minutes later, they were seated at Pizza Palace, simply enjoying being together. "I'm really glad you talked me into this. I think I needed it."

He grinned and leaned a little closer. "I like it when a woman admits she needs me."

Sabrina just laughed. It felt good to laugh for a while.

"So, tell me about this trip to Atlanta. Where are you staying?"

"Some friends of my father keep a high-rise condo in downtown Atlanta that they rarely use. They're letting me stay for free, so I'm going a couple of days early. It'll give me time to get some things ready, and to make certain I know how to navigate. I don't want to be late to my interview because I'm lost."

"Does it make you nervous, staying by yourself in a strange city?"

"Nah, I got used to it when I was . . ." Sabrina shook her head to remove the memories. "I used to travel a lot when I was younger."

"I see." His eyes narrowed. "Another clue to this mysterious past of yours."

And just like that, with the mention of what used to be, the wall that Sabrina had built so carefully against all that was going on cracked, then burst. She felt tears stinging her eyes but blinked them back, hard. The last thing she wanted to do was cry in front of Koen.

He put his hand on hers. "You okay?"

"Yes." She tried to focus on the picture of the Leaning Tower of Pisa hanging over their booth. She concentrated on the rows and rows of white columns, each joined together by an arch, and the difference in the size of the top floor. It was no use, although the distraction did at least help regain control over her outward display of her inward turmoil. At least she wasn't going to cry. "I need to walk outside for a minute—there's a phone call I forgot I was supposed to make."

"O-kay."

Sabrina hurried outside before she changed her mind, opened her list of contacts, and pressed the Call button. She supposed she shouldn't have been surprised that the call wasn't answered. When it rolled over to voice mail, she started to hang up, but for some reason, she didn't. "You know, I've been thinking. Maybe you coming to Atlanta isn't such a bad idea after all. Be ready to go by eight o'clock Saturday morning." She pushed the button, wondering if she hadn't just made a huge mistake.

No matter. Brandy would probably refuse to go now anyway. Sabrina turned back toward the restaurant, wondering if she hoped that were true.

20

Sabrina looked at her packing list again, then looked at the neatly rolled clothes in her overnight bag. Tomorrow morning, all she would have to do was throw in her toothbrush and she would be good to go.

Her cell phone vibrated on the bedside table. In spite of the fact that she'd already talked to him twice this evening, she hoped it was Koen again. She hurried over, already smiling at the prospect. The caller ID read Brandy Philip.

Great.

Brandy had shown up at that morning's training session sullen and grumpy. She didn't mention the message about Atlanta, and neither did Sabrina—she'd made the offer, she certainly wasn't going to beg. There was a strange awkwardness about their interaction, but as far as Sabrina was concerned she had done her part.

"Hello?"

"I want to show you something. Will you come on a ride with

me?" Brandy's voice was low, her words fast, like floodwaters rushing over the wall of a dam that was not used to being breached.

"Tonight?"

"Yes."

"Where to?"

"The place I went camping the other night."

As a method for breaking down barriers, this was definitely over the top. Time to refocus. "Brandy, it's late and I've got a long drive in the morning."

"Please. Just come with me. There might be some things about me that you would find surprising, too."

There was an urgency in Brandy's voice. For whatever reason, and against her better judgment, Sabrina said, "Okay. I'll be over there in a minute."

"No need. I'm parked in front of your house. Come on out."

The upholstery in Brandy's beat-up old Grand Prix hinted of the smell of tobacco, alcohol, and a sort of skunk mixed with burnt lawn clippings that could only be marijuana. "Tell me again why we have to take this trip in your car instead of mine?"

"You'll see when we get there." Brandy said no more. She kept both hands on the wheel and paid close attention to her driving, showing no hint of recklessness as she drove further and further from town.

"How far, exactly, are we going?"

"Nashville."

"Say what? I don't have time for a trip to Nashville. Does your grandmother know where you are?"

Brandy shrugged. "You're with me."

Sabrina opened her mouth to protest, to demand that Brandy

turn the car around right now, but then stopped herself. She'd come this far, she might as well see this thing through. "Your grandmother will be worried."

Brandy shook her head. "I told her I was going over to see you and that I might be late. And I brought my cell phone with me so she can call at any time."

"All right." Sabrina had told Nana she was going for a ride with Brandy, although she'd had no idea at the time it was going to take this long.

They made the rest of the ride in complete silence, until Brandy pulled off the interstate near downtown. She pulled to a stop in the parking lot of a Superama, turned off the car, and got out without a word. Sabrina opened the passenger side door and stood up. "What are we doing here?"

"It's a grocery store, what do you think we're doing here?"

Sabrina hurried after Brandy, who went inside the store, grabbed a hand basket, and made for the dairy aisle. In just a matter of minutes, they were standing at the self checkout with a gallon of milk, a loaf of white bread, peanut butter, jelly, apples, bananas, and assorted granola bars and protein shakes.

"Brandy, this is crazy. We are not going camping—we don't need supplies."

"You think?" The total came to just over forty dollars. Brandy reached inside her pocket and pulled out some folded bills. She peeled off a twenty, then proceeded to count out the rest one dollar at a time. When she finished, she had one dollar and change left over. She grabbed one of the plastic bags, Sabrina took the other, and they started for the car.

"Weren't you getting worried that you didn't have enough money? That was really close."

"I'm not stupid." Brandy cast a disdainful glance over her shoulder. "I knew how much I had and I checked the price of everything before I put it in the basket. I always leave it just a couple of dollars short in case I want to stop at the Quick Mart on my way home for a Coke."

Sabrina studied the girl's face. What she was saying had to be bravado. For her to have added up that many items and cut it that close would have been a pretty amazing mathematical feat for anyone, much less a troubled kid like this one. Brandy looked at her with a bland expression, as if she didn't care whether Sabrina believed her or not.

"All right. Now that we've gotten these groceries, are we heading to this elusive campsite, which apparently exists somewhere in the middle of Nashville?"

"You'll see." They put their bags in the back seat and drove further into the heart of the city. It wasn't that part of downtown that Sabrina sometimes ventured into, with restaurants and theaters and country music saloons. This was the part of town they didn't show in tourist magazines.

The homes became more ramshackle, the yards unkempt, with pieces of equipment, old cars, and various broken toys littering the yards. In spite of her determination not to let Brandy see that she was afraid, Sabrina couldn't help but glance over her shoulder to make certain her door was locked.

Brandy pulled to the curb in front of a tiny home with ancient gray shingle siding, a sagging front porch, and tattered curtains visible through the light coming from inside the front room. "This is our stop." She reached into the back seat and took both bags of groceries. "You stay in the car and lock the door behind me. I'll be right back."

"You can't get out here, it's not safe."

Brandy didn't acknowledge Sabrina's comment in any way. Instead she climbed out of the car and started for the house, bags in hand. She moved slowly up the front porch steps, stopping after each upward movement. Maybe it was because she was listening to something inside, or more likely, because she was afraid the boards might break through with any sudden movement.

Sabrina tried to imagine who might live there that would inspire these strange actions on Brandy's behalf. She couldn't help but fear the possibility of a crazed man coming to the door with a shotgun in his hand, ready to kill anyone who dared to trespass on his front porch. She cradled her cell phone in her palm, prepared to dial 9-1-1 at the slightest provocation.

By now Brandy was moving across the front porch and Sabrina's anxiety was growing with each step she took. She heard some raucous laughing and looked ahead to see a group of boys walking down the street toward her. Long T-shirts and baggy pants.

Thugs. Out looking for trouble, and they were walking right toward her.

Sabrina sank down lower in the seat in spite of the fact that she was more than certain it was too dark where she was sitting for them to see her. She lifted her head just enough to chance a peek toward Brandy.

The two grocery bags were sitting on the porch directly blocking the front door, and Brandy was making her way down the steps. She turned her head in the direction of the boys, stopped walking, and slid back into the shadows by the side of the porch. Sabrina sank all the way down into the floorboard and waited. She could hear the boys cutting up as they walked by. After what seemed like an eternity their voices began to fade further away.

Sabrina let out the breath she hadn't realized she was holding. Perhaps it was safe to sit up now.

Boom. Boom. Boom. A fist pounded on the driver's side window. "Let me in. Hurry up."

Sabrina made quick work of unlocking the door. Brandy sat

down fast and locked the door behind her. "See now why I didn't want to bring your car? It would have stood out like a shiny new toy in this neighborhood—no way those guys would have left it alone." She turned the key and pulled away from the curb.

"Whose house is that? And I still don't understand what this has to do with your camping trip." Sabrina looked back over her shoulder as the home grew smaller behind them.

Brandy didn't answer. She turned onto the next street and the next, looking in her rearview mirror from time to time as if to make certain they weren't being followed. When she turned back onto the interstate on-ramp, she said, "My mother."

"Your mother what?"

"You asked me whose house that was. It is my mother's."

Sabrina looked toward her to see if she was serious. She seemed to be. "Then why didn't you knock?"

Brandy turned her head completely toward Sabrina, in spite of the fact that she was hurtling down the interstate at seventy miles per hour. She just looked at her, not saying a word, until Sabrina said, "Brandy, watch where you're going." Brandy did turn her attention back to the road, but she didn't say anything.

"Why didn't you at least knock on the door and tell her you were bringing groceries?"

"She'll find them. She always does. I usually hide and watch—that's where I was when I said I was camping, at least for most of the time. I did go to the campsite with my friends, but they weren't thrilled about my lack of, shall we say, recreational participation. It was too much of a drag to listen to them going on and on about it. I mean, if I want to be told how wrong I am, all I've got to do is talk to a grown-up, know what I mean? I don't need it from my posse."

"So you left and went to your mother's?"

"Yes."

"Why didn't you answer your grandmother's calls? It's not like Nashville doesn't have cell service."

"My battery died. But I didn't want to leave until I saw her, you know, just to see if she seemed okay and to make sure she saw the food. It was almost noon before she came stumbling home." She drove on for a little while. "And you have no concept of life on the other side."

The words stung. In spite of an upper middle class upbringing, Sabrina had never considered herself naïve. "I guess not." She murmured the words, more to herself than Brandy. She thought about what Brandy's life must have been like. "How long has it been since you lived with your mom?"

Brandy shrugged. "A while. I lived with my aunt and uncle for a couple of years. They took me in the last time my mother got arrested."

"How did you end up with your grandmother?"

"My aunt became concerned that I was corrupting her kids." She paused, changed lanes, and remained silent for a couple of minutes. Finally, she said, "I guess I can't blame her. Truth is, I probably was corrupting them. My uncle is my mom's half-brother—he was nice enough to fight to keep me for a while. He and my mother don't have any kind of a relationship, so he really didn't owe me anything. Finally, he asked me to find somewhere else."

"Is that when you came to live with your grandmother?"

"Yeah, right around Christmastime." She kept her eyes focused on the road. "That's why I didn't like you so much. You have a mother and a father who are still together, and from what Grandma has said, they make a good living and love you to pieces, but she says you never go home for a visit, even in the summer. Don't you appreciate what you've got?"

"I live with my grandmother because I go to school in her

143

town and because she can use the help around the house. Besides that . . ." Sabrina stopped. There was no reason to go there.

"Besides that, what?"

Sabrina shrugged. "It's hard to be in my hometown, you know. Everyone there had such big expectations for me. Including my father. It's like every time I see him, or one of my old teachers or coaches, well, it's too much a mixture of pity and disappointment. My father, especially. I think he's upset that I lost my scholarship."

"One of the girls who was mean to you while you were at UT, was her name Kayla?"

Sabrina turned to her, stunned to hear that name after all these years. "How did you know that?"

"She spoke to the Fellowship of Christian Runners a few weeks ago. She told her side of that story, about how some slacker got the scholarship that she should have gotten."

The same old pain welled up through the center of Sabrina's chest. "She never did believe it was anything other than me just being lazy and not being fast enough. She was pretty ruthless at times."

"Well, she's coaching up here at Samson Academy and she was talking about how her runners have been dominating at the local races. I say, let's make a plan to beat her in that big Columbia 5K in a couple weeks."

Sabrina looked at Brandy, and for the first time she felt something like a true partnership might be beginning to form. "Sounds like a plan."

"Cool," Brandy said, nodding. "What time do we leave for Atlanta in the morning?"

21

People milled about in groups almost as far as Brandy could see. Some chatted, others stretched. "Who knew there were so many people who like to run?" She shook her head, trying to make sense of it. "What motivates these people?"

Sabrina didn't look around at all—she focused her attention on Brandy. "Lots of reasons. Some people are out here because they're trying to get in shape, some are here because they have a competitive nature, and a few just actually enjoy the process of running."

"I guess. I don't know that any of those reasons would have me out of bed at seven on a Sunday morning."

"So what about you, then? You certainly went far enough out of your way to be here. You can't even blame this one on me—it was your idea."

Brandy had to stop and think about that one for a minute. Why did she fight so hard to get here? Was it so she could have a chance to try this away from the prying eyes of other track team kids? Was it because she needed to prove herself after the last race? Either way, she wasn't going to tell Sabrina all that, so she simply said, "I'm in training, remember?"

"That's another reason there's such a large crowd, I'm guessing. Probably, a lot of these people are here because of the upcoming Peachtree Road Race." Sabrina did look around the crowd now. "Either trying to get in shape so they can actually do it, or maybe looking for a good finish time that will move them into a better start group."

"What's the Peachtree Road Race?"

"The world's largest 10K. It happens right here in Atlanta every Fourth of July. The last number I heard was over sixty thousand runners, so if you think this morning's race is crowded, you haven't seen anything."

"Sixty thousand runners, really? How can you even move?"

"They have different waves. The first group, the runners who might actually win the thing, are released first. Then the next and the next. Still, it's pretty insane." Sabrina was smiling now, shaking her head.

"So you've done it?"

"Yeah." Her smile disappeared. "A few times. I got second in the women's fourteen and under division the year I was fourteen. Then when I was seventeen I got first in the fifteen-to-nineteen-year-old women's division."

"Really?" Brandy looked at Sabrina, wishing she could have known her back then, back when she was at the top of her game. "What was your time, do you remember?"

"Forty-six minutes and something when I was fourteen—I can't remember the seconds. When I was seventeen it was thirty-eight minutes fifty-two seconds."

Brandy paused and then said, "That's about a six-minute mile for the entire course!"

Sabrina cocked her head to the side as if surprised by Brandy's surprise. "I told you I used to be fast."

"I guess." Brandy doubled over and touched the sidewalk,

stretching out her hamstrings, but she was still thinking about Sabrina and what her life must have been like. She decided she had a new respect for someone who could be that good at something and then lose it all, but still go on with life without drowning her sorrows in self-pity or pills. The girl was stronger than she appeared to be on the surface.

"Everyone make your way to the starting line, please." The woman held the bullhorn in one hand, a clipboard in the other. She wore wraparound sunglasses and a yellow visor, in spite of the fact that the sun had barely broken through the overhead cloud layer.

Brandy followed a thousand of her new best running buddies toward the starting area. This was the second when she realized how much she wanted to do well in this race. Not just good enough, but really, really good. Was it because Sabrina had actually brought her here for the weekend, or was it because she was only now beginning to realize what a good runner Sabrina had been? Somehow she felt she owed it to her.

"Pace yourself. Stay steady. Don't overdo it in the beginning no matter how strong the rush of adrenaline." She kept whispering these pieces of advice to herself, hoping it would actually sink in. Maybe this time, without the pressure of performing for anyone she knew, she could pull it off.

Her stomach churned until she had to take deep slow breaths in an effort not to puke right there in front of everyone. Breathe. Relax. Breathe. Relax.

"Well, hello. What are you doing here?"

Brandy couldn't believe her ears, until she turned to see the owner of the voice. Sure enough, same perky smile, same bright eyes, same swinging ponytail. "Erin? What are you doing here?"

"My aunt lives in Atlanta, so she invited me over. This race counts as a qualifier for the Peachtree, and I want to get a good time so I can get in a good starting wave. What about you? Why are you here?"

Brandy shrugged. "Same as you, I guess." There just wasn't any reason to explain it all to her.

"You're going to run in the Peachtree? That's great. Maybe we can drive over together. Wouldn't that be fun?"

"Runners take your marks."

Brandy looked over to Erin. "I'm going to try a different pacing method this time, so I'll just see you at the finish. Okay?"

"Sounds good." Erin nodded, causing her ponytail to swing in agreement.

The horn sounded, and in spite of her perky agreement, Erin stayed right beside Brandy. The first mile came and went, and still Erin remained. Every instinct inside of Brandy wanted to run faster, to push herself past this girl and leave her in the dust. But, she'd learned that lesson the hard way. She was going to stick with a steady pace until it got closer to the end, then she would burn up whatever reserves of energy she had left.

Sabrina always said a runner should use her very last ounce of energy, so there's not even enough left to take another step. The trick was accomplishing this the very second you crossed the finish line. That's what separated a good runner from a great runner.

Just past midway, Erin surged forward. Brandy knew that she could keep up with her if she pushed, but this time she was going to do what Sabrina had told her to do. It grew more and more difficult as Erin's ponytail got further and further ahead in the pack.

Brandy began to strain to see the sign post that was her signal to let go and run hard. She and Sabrina had driven the course yesterday, noting mileage, and then they'd walked the entire length. Sabrina had pointed out things to be aware of: *"Just ahead, the course narrows for a couple dozen yards. So tomorrow, when you see this sidewalk mailbox, I want you to immediately look at who is just ahead of you. Is it someone who's losing steam? If it is, you need to do what it takes to get around them, to make sure you don't get caught behind them for any length of time.*" They'd continued on their journey, with similar tips.

Finally, Sabrina put her hand on the post of a pedestrian crossing sign. "*When you see this, it mean's there's about a half mile to go, so start picking up the pace. Lots of people will have pushed too hard by this point, and you'll be able to blow past them without a lot of effort. Don't push to the point where you won't be able to finish, but push until your leg muscles are burning and begging you to stop.*" Then they'd walked just a little further. "*From here on out, give it everything you've got.*"

The pedestrian crossing loomed just ahead. Brandy quickened her pace. She could still see Erin's ponytail ahead of her, and instead of focusing on the pain or how much course she still needed to eat up, she focused all her thoughts on catching that ponytail. Coach Thompson always said to find someone in front of you and reel 'em in . . . well, that's what Brandy was going to do. Her feet pounded against the pavement faster and harder. Her breathing became loud, but with each exhale she grew just a tiny bit closer to the ponytail. And by the time Brandy reached the give-it-all-you've-got spot, Erin's ponytail bobbed only twenty yards ahead of her.

Every stride hurt more than the last one, but now, with a goal so firmly within her reach, Brandy had reached familiar territory. Her legs burned like fire, but she knew if she pushed through the pain for just a little longer, it would be so worth it. So she concentrated on long strides, standing straight, landing on the ball of her foot, arms straight up—all the things that Sabrina harped about.

The finish came into view with Erin still ten yards in front of her. It was now or never, so she pulled up her last shred of courage from deep inside her and concentrated on moving faster. Wavy lines began to form around the edges of her vision, but still she forced her legs to move faster. With every few strides she was rewarded with a closer view of that ponytail, until she was close enough to reach out and touch Erin's shoulder. Three more yards to the finish, she thought of Sabrina's finish time at the 10K and vowed to make her proud. At the last possible second, she leaned toward the finish line to cross a mere two inches behind Erin.

They made their way through the finish chute, and at the end, Brandy finally collapsed to the ground. Erin leaned over and grabbed her knees, taking deep breaths. She looked up, and when she saw Brandy she sort of laughed—as best a person could laugh with oxygen-starved lungs. Brandy's vision was still wavy, and she wondered if she would ever be able to breathe normally, or even walk on her spaghetti legs again.

Finally, Erin said, "I heard someone coming up behind me. I didn't know it was you, but I'm so glad it was. The clock said 18:16 when we crossed. That's my best time ever—thanks to the sound of you coming from behind. I was determined not to get passed at the end."

"And I was determined to pass you." Brandy managed to get off the ground, although it was difficult. She bent over, pretending to stretch, but it was less about stretching and more about exhaustion. After a couple of minutes, she was able to walk off a cooldown. There were hundreds of people milling around the finish area, but Sabrina did not appear to be among them.

"There's my aunt." Erin waved over to a middle-aged woman whose tailored pants and jacket seemed a bit out of place in this setting. The woman waved back and started toward them. "Do you need us to give you a ride anywhere?"

Brandy shook her head. "Nah. My . . . aunt is here, too. I'll just go find her." Brandy made a quick getaway before Erin asked to meet this nonexistent aunt. She hurried through the crowd, not daring to look back for quite a while.

Finally, on the very outskirts of the crowd, she saw Sabrina sitting on a bench. She had her back turned to the race crowd and was faced toward the distant skyline of downtown Atlanta. "What are you doing way out here?"

"I saw your running buddy from school. I figured she'd be suspicious about me coming to Atlanta to watch a race to write my paper, so it was just easier to blend into the background until she moved on her way."

"You have the natural skill set of a criminal. If your interview doesn't go so well tomorrow, let me know. I could set you up with some people who could have you working in no time."

"Thanks, I'll keep that in mind." Sabrina quirked one eyebrow and grinned. It was a nice change from her usual serious expression. She looked down at her watch and the grin faded. "We need to get moving. We're going to have to hurry to get showered and changed before the second service."

Brandy's legs still felt wobbly and weak. "We could just go back to the condo and take a nap. That sounds good to me."

"Nothing doing. I promised your grandmother if she'd let you make this trip, I would see to it that you made it to church today."

"I won't tell if you don't."

"Not happening. Now get moving." Brandy followed Sabrina toward the car. As much as she really wanted to go back and just lie down for a while, something about the fact that Sabrina kept her word at all costs made her feel a strange warmth. There weren't many people left who were like that. At least not in Brandy's world.

22

Sabrina splashed some tepid water on her face and groaned. Of all the times, why did this recurring cold have to show up the morning of the most important interview of her life? She dried her cheeks with a towel and looked in the mirror to see just how terrible the dark circles under her eyes might be. "You are kidding me."

She dropped the towel on the sink and leaned closer to the mirror. And why, of all mornings, would there be a large zit on the left side of her nose? She shook her head and pulled out her face scrub, determined to minimize the damage in any way she could. She popped a couple of Tylenol and got busy getting ready.

By the time she opened the tall glass doors of the Kershaw Building, the Tylenol had kicked in, clearing her head slightly, and the side of her nose was a little less like Rudolph the Reindeer and a little more like pink bubblegum. Neither situation was perfect, but she intended to make the best of it.

She rode the elevator with a dozen other people, none of them looking at one another. By the time she reached the twenty-fifth floor, there were only three people left: two middle-aged men in business suits and an older woman with a cane. Sabrina doubted these were her competition.

The doors opened with a ding, and she walked through to find herself standing before a large reception desk, all done in glass and blue granite. Original pieces of art hung on every wall, a couple of life-size sculptures flanked the doors on each side of the lobby, and an exquisite chandelier of blue and green glass curling out in every direction hung directly above her. Remembering similar works from an introductory art class, she had no doubt it was a Dale Chihuly. Everything about this place screamed modern, meticulous, and successful.

She thought about the brochure she'd brought in her bag and suddenly it seemed old-fashioned and amateurish. Why hadn't she spent just a little longer on it? By the time she'd taken the dozen steps to the receptionist's desk, she could feel little trembles that started in her fingers and moved all the way down to her toes. "Hello. I'm Sabrina Rice, I have an appointment with Ms. Davenport."

The woman at the desk, her glossy black hair pulled back in a sleek ponytail, didn't bother to consult a computer screen or even a handwritten list. She simply nodded and smiled. "Yes, welcome, Ms. Rice. We're expecting you. Come with me, please." She stood and walked around the counter, her footsteps silent in spite of the fact that when she emerged into full view, Sabrina could see her four-inch heels.

The trembles increased, and a dull, churning nausea began to burn at the pit of her stomach. While Sabrina had researched all about the work and scope of Grace Rose, somehow she had never fully understood the utter magnificence of this place. What had possessed her to believe that she could fit in here?

"This is your stop." The receptionist opened the door to a

small conference room. A rectangular mahogany table surrounded by leather chairs filled the space. At each seat there was a water pitcher and a heavy glass with the GR symbol engraved on it. "Take a seat at the end. They'll be with you in just a moment." And with that, she closed the door, leaving Sabrina alone with all her inadequacies.

Two hours of information blast had taken its toll until Sabrina wasn't certain she could even string one more sentence together. Her head was swimming in a sea of questions, discussions, tours, and company facts. Various people of varying positions in the company had come in and out all morning. Some to ask questions, some to simply convey information. Their names and faces were starting to blur, but Sabrina struggled to keep them all straight—at a place like this it would be expected that you could remember names.

Candace Davenport reentered the conference room, prompting Sam . . . Sal . . . no, Sage from accounting, to stand up. He reached out to shake Sabrina's hand. "Nice to have met you."

She concentrated on keeping a firm handshake. "Nice to have met you, as well." She tried to smile, but her whole body ached and she wasn't certain the muscles in her cheeks were fully cooperating.

Candace, as she'd insisted that Sabrina call her, took the seat beside her. "Have we managed to overwhelm you yet?"

Again, Sabrina attempted a smile. "Almost."

"Well, we've just about finished up here. There is one other question I wanted to ask before you go. There's something in your resumé that I feel certain will come up during our intern-hiring discussions, and I want to get the facts directly from you."

"Okay." The nauseous feeling kicked up again.

"Your freshman year of college you went to the University of Tennessee, and as I understand it, you were on a full-ride, four-year scholarship."

Oh no. Not this, anything but this. "Yes, that's true."

"Might I ask what provoked you to switch to Southern Tennessee State your sophomore year?"

"Well . . . I . . ." Sabrina knew she was stammering, an absolute point killer, but she hadn't counted on this question and had not prepared herself to answer it. She studied her hands, locked together on the table in front of her, then forced herself to look back up at Candace. "I had some . . . physical problems that prevented me from being able to fulfill my obligations to the track team."

"I see. But you don't see those—physical problems, did you call them—as something that would prevent you from fulfilling your obligations here? Is there anything about you that we need to be aware of?"

Sabrina shook her head. "I have rheumatoid arthritis. That keeps me from running, but it doesn't keep me from being a hard worker."

Candace looked long and hard at Sabrina, her hazel eyes squinted. "All right, then." There was nothing in her tone that revealed whether this last statement was said in acceptance or outright dismissal. She reached out her hand. "Nice to have met you. We'll be making our selections in the next couple of weeks. You'll hear from us soon after."

"Thank you."

Sabrina walked back down the hallway, out through the reception area, and down the elevators, having no idea what kind of impression she might have just made. She could only hope it was better than she felt.

23

Sabrina awoke, happy to have slept in her own bed again. She wanted to hurry and get to school a little early. Even though they'd talked multiple times, she hadn't seen Koen in several days and she missed him.

She made her way to the bathroom and looked in the mirror. *Oh no*. The pimple from yesterday was back, and it looked worse. She leaned closer to get a better look. This seemed more like a blister or an infected sore. Strange. And gross. And why now?

A few minutes later, she went downstairs and found Nana sitting at the breakfast table.

"Morning, dear. It's good to have you back home again."

"It's good to be back." They chatted about the trip and how the interview went as Sabrina poured herself a glass of milk, Nana positive as always. Sabrina grabbed a banana from the fruit bowl and then settled herself at the table.

"Well, Sabrina, what happened to your nose?"

"I don't know. It's weird, isn't it? I must have scratched it or something."

Nana leaned closer and looked over the top of her glasses. "I do believe you've got a case of impetigo. Haven't seen it in years, but I'm sure that's what it is."

"Impetigo?"

Nana shrugged. "A skin infection that pops up on the side of the nose—happens a lot to kids. Best I remember, you put some Neosporin on it and it'll clear up."

"Hmm." Sabrina reached up and felt the blisters on the side of her nose. "Hopefully it will clear up fast."

"Doesn't take too long, best I remember."

Sabrina hoped she was right.

She did her best to minimize the apparent damage with a liberal application of Neosporin and some makeup. Not a great way to start her day, but things could only go up from there.

When she arrived, a little less early than she'd hoped, to psych class, she immediately spotted Koen on the back row of the stadium-style classroom. Since the doors were in the back of the class, he would have no idea she'd entered the room. He was leaning forward, talking to one of his friends in the next row until they both erupted in laughter. Sabrina started toward him and just then he turned. He rewarded her with his most winning grin, and reached over and turned the chair beside him out to face her.

"Attached chairs make it impossible to be a gentleman in this particular case. I hope you'll accept my best attempt."

She slid into the offered seat and noticed again just how perfectly his blond hair swept across his forehead and framed his perfect face. "I'll take it."

"I'm saying you're not allowed to go away for the weekend again. It's far too boring here without you. I'm beginning to find out that my guys just aren't as much fun as they used to be."

"Are you saying you prefer me to Jared?" Koen's best friend

was a hulking, adorable goof-off that was universally loved across campus. "Wow, I think I'm flattered."

"And you should be." He reached over and tucked a stray hair behind Sabrina's ear. "And speaking of Jared, he is having everyone over on Saturday to watch March Madness. I told him we'd bring the chips and some two-liters. So, I'll pick you up around two. Okay?"

Sabrina hesitated. She knew that the Tennessee men's basketball team was playing in Saturday's game. "I . . . uh, well, I'm not sure. I want to, it's just that I think I might be helping my grandmother with some yard work on Saturday afternoon."

He cocked his head, looked at her for a minute, then nodded slowly. "I see." He turned toward the front of the classroom and shook his head a single time, as if just figuring something out.

"What? What do you see?"

"I guess I've been taking a little too much for granted here. Sabrina, if you don't want to see me anymore then just say so."

"No, that's not what I mean at all, it's simply that I . . ." She started to try to explain her way out of it, but she knew it was a flimsy excuse. She supposed she could tell him that she didn't like to watch basketball on TV, but that sounded even weaker. "I . . ."

He was looking at her, waiting for an answer. His expression clearly said that he wouldn't believe her, no matter what sort of excuse she came up with.

"I just meant that, you know, my grandmother has been wanting to get her vegetable garden started, and since I was out of town last weekend, I don't want to just leave her to do it all herself. Maybe I could meet up with you later, huh?" And there it was. The brilliant idea that would solve her problems. She would stay busy until the game was over, then join them at Jared's.

"Really? That's really all it is?"

"Of course. I can't wait to spend some time with you that

doesn't involve studying or quick bites of dinner between studying."

"I have to admit, you scared me there for a minute." He smiled again, just enough to show his dimple. "Hey, I've got an even better idea. What if I come over a little early and help the two of you? Since I grew up on a farm, I make quick work of vegetable gardens. Then we'll be able to go over to Jared's together in time for the game."

Great. Just great. Sabrina knew that if she refused now, it would be a direct slap to Koen. So she took a deep breath, and in spite of everything that she did not like about his plan, she simply smiled and said, "What a wonderful idea."

"Okay everyone, game starts in sixty seconds. Get your boo-tays inside." Jared's booming voice not only caught the attention of the twenty-some-odd college kids present, but likely was heard by the neighbors across the parking lot, and maybe even the Quick Mart on the other side of the street.

Sabrina began to panic when Koen pulled on her hand. "Let's hurry inside and get a good seat. Last time I ended up on the floor, and believe me, Jared's carpet is something I don't care to be up close and personal with ever again."

"Uh, why don't you go on inside. I'll stay out here and make sure they don't need any help."

"Hey, Jar, you need any help out here?" Koen called over to his friend.

"Nope. I'm going inside to watch the game. I'll fire up the grill just before halftime."

Koen smiled at her. "There you have it. No help needed here." He tugged her toward the sliding door that led from Jared's patio area to his living room, and before Sabrina could think of another protest, she was seated on the couch beside Koen, front and center for TV viewing.

A couple of announcers in dark sports coats and ties were talking about the upcoming game and the match-ups at point guard. Sabrina turned away from the screen, trying to find anything else at all to focus on. The carpet was dark brown shag, and looked as though it might have been installed when these apartments were built—some fifty years ago. The walls were probably painted white—it was hard to say for sure with probably a decade's worth of smudges and scrapes. Several posters hung around the room—a guy flying through the air on a dirt bike, jet skis sending up a spray of water, and a couple of bikini-clad girls on a sunset beach. Jared's popularity, plus the location of this townhouse unit with its large backyard, made this the gathering spot for most notable social occasions for Jared's circle of friends, in spite of the run-down condition of the place.

"Tip-off time. Yeah!" A large athletic-looking boy who was sitting in one of the vinyl recliners thrust his hand in the air. "Come on, Tennessee." A chorus of cheers and general agreement sounded around the room as the game was ready to commence.

Sabrina turned toward the television just in time to see the flash of orange jersey, as the center reached higher than his opponent and knocked the ball toward his teammate. In a flash, the men in orange worked their way down the court, passing it a few times, before the ball whipped to number 33 just outside the three-point line. He rose up for a shot and nailed it. Everyone cheered and instantly the TV went to replay, this time zooming in on the shooter as he released.

Sam.

They had shared a couple of classes freshman year. Although *friends* might be too strong of a word, they had studied together and run in a similar circle of friends. The sight of him now, wearing the colors that were so familiar . . .

Sabrina turned her attention to the window, its metal casing even grimier than the glass, and began to concentrate on her breathing. This was the one thing that had remained useful past her running years. Breath control could get you through seemingly unendurable pain.

The room erupted into cheers. "Yeah, that's what I'm talking about."

Sabrina didn't look back to the TV; it wasn't necessary. She looked at some birds perched on the electrical wire just outside the window and started counting them. *One, two, three, four*, one flew away but another two landed, *five, six, seven, eight*, but wait, had she already counted that one?

"Oh man, did you see that?" Koen leaned toward the TV. "I can't believe that, can you?"

Sabrina looked at him. "Huh? Oh, no, I sure can't."

"Miss Rice, are you daydreaming out the window? In the middle of the game?" Koen grinned at her, and it took every bit of her inner strength to smile back.

"Uh, guilty, I guess."

"You better play closer attention, because there'll be a quiz at halftime." He put his arm on the couch behind her and turned his attention back to the game.

Somehow she managed to stare blankly at the TV, send her thoughts elsewhere, and mostly ignore what was happening in the game. She focused her attention on Koen sitting this close, on how right it felt to have him near. This worked pretty well until the band started playing "Rocky Top." The sound of the fight song that was so much a part of her past broke through the last of her strength. She jumped up from the couch, mumbled something about coming right back, and bolted from the room to the backyard.

She made it around the far corner to the side yard before she lost the battle to blink back the tears. There, standing in the narrow area between the fence and the side of the building, sharing the space with a large recycling container and two trash cans, she leaned against the wall. *Get a grip, Sabrina. Get it now!* Through sheer force of will, she somehow regained her composure within the course of the first minute, maybe two.

She stared at the beige paint on the wood fence separating this backyard from the one beside it, feeling stronger with each breath. All she needed to do now was to formulate an excuse to give Koen about what had happened. She got the sudden urge to see the sky? She was claustrophobic? She couldn't think of one single plausible explanation that didn't make her sound like she was a nervous and emotional wreck—which she more or less was, she supposed.

Might as well go face it. She pushed away from the wall and turned toward the backyard. Maybe she'd tell him she thought she'd left her cell phone out here and had come to look for it. It was a weak excuse at best, but it was all she had. Yes, that might work. She rounded the corner, thinking through details she could add to make it more believable.

"Hello there." Koen was leaning against the wall on the other side of the corner, his arms folded across his chest, his left foot propped against the building.

"Hi." Sabrina stopped walking and stared down at her feet. "Sorry about running out like that. I thought I'd left my cell phone out here, so I came looking for it."

"You thought you'd left your cell phone on the recycling bins?"

"Well, sometimes I—"

"Sabrina." He cupped her chin with his left hand, lifting her head until she had no choice but to look at him. His perfect face, his complete and utter perfection in all things . . . She tried to pull away but he held her. "It's time that you told me what's going on."

"It's nothing really. I'm sorry I interrupted everything. . . . Please, let's go enjoy the game with your friends. We can talk about it later."

"No, I want to talk about it now." He reached down and took her hand, then led her back through the side yard, out the gate, and around to the front of the apartment complex. "Let's go for a walk."

"But you'll miss the game."

"Doesn't matter. Now start talking."

The humiliation of what she had to tell him was almost more than she could bear, but she supposed it was best to just get it done. "I've known since I was twelve that I wanted to be an Olympic runner. . . ." Once she started, the story just tumbled out of her until there was nothing left to say, no tears left to cry. Just nothing. Or so she thought.

"I think you left out a few details." His voice was soft.

Sabrina looked at him, sniffling. "What do you mean?"

"You didn't mention breaking any records. I happen to know for a fact that you broke several."

Sabrina planted her feet on the sidewalk, too stunned to keep moving. "How do you know that?"

He ducked his head and grinned. "I . . . uh . . . sort of Googled you last week."

"You what?"

He shrugged and looked at her. "You were so secretive about everything, but it was more than obvious that there was some sort of weirdness with you and running. When I finally couldn't take the not knowing anymore, I decided to do some Internet creeping."

"So you knew everything already?"

"No. I knew about your running. Lots of wins. Several records. I didn't know why you'd stopped. Until now." He kissed her forehead. "Are you mad?"

Was she? She pictured him sitting at his computer, typing in her name, clicking on Search. Reading through page after page of her life, eyes squinted in concentration, head shaking because it made no sense. And of course it made no sense to him because she'd been so defensive anytime running had come up. At least he'd cared enough to look for answers instead of just walking away in frustration.

"No. I'm not mad." She smiled up into his blue eyes. "Just don't do it again."

"Deal." They started walking again, until they reached Koen's truck. He stopped, leaned against it, holding onto her hands.

"So, about the game . . . I know I'm being a baby, but somehow it bothers me to watch college sports on television now. Especially Tennessee sports. I'm happy for all of them who are doing so well, really I am, it's just . . . like having an in-my-face reminder of what I've lost. It makes me sad." Sabrina knew it sounded weak, and pathetic, but he deserved to hear the truth for all its ugliness. She was every bit as needy and whiny as Lindy had ever been, that much was certain.

"So, that's it then." Koen pulled her into his arms and kissed her, long and soft. Finally he pulled away and said, "Let's drive out to the lake and go for a walk."

"What about the game?"

"What game?" He grinned at her, that irresistible dimple working its usual charm.

"Really, I'm fine. I promise, we can go back in. I don't want you to miss it."

"And I promise if we go for a walk around the lake right now, I'll be fine. Now, let's go." He opened the passenger door to the truck and held it for her.

"Are you sure?" she asked as she slid into the seat.

"Never been more sure about anything." He leaned in and kissed her again, then closed the door and walked around to his own side.

24

Brandy more or less stumbled down the front porch steps, and although her feet moved her in the general direction of Sabrina's house, every step felt like a million pounds, and achy, and like something she didn't want to repeat. When she turned the corner, Sabrina was, as usual, sitting on the retaining wall with her laptop open, working on some sort of school project or other. She looked up as Brandy approached.

"Hmm, you seem a bit sluggish today." She closed the computer. "Everything all right?"

"Yeah, I don't know what's wrong with me. I just woke up this morning and everything feels dead and sore, and I just want to go back to bed." Brandy looked at Sabrina and braced herself for the "you've got to push through this" talk that she was certain was coming.

"I remember those days. I called them my heavy days. There was never a pattern that I could figure for why they showed up when they did. It wasn't necessarily after a hard day of training.

A lot of coaches will tell you that you've got to push extra hard on these kinds of days."

"That's what I was assuming you were going to say." With the Columbia 5K less than a week away, Brandy's training sessions had grown longer and more intense. Part of this was Sabrina's doing, but now that she understood more about what was at stake, Brandy had refused to settle for only Sabrina's plan. She was going to do whatever it took to beat that Kayla girl's stable of overindulged runners. She always forced herself to go one more lap, or two more sprints, or whatever the torture of the day was. "We're short on time. I can't afford to slack off now."

"I've never been much of one to hold to that theory. It seemed to me, when I had a heavy day, I knew I couldn't let myself go back to bed, because that was setting up a precedent of quitting. But what I would do is run my course, but not even bother to keep time. Instead, I would try to remember what it was I liked about running in the first place. I would take it slow, sometimes even stop and walk a little if things were all that bad. Usually, by the next day, I felt fine again." She made a show of putting the stopwatch away in her sweatshirt pocket. "Just take some slow laps around the block. Don't push unless you feel like it."

Brandy stretched for a few minutes, happy that Sabrina was going to back off for today, but somehow frustrated by it, too. What if today's slacking was the thing that made her do poorly in the race? She took off in a slow jog toward the corner. What must Sabrina have been like back in her running days? Did she really wake up feeling sluggish and take it easy for a day? It didn't seem likely—she was always so overly motivated about everything.

Brandy's hips ached and so did her lower back as she took the next corner, and she *really* wanted to stop. But she didn't, not yet. Did Sabrina's joints ache like this every single minute of every single day? Once again, the urge to stop pulled hard at her, but once again, she forced herself to keep going. Step by step, just a little at a time, she was going to get through this. She supposed this is how Sabrina survived from day to day.

Now, for the first time, it occurred to Brandy—she wanted to be like Sabrina.

Sabrina attempted to take a sip of Diet Coke, but she'd chewed on the end of the straw to the point where it would no longer conduct liquid. She observed the mangled piece of plastic, all the little tooth-sized craters crushing the top, and knew it was a hopeless cause. She pulled out the straw, flipped it upside down, put it back in her drink, and resumed chewing.

"So, are you going to tell me what's got you so worked up, or are you just going to leave me to wonder?" Koen pulled the back of Sabrina's right hand to his lips.

"Hmm?" She reached up and touched his cheek, the very touch of him calming her, if only a little. "Oh, sorry, I guess I'm a little out of it."

"Not out of it, I'd say freaked out is more like it. What's up? I mean, you're always uptight—in your cute and adorable way, of course—but tonight you've been way beyond the usual. Are you nervous about the race this weekend? I'm sure Brandy will do fine."

"No . . . yes . . . no . . . it's not the race, exactly. It's my parents."

"Your parents?"

"Yeah, Mom called this afternoon. It seems that Nana has been waxing eloquent about what a great job I'm doing coaching Brandy, etcetera, etcetera, and they've decided to come spend the weekend here and go to watch the race."

"Really? Cool." Koen continued to look into her eyes, as if searching for an answer there but not finding it. He finally wrinkled his forehead and leaned back a little. "You like your parents, right? Why has this got you so wound up?"

"I love my parents, they are terrific." Sabrina looked at their hands, entwined across the table. "My mom is my best friend. And my dad, well, he's great, a terrific father really."

"Sounds good. I'm still not seeing the problem here."

"My dad is very type A."

Koen snorted. "That's one trait that runs in the family."

Sabrina looked up at him, surprised "What do you mean?"

He took on a high-pitched voice and waved his hand in a feminine sort of way. "I have simply got to make an A on this test, so I do not have time to do anything but study. Okay, a five-minute break with lighthearted conversation is allowed every three hours, but other than that, I must study."

Sabrina laughed. "Okay, maybe I'm type A in the driven sort of way. Dad is type A in the "nothing is ever good enough" sort of way. It's his way of showing his love, of pushing me to achieve more than I would achieve on my own, I know this. But it just puts a lot of pressure on me when he's here, because I'll be looking over my shoulder the whole time, wondering what more I should be doing, or wondering what it is I'm doing wrong."

"I see." Koen nodded and leaned toward her across the snack shop table. "Well, I'm just going to have to spend extra energy this week reminding you of how fabulous you are."

Sabrina smiled and leaned toward him. "I'm so glad to have you on my side."

"I'm glad to be here."

She sighed. Koen's nearness, his warmth, his beautiful blue eyes looking into hers. Nothing else mattered. Sabrina wanted to stay just like that forever. Unfortunately, her practical nature eventually overrode the perfection of the moment, reminding her of the rest of reality. She leaned back against her seat but continued to hold his hand.

"Hopefully you'll still be glad after this weekend. I'm counting on you to join us for dinner at Nana's house on Friday night?"

For the briefest fraction of time, a look of alarm flitted across his face, but much to Koen's credit he immediately put on his most winning grin. "I can't think of anywhere else I'd rather be."

"Yeah, we'll see if you still say that after Friday night."

"Sounds like an interesting challenge."

"I think so." She pulled the straw out of her cup and took a sip directly from the styrofoam cup. "But for now, we need to refocus on our psych paper. After all," she said in a fake high voice, imitating the one he'd just used, "I simply must get an A on this project."

25

Sabrina threw her backpack over her right shoulder and made her way toward Campus Eats. Today she was thankful for the part-time on-campus job. To go straight home now and just wait for tonight's gathering, well . . . just the thought made her shudder. In years past, she would have gone for a long run, kept going until every twitch of anxiety dissolved into muscle exhaustion so complete she couldn't even feel the tension. For now, she had a job to do and she was glad for it. Busyness was her friend.

Brandy *had* to do well in the race tomorrow. If Sabrina's father was coming all the way out here, he expected nothing less than first place. Her mother would have more realistic expectations, but clearly, everyone expected Brandy to be amazing, thus demonstrating Sabrina's effectiveness. If Brandy failed to perform, it'd be chalked up as Sabrina's failure. She walked behind the counter and put her backpack in a bottom cabinet. The line at the counter was five people deep and that was a good thing. Hopefully they would be followed by many others.

Three hours later, her hope had been realized. Her back and knees hurt from standing, and her muscles ached with exhaustion from constant motion. It couldn't have been better. Sometimes things just worked out right.

Sabrina had retrieved her backpack and started for the door, thankful for those hours of blissful escape, when little nervous twitches started in her stomach. Apparently she wasn't completely exhausted. Every step she took toward the door increased the nerves. Maybe she should check to see if her journalism professor had posted grades from this week's project yet. Mostly in the interest of stalling, she walked over to the nearest booth, sat down, and opened her laptop.

No grades were posted. Might as well check email while she was here. She opened Outlook, which loaded a dozen or so new emails. She scanned the list, and when she saw another message from Rita Leyva she clicked on it.

Dear Sabrina,

I hope you are still prayerfully considering the position I spoke to you about. I'm currently in South Africa and God has brought you to mind a number of times. Would you be open to another phone conversation next week? I would be happy to talk through any additional thoughts or questions you may have encountered since we last spoke. Anytime Tuesday or Wednesday of next week would work for me. Let me know your availability and we will set it up.

Looking forward to speaking with you!

In Him,
Rita Leyva

Rita Leyva was persistent, Sabrina had to give her that. She was so utterly convinced that Sabrina was the right person for this job. Sabrina tried to remember the last time she'd been so completely convinced of anything being absolutely true. She didn't have to think long. She knew it was back when she thought she was headed for the Olympics.

But she'd been wrong. Dead wrong. Strength of conviction didn't make something true.

For just a second, a vision of Brandy running in red, white, and blue flashed through her mind. Sabrina snorted at the thought. Wouldn't that be ironic?

She walked out to her car, supposing that she should be grateful for the mini distraction. It was all silly, really, her being so worked up. It was going to be fine, of course it was. What could go wrong? Nothing. Nothing at all. It was going to be fine.

The short drive home was long enough to give herself a little pep talk. At least she'd have Koen at dinner tonight. With him around, she'd be somewhat distracted, and she knew her parents would like him. What wasn't to like?

As she pulled into the drive, she wondered if he'd called that afternoon. She dug her phone out of her backpack. According to the screen, she had three missed calls and one new voice mail, none from a number she recognized. She pressed the button and listened.

Hi, Sabrina. It's Candace Davenport from Grace Rose PR. I am pleased to let you know you've made the short list. There is a slight possibility that we will do one more round of interviews in the next few weeks, but this is unlikely, and at most a formality. I was hoping to give you this news personally, but as we have a client event tonight and I didn't get you live, I wanted to at least let you know. Please call me on Monday and we will talk through details. I look forward to working with you.

Sabrina stared at the phone in her hand in numb disbelief. The unbelievable had happened, and what perfect timing. *Wow. Wow. Wow.* Her dreams, her new life, it was all falling into place. She climbed out of the car and ran toward the house. This would be a great way to start this weekend off. She pulled open the front door and ran into the living room. "I have the most amazing news."

The room was empty and dark. "Hello?" She went through the house until she finally saw Nana and her parents in the backyard, checking out the fledgling vegetable garden. She started to run out and scream her news at the top of her lungs. Then she had a better idea.

She'd wait until tomorrow. Until after the race. It would give them twice the reasons to celebrate.

Or soften the blow if things didn't go so well. Oh, how she hoped and prayed that would not be the case.

26

Brandy took another bite of spaghetti, sneaking another glance as she did at Sabrina across the table, talking with her father. She seemed really uptight tonight. In fact, she'd been like this ever since she'd found out her parents were coming this weekend, but even after an hour Brandy still couldn't figure out what made Sabrina so tense. They smiled a lot. Dressed nice. Nobody yelled. She couldn't imagine them disappearing to go on a major drug binge overnight, or vanishing with the last of the food for the next week. She shook her head at the thought; upper-middle-class families had no concept of true stress.

That Koen guy seemed all right. He was chatting with Sabrina's grandmother, talking about some old movie or other that they'd both seen. He seemed pretty genuine about it—not like he was just kissing up to get on her good side or anything, although maybe he was. One thing for sure, he was hot. Not in the buff football player kind of way, but more like a pop star. Sabrina had good taste in men, which surprised Brandy more than a little. She was pretty enough and all, but she seemed so . . . dull. Everything was work, work, work.

"So, Brandy, tell me about you. What kinds of things do you enjoy besides running?" Sabrina's mother was the word *cute* wrapped up in a tiny middle-aged package. Her black hair had just a hint of red to it, and just enough curl that it made her ponytail a bit frizzy—which totally suited her. She was thin, pretty, and stylish in an understated sort of way. Brandy wondered what it would be like to have a mother like this—one that you never had to hide from your friends.

"Oh, you know, the usual." Brandy didn't think Sabrina's mother would approve of what she enjoyed—not that she'd enjoyed any of it in the last couple of months.

"What kind of music do you like?" Her southern drawl was just like everything about her, understated and perfect.

"Rock. Hip-hop." Again, answers she doubted would meet approval. Time to turn the conversation. "How about you, Mrs. Rice?"

"Please, call me Cookie. Mrs. Rice sounds old." She cupped her hands around her mouth and leaned closer to whisper, "And makes me think of my mother-in-law, whom I prefer not to be compared to."

"Cookie? That's your name?" Brandy knew the question was probably rude, but how could she not ask it?

"That's what everyone calls me. My real name's Bernadette, of all things. When I was little I couldn't pronounce it, and neither could anyone else under the age of ten. It seems I always walked around with a graham cracker in my hand—I called them cookies—and it stuck."

"Nice." Brandy realized that it really was nice. A vision passed through her mind of Cookie standing on the sidelines, cheering Sabrina on, smiling and clapping the entire time. How nice it must have been for Sabrina. "I bet you've watched more than your share of 5Ks over the years, huh?"

Cookie glanced toward Sabrina and took a sip of her ice water. "You know what? It never really occurred to me until you asked the question, but I guess tomorrow's race will be the first one I've ever watched."

"Really? I guess I just assumed . . ." Brandy felt an odd sense of loss as her dream of the perfect family dropped a few degrees. "I just thought with Sabrina being a runner and all . . . Well, I suppose they're not that exciting to watch from a single spot on the sidelines."

"Oh, I watched her school races, yes, if that's what you meant. But never something like tomorrow's run. I was too busy running in them."

This answer more than surprised Brandy. "Really? You *ran* in them? With Sabrina?"

She laughed. "Technically, yes, I guess you could say we ran together. But she always finished fifteen or twenty minutes ahead of me. She would then plant herself near the finish line, and when she saw me coming, she'd run out to join me and cheer me on to run a little faster to the end." She smiled as she recounted this, but her eyes grew misty. "I always loved that."

Brandy could picture the scene. It made her . . . homesick . . . for something she'd never had. What would that feel like? "Do you still run sometimes?"

Sabrina's mom shook her head. "Never."

"Really? Didn't you enjoy it?"

"Oh, I enjoyed it. Quite a lot, actually. But, after Sabrina . . ." She shook her head and looked toward Sabrina then, confirming that she was involved in another conversation before continuing. "Well, when it became apparent that things weren't going to work out for her and running, she and I entered a local 5K together. By that point, one of her knees was bone on bone, so she couldn't do anything but walk. I wanted to walk with her, but she insisted that

I go on ahead and get a good time. So I went ahead and ran my race, then stood near the finish line like she'd always done for me.

"When she finally rounded the corner, dead last, I could tell, by the look on her face she was near tears. She told me later that a car had driven past her, and a young man had leaned out the window and yelled, 'Hey slowpoke, need a ride?'" She wiped at her eyes and looked at Brandy. "She was so devastated, she's never done another 5K since. And I've never run another step. I'm sure that young man has no idea how badly his words hurt, how much they still hurt, but it does make me wonder what would possess a person to say such a thing."

Brandy focused her attention on rolling a meatball around on her plate. It sounded just like something she and her friends would do and she knew it. She looked toward Sabrina and thought about all the things she had gone through. It was so unfair in so many ways—different ways than Brandy's life was unfair, but unfair just the same. "The thing is, to look at her, you'd never know anything was wrong with her. I'm sure that guy had no idea."

"You'd be amazed at some of the comments that poor kid has endured for just that reason." Cookie shook her head, then looked toward Brandy and reached out to touch her arm. "I'm so glad she has you. She needs running in her life, although she's never realized it. It's been a part of her for so long, then it was just gone. I'm glad you're here now to give that part back to her."

Brandy had never felt more unworthy in her entire life.

Brandy paced back and forth in her room, nerves zapping through her and making it impossible to think about lying down, much less sleep. She'd seen the look on Sabrina's face when she was talking to her father tonight and had heard her mother's story. How was it even possible to begin to measure up to the expectations they all placed on her—that she placed on herself? "I can't do it."

Of course she couldn't beat the Samson Academy kids. She couldn't even beat Erin Methvin from her own team. What if she got nervous and ran too fast in the beginning again? What if she completely fell apart? What if . . .

Unable to stare at the shabby wallpaper in her room for another minute, Brandy did something she hadn't done in a couple of months. She slid open the window, taking care to do it quietly, and climbed out. Maybe a walk around the block would help. Or just a slow jog? That's what a real runner would do, right?

Yes. That had always calmed her nerves in the past.

She stretched out for a minute or two, not wanting to do something stupid and pull a muscle at this point. Finally, she stood up and began a slow pace in the opposite direction from the house where Sabrina and her family were all sound asleep by now. They were warm and comfortable in their beds, dreaming of fast times and victory and glory for tomorrow. It was best to avoid that area altogether.

After three or four blocks, she felt a little better and since she was headed in the general direction of town, she felt safe despite the late hour. There were plenty of cars driving past, and on the next street over she knew the parking lots were still half full at Walmart and a couple of fast-food places.

She heard a car coming up behind her. The headlights lit the path before her, showing her the cracks in the sidewalk. She sensed the car was slowing, and the fact that it didn't soon pass her only confirmed her suspicion. The skin prickled at the back of her neck, but she told herself she was being silly. It was likely just a family pulling up in front of their house after dinner or a movie. Then she heard the engine almost idling, it was going so slow behind her.

Finally, she couldn't take it anymore and she ventured a glance over her shoulder, prepared to make an all-out run for it if necessary.

When she saw the jacked-up blue Camaro just over her left shoulder she almost wept with relief. She stopped running and approached the passenger-side window, taking deep breaths. "Hey."

Samantha was in the passenger seat of Janie's car. She lowered the window. "Kind of late for a run."

"Yeah." Brandy tried to act nonchalant. "Bored, I guess."

"We can fix that. We're just heading out to Charlie's house for a little while. Hop in."

"Nah, I've got to get back."

"What, you've forgotten all your friends now? What's the deal?"

"I'm training, all right? You know that doing this running thing is keeping me out of juvie right now. I got a race tomorrow, so I'm just out working off a few nerves."

"Come on. Just for a little while. A couple hours at Charlie's and I guarantee you that your nerves'll feel better."

Brandy knew what she should say. She knew exactly what she needed to do. But the offer of almost instant relief . . . it wasn't like she had to do anything. It would be good to see everyone again— just a distraction, that's all she needed. "Maybe just for a half hour or so. I can't stay long. I've got to get up early tomorrow."

"Not a prob. You let us know when you want to come back, we'll bring you right up to your doorstep. Promise." Samantha opened the passenger side door, stepped out, and leaned the front seat forward.

Brandy looked into the darkness of the back seat, knew what was waiting for her if she didn't turn for home right now. *Go back, go back.* She glanced down the road in the direction from which she'd come, knowing what awaited her there. More pacing. More nerves. No sleep.

She climbed into the back seat. "Crank up the tunes."

27

A long yellow banner announced *Sign-ins Here* in bright red letters. Beneath that, in a smaller font, there were three distinct groupings, A–G, H–O, P–Z. Beneath each sat a smiling race volunteer who marked off names and handed out numbers, the lines three or four people deep at all stations. Sabrina found herself frantically scanning the entire scene, desperate for a glimpse of Brandy. Where was she? And why wasn't she answering her cell?

Since there were several hundred people here, it was possible that she'd just missed her in the chaos, right? She meandered through the crowd, spotting several kids that she recognized from the local track team. Over to one side waited a group of maybe a dozen runners, all dressed in cardinal-red shirts and black running shorts. Sabrina didn't have to see what was written on their shirts to know exactly who they were. Samson Academy kids.

Sure enough, Kayla was standing at the front of the group, directing pre-race stretches, giving a pep talk. Today would be a big day for her.

Sabrina knew the thought was wrong, selfish even, but what she wouldn't give to see Brandy beat a few of those kids. That would take Kayla down a notch.

She looked at her watch again. There was still a half hour before the race, but Brandy knew that she was supposed to be in Columbia before now. You never arrived at a race at the last minute. You got there early, signed in, stretched out, and took any of the late arrival kind of stress out of it. They'd talked about it numerous times.

Coming in separate cars had been a bad idea. Sabrina should never have let them talk her into this, in spite of the fact that Brandy and her grandmother were going to visit some cousins after the race. She should have insisted that Brandy ride with her and let Mrs. Jenkins ride with her family, then they could switch after it was all over.

Sabrina walked through the crowd again, searching, but finding no one. She called Brandy's cell phone again, which went directly to voice mail. Again. Her parents and grandmother were standing together over near the start line, so she walked over to join them. "I can't find her."

"I'm sure they're here somewhere. Maudie is always on time." Nana's tone didn't quite match the confidence of her words.

"Your grandmother just hasn't stopped talking about what a good job you're doing with that young lady." Dad looked at his own watch, but then put his arm around Sabrina. "I'm thinking, how about I take the entire group out for a big victory celebration? We can go to the nicest place in town—your pick."

"Dad, victory sounds like a bit high of a goal. A good finish is what we're hoping for here. Brandy is still new to all this."

"Bah. I know you better than that. I'm sure you've got her trained up and ready to take this race by storm."

And there it was. Dad's expectations spelled out, with him

seemingly the only person who didn't realize how unattainable they were. At this point, Sabrina's only goal was Brandy's arrival in time for the race.

The minutes ticked by. The line at the sign-in table began to dwindle, so Sabrina made her way over. "Can you tell me if Brandy Philip has checked in yet?"

The woman at the table flipped through a couple of pages on the clipboard in front of her, then ran her finger down the page. "Philip, Brandy. Nope. Not checked in yet."

"Make your way to the starting line, please." The announcement crackled over the makeshift loudspeakers, and the group as a whole began to move toward the large banner that stretched across the street. "We'll be starting in just a couple of minutes."

There was nothing for Sabrina to do now but go back over there and admit the truth to her family. Brandy had failed to show.

"Oh, sorry I'm late," a voice said. "Brandy Philip."

Sabrina turned to see Brandy at the check-in table. Her face was pale, dark circles under her eyes. "Where have you been?"

"I made it, okay? I don't have time for a lecture now." Brandy took her race number and some safety pins, then threaded her way through the crowd toward the starting line and away from Sabrina.

Maudie Jenkins was standing with Sabrina's family when she made it back to where they were. "Oh, Sabrina, I'm so sorry. She . . . well, she ran into some trouble last night." The way she said it left no doubt what that trouble involved. "She's been sick to her stomach all morning. We were barely able to get her here."

"I'll just bet." Sabrina looked toward her father. He wasn't looking at her at all, but he'd heard the conversation. He was shaking his head slowly from side to side. It seemed that once again, she'd failed to live up to his expectations.

The starting gun cracked and the throng of runners surged

forward, leaving Sabrina and her family helpless to do anything but watch what was going to happen next. It was not going to be pretty.

"Sabrina? Is that you? I thought so." Kayla's overly perky voice sounded from somewhere behind her. "What are you doing here?"

"I . . . just came to watch the race."

"I see." Kayla looked around at the assembled family. "Your whole family, too, huh? Do you know someone racing?"

With everything inside her, Sabrina wanted to deny everything. She couldn't face the humiliation of what was going to happen today, not if Kayla had the chance to gloat about it. She knew that everyone was looking at her, waiting for her answer, including Maudie Jenkins. Finally, she managed, "A friend of the family is running today."

"Oh, that's great." She paused a moment, touched the bottom of her chin as if in thought, then said, "Wait a minute. I remember now. Someone told me you've been helping coach a girl. Is that it?"

"I've been helping the high school coach get her ready for cross-country season next fall."

"Right. I've heard she's a true running prodigy. What's her name? I'll look for her at the finish line. I hope she'll give my kids a run for the money—they've been needing a good challenge but it's hard to find. There aren't that many young runners with that kind of talent and work ethic around these days. You know what I mean?"

Sabrina knew exactly what she meant. And it had nothing to do with today's race.

🍁

The wait at the finish seemed to drag on forever. At last, a single runner emerged around the final turn. It was a teenage boy, followed closely by another. Both of them wore red shirts and black shorts.

Kayla was by now standing among a group of supporters just a bit further down the race course. Sabrina could hear her voice as she cheered her runners on to victory. The clock passed seventeen minutes and it wasn't long before the first female runner appeared around the corner, also wearing red and black. There was a twenty-something woman tight on her heels and they raced up until the very finish, the Samson Academy girl just eking out a victory. Another girl from her team followed soon after, making an amazing showing for Samson Academy. The clock passed eighteen minutes and then nineteen minutes with no sign of Brandy anywhere on the horizon.

More and more runners rounded the corner, clumped into groups now, making their finish places a bit more difficult to determine, not that it mattered. Brandy was nowhere among them.

Finally, at twenty-six minutes, Brandy slogged around the corner. She was partially bent over and had one hand across her abdomen. She stumbled across the finish line without ever looking toward Sabrina, hobbled over to a nearby tree, and vomited white foam into the grass.

A woman wearing a race volunteer T-shirt handed her a water bottle, which she took and went to sit on the curb. After a couple of sips, she looked as though she might vomit again. Her time of 26:15 was at perhaps the fiftieth percentile for the race participants, which included grandmothers and young mothers pushing double strollers. Brandy put her head in her hands, refusing to even look at Sabrina, much less speak with her.

When it was finally all over, the group in red giggled and squealed, gave out hugs and high fives all around. Kayla looked over the shoulder of her bouncing third-place finisher and smiled a fake sweet smile at Sabrina. She waved, one finger at a time. Sabrina simply nodded a response.

Maudie Jenkins petted Sabrina's arm, murmuring something about thanks and being sorry. She leaned over and said something to Brandy. Brandy didn't respond at all, but about a minute later, she slowly stood and took a couple of steps toward Sabrina.

"Thanks." She mumbled the word in Sabrina's general direction without ever actually looking at her, then turned and walked to the parking lot with her grandmother. It was that sullen complete lack of gratitude that finally pushed Sabrina over the edge. She pulled out her phone and sent a text message to Brandy.

Find someone else to train you. I'm done.

Sabrina's parents were standing off to the side, behind a large oak tree, having a conversation of their own. She had to face the music at some point, might as well do it now. As she neared them she could hear her father's voice, raised in anger. "You told me to come here and be supportive, and that's exactly what I did. I told her I was proud, offered to buy a celebration lunch, but I mean, come on. . . . That girl hardly looked like she'd run a day in her life. And speaking of coaching, have you noticed the way Sabrina looks?"

Sabrina's mother said something that Sabrina couldn't quite hear, but his response was loud and clear. "Gained a little weight? She's completely out of shape. I'm thinking it's time she got some coaching of her own.'"

Sabrina stopped dead, her feet unable to move and on the verge of getting as sick as Brandy. She looked down at her body, thinking about what she'd just heard her father say. She knew her jeans had gotten a little tight, but really? Looking down, she knew her father was right. This was not the same person she'd been for most of her life. How could Koen possibly be attracted to someone who looked like this? She knew the answer. He wouldn't be for long.

She turned around and walked back to her grandmother's

side. Nana lifted her hand to Sabrina's cheek. "This wasn't your fault, dear. You did everything you could have done and more."

"I guess." She just couldn't think about it anymore.

"Did you find your mother and father?"

Sabrina glanced toward the tree where her parents were still arguing and shook her head. "No. Couldn't find them anywhere. I'm sure they'll meet us here if we just stay put."

Her cell phone vibrated in her pocket. She pulled it out to see Koen's name in the display. She pushed the button, taking a step away from her grandmother.

"Hey."

"How'd it go?"

How did it go? There was a question that Sabrina couldn't bear to answer truthfully. "Pretty well."

"Great. How'd she finish? What was her time?"

"I'm, uh, not sure."

"Huh? When have you ever been not sure of Brandy's run time? Come on, I've seen your spreadsheet. I know better."

"I don't know, all right?"

"O-kay." He paused for a moment. "So are there family plans tonight? Jared was talking about round-robin tennis. You up for it?"

"I'm pretty sure we'll just be sticking close to the house for the rest of my parents' visit. You go ahead and have a good time. I'll see you in class on Monday." Sabrina hung up the phone, not waiting for a response. It would be better for all of them if he wasn't around this weekend.

The family drove into Nashville for lunch and then walked through the Opryland Hotel conservatory in almost complete silence. Nana tried to make small talk, but her words disappeared into the thick fog of awkward silence that encompassed them. By the time evening rolled around, the car ride home occurred with less than a dozen words spoken between them.

They were driving past the university, almost to Nana's house, when Sabrina's father said, "Hey, isn't that your friend Koen?"

A group of about a dozen people, tennis racquets in hand, were heading toward the school courts, talking and laughing. Koen was in the middle of them, as were Jared and some of the others. But the one that caught Sabrina's attention was standing on Koen's left side. Her tennis dress was cute, white, and short. Lindy Stewart.

"Yes. . ." Sabrina's chest had squeezed so tight it was hard to say the word, but she knew not to leave it at a single syllable. She tried to sound upbeat, "and a group of our friends."

Sabrina looked at the beautiful Lindy, her entire attention focused on Koen, smiling as she swatted toward him with her racquet. Everything about her was so perfect. Her beautiful blond hair, her long limbs, her completely flat stomach. Sabrina looked down at her own midsection and thought about what she'd overheard her father say that afternoon. She touched the side of her nose and the puffy red blisters that seemed to be growing larger every day. Of course Koen would prefer Lindy. Who could blame him for that?

28

Sunday morning dawned bright and sunny. Sabrina peeked between the metal slats of the blinds and noted there wasn't a single cloud in the sky. It was early yet, but since she was awake, she might as well get going.

She caught a glimpse of her father walking down Nana's driveway toward the sidewalk. He was dressed in a gray T-shirt and black running shorts, his favorite glow-green Nikes on his feet. He spent some time stretching, then pushed a button on his watch and took off jogging toward town.

Now would be a good time to go downstairs and get a glass of water, when she wouldn't see him trying to hide his disappointment. She had to give him credit, he'd said very little in a negative frame—not to her face at least. But fact was, he had said very little about anything. This had to be her mom's doing—telling him not to say anything if he couldn't say something encouraging, or some such mom-ism. It didn't matter. There was no need for words. His sighs and the fact that he could hardly look at Sabrina said more than any amount of words could.

Sabrina made it to the kitchen. She pulled out a glass and pushed it into the ice dispenser on the refrigerator door, thinking of the last part of the evening that made everything worse. Koen. With Lindy. She looked down at her stomach and shook her head.

"Good morning."

Sabrina jumped at the voice, then turned and smiled. "Morning, Mom."

Her mother reached over and patted her on the arm. "How'd you sleep?"

Sabrina shrugged. "Not great."

"I suspected as much." She reached inside the cupboard for her own glass. "Let's go sit on the porch, shall we? It's a beautiful morning."

"Sure. That sounds nice."

There was a white wicker porch swing on Nana's front porch. The seat had a blue and green striped cushion, with solid blue square pillows scattered around the back rest. Mom took a cushion, placed it in the small of her back, then leaned against it. "I can't tell you how long it's been since I sat in this thing. I've always loved it. So many happy memories."

Sabrina took another pillow and sat beside her mom. They slowly rocked back and forth, barely moving really, neither saying anything for a long time. Finally, Mom said, "It wasn't your fault, you know."

The swing went back and forth and back and forth. Sabrina took a breath and started to answer, then choked and had to rock a little more. Finally she managed to say the one word that had been ringing through her mind for the past twenty-four hours. "Why?"

Once she had spoken the word she'd been holding inside for so long, the rest just spewed out in an inevitable release of pressure. "I don't understand, Mom, I just don't understand. Why? I was so sure I heard God's call on my life. Everything that happened seemed to confirm it—you felt it too, I know you did. I don't understand why He did this to me, why He would issue such a strong call, then take it all away like this. I would have been fine if I'd never run the first step. Why?"

Sabrina allowed herself to sob out some of the pain for just a moment. "I know I should be grateful for all the wonderful things that I do have, and I am, really I am, it's just that I don't understand why God would not only take away my running, but also give that gift for it to someone like Brandy, who clearly will never use it like I would have.

"And then, after I got past all that, and started helping her—bam! Right back in my face again. Just more failure."

"Sweetie, one race is not a failure. I'm sure she's embarrassed and devastated right now. I talked to her on Friday night. I know that she was putting lots of pressure on herself to do well *for you*. I think the fear of not measuring up when it counted just got to her. She's not used to success. She's used to criticism and failure, and having no one to catch her after she falls. I think Brandy may be part of your new calling, whatever it is. You need to help her pull herself back together again. It would be so easy for her to dive off into the deep end now and never come back out. You've got to let her know there is someone who cares enough to try to catch her now."

"I can't, Mom, I just can't help her anymore. I've been having nightmares about running almost every night since we started. I wake up covered in sweat, usually soaked in tears. I can't handle it anymore."

"Sabrina"—her mother took her hand—"I think that might be the problem. You never handled it in the first place."

"What do you mean? I moved on. I started on a new path without sitting around and whining about what I couldn't have."

"That's true, and there are plenty of good things to be said about that, but pretending that the pain is not there doesn't make it go away. It just hides it beneath the surface until something forces it up—like when Brandy came along. To tell you the truth, I think you let the suffering deflect you from the path you were supposed to follow. You turned your back on your former dream and chose a completely different goal. What if your true calling lies somewhere back behind you? What if that's the only thing that will ever make you truly happy?"

"God took my running away from me. I don't think He's all that interested in whether or not I'm happy about it."

They sat silent for a moment.

"Honey, I wish you could hear what I hear. You're angry. Angry toward God and I think you're trying not to be, but right there is where you need to start. Do some digging and work through this pain. Maybe once you do that, you'll see that He does indeed have a call on your life, and running is still a part of it—whether it's your past running or coaching a current runner."

Sabrina shook her head. "You're wrong. I'm not angry."

"Am I? Wrong?"

"Of course."

"Let me give you one last thought, and then I promise I'll leave this topic forever. Eric Liddell was always your role model, I know that. He won an Olympic gold medal, that is true. But there are lots of men who have won gold medals since then, men with names we do not know, whose faces we can't remember. What made Eric Liddell so special that all these years later so many people still know his name?"

"I guess most people know his name because he refused to run that heat on a Sunday."

"Right. And in spite of what the movie did or did not show, you know that he was strongly criticized for it, hated for it, even."

"Yes." Sabrina knew that the newspapers at the time had called him a traitor and worse.

"Eric loved to run as much as you did. He had earned his spot on the Olympic team, but he was willing to give up his dreams of a medal—in fact he *did* give up his dreams of a medal, when it would mean doing something that He didn't believe God wanted him to do. In spite of the fact that he worked so long and so hard, he counted it nothing. Right?"

"Yes."

"He could only do that because what he wanted more than that dream was to follow God in the very best way he knew how. For him, that meant not running on Sunday. For you, maybe that means living through old pain so that you can save a girl from a lifetime of pain. You need to go comfort Brandy."

"How can I, when I can't even comfort myself?" Sabrina shook her head. "I cannot . . ." The words died on her lips. In that instant, she knew that her mother was right. About all of it. She had been doing nothing but pretending for the last three years. Pretending to be happy. Pretending to be strong. Pretending all through church and Bible studies and every bit of it that everything was okay.

"I promised I would change subjects, so now I am. Have you decided what to do about the job?"

"It's still not a firm offer, but the chance to work at Grace Rose is a dream come true. I don't see how I could not do it."

"Is it your dream come true, or the dream you think you're supposed to have?"

Sabrina thought about that for a minute. "I thought it was mine, but now I'm not sure I understand anything anymore." Sabrina thought about Bridges and the offer there. She thought about what her mom had said about her turning her back on the past.

Just then her father came up the front porch, still breathing hard from his run. "Good morning, ladies."

"Morning," Sabrina and her mother replied in unison.

Sabrina looked at her father and knew exactly what he would think about her job situation. Likely, the fact that she had this opportunity was one of the things helping him to remain so silent about yesterday's epic failure. He believed that Sabrina was going to redeem herself with this amazing job and go on to greatness. And maybe that was the answer right there. Maybe taking that job was the only way to regain any semblance of worth again. Or maybe she needed to rethink her life and, like Eric Liddell, look for where God wanted her to be great.

"Girl, you've got to get up and start moving. You can't go on like this." Grandma's voice hovered somewhere outside the covers, which were drawn up over Brandy's head.

"I can't. I'm too tired." Brandy closed her eyes and tried to will herself back into the oblivion of sleep.

"You've been buried here in this bed ever since we got home from the race yesterday afternoon. It's time for you to get up, eat and drink a little, and get moving around. This isn't good for you, all this lying around and wallowing."

But that was all Brandy wanted to do. Lie there and wallow. What kind of an idiot had she been? After everything that she'd planned to do, every bit of all that hard work, it all came to nothing. Brandy's one chance had been handed to her, wrapped in cellophane and a big red bow, and she'd somehow managed to throw it all in the trash.

The covers were suddenly lifted from her head. "Now, you listen to me, young lady. It's time for you to get out of your bed and I mean right now. You made a mistake, a big one, and there's no doubt about that, but what you've got to do now is to keep moving on. You can either let this one mistake ruin your life or you can learn from it and make the decision that next time you'll be smarter."

"There won't be a next time for me."

"I'd say that's entirely up to you."

"Grandma, Sabrina isn't going to train me anymore. When Mrs. Lauderdale doesn't get her paper work on time they're going to send me to juvie and there's not a thing I can do about it. I guess most people'd say I deserve it, and I probably do. We all knew it was going to happen sooner or later." Brandy grabbed the covers and pulled them back up over her head. "Sorry, Grandma. I give you credit—you hung in there longer than anyone else, but it's time to give up."

The bed shifted as Grandma sat on the edge. She put her hand on Brandy's knee. "Darling, I won't ever give up on you as long as there is breath in my body. I love you more than anyone else on earth, and I'm going to keep on loving you no matter what you do or don't do. You might as well get used to the idea, I'm here for the long haul."

Not another word was said, and in fact Brandy would have almost believed that her grandmother had left the room if it weren't for the gentle pressure of a hand on her knee and the slight lean of the mattress.

After some time, Brandy had no idea how long, she pulled the cover back from her face. Her grandmother was sitting there, head bowed, eyes closed, lips moving in some sort of silent plea to God.

Maybe sometimes you have to lose almost everything to realize that there is something valuable that you've had in your possession all along. In Brandy's case, she was sitting right there beside her. "Grandma?"

Her grandmother opened her eyes. "Yes, darling?"

"You want to make some dinner together?"

"I can't think of anything that sounds better."

29

The sound of ocean waves grew louder and louder in Sabrina's room, until it seemed as though the churning water would soon overtake her. She finally managed to roll over and hit the Snooze button, thus quieting her nature sounds alarm clock, and pulled her pillow over her head. Her joints all ached this morning, every single one of them. This was going to be one of those mornings that took a while before the stiffness eased up. She knew that she needed to get up and get going, but she was just so tired.

She hobbled down the hall, hoping a warm shower would help loosen things up a little. As she took deep breaths of the steam and let the hot water flow around her, she waited for relief, but it was slow in coming. Ten minutes later, she managed to get some shampoo into her hair and rinse it out. Conditioner would not be an option today. Apparently today's look would involve a frizzy ponytail.

She pulled on her yellow ducky bathrobe and walked over to the sink to wash her face and at least try to make herself presentable.

Her nose looked worse. Much worse. In spite of the fact that the school doctor had put her on an oral antibiotic last week. Maybe she should see her again. Great. Just great. Frizzy hair and a bright red nose—not the way she wanted to start the week.

Right after breakfast she'd return Candace Davenport's call about that internship. She would . . . accept the position . . . right? Not that the offer was 100 percent firm yet. But if it did turn into a firm offer, it would be a dream come true. A long shot that had been realized.

Out of the blue, Rita Leyva's words from their last conversation returned to her and she suddenly felt awash in confusion. Was Bridges the right choice for her? Her mother would likely think so. Her father most certainly would not. She took a deep breath. In this particular case, he'd be right. She'd be crazy not to take the opportunity at Grace Rose. She could do something like Bridges work later on, after she'd established herself. Right now, she should do what she did well and do it as well as possible.

A brief flash ran through her mind of her younger self. She'd designed an ad campaign for Dad's company as part of a school project. His face had beamed. "This is amazing. We pay professional firms for plans that aren't as good as this. You should major in public relations."

"Dad, you know I'm going to be a missionary."

"Honey, no one majors in being a missionary. Besides, most of that life is getting the word out about your work to the right people. You've got a true natural gift for that. It's definitely what you should do."

It was one of the few things that Sabrina could ever remember doing without her father making suggestions for improvement. She'd decided on her college major that very day.

That's the only thing that has stayed the same from my former life. For some reason, in spite of the fact that she didn't want to do it, in spite of the fact that she had no time for this, she opened the drawer of her bedside table and pulled out her old journal. She flipped it open, a little further than the last time.

Oct. 21—Every time things go wrong or get hard, the children of Israel keep repeating that they were better off in Egypt, sometimes they even start appointing leaders to take them back. To slavery! Why would anyone want to go back to slavery?

It couldn't have been that they were well treated, because God said their cries came up before Him and that's why He was freeing them. Why was it, then, that they would want to return?

I think maybe it's because it was familiar. They knew what to expect and what was expected of them. Now, when things kept happening that they didn't anticipate, they quickly lost sight of the goal and turned back toward what they could understand. Walking forward in faith, into the unknown, had proven too scary.

I hope that if my course should someday look less certain than it does now, my faith will not be proven to be so easily swayed and my heart so easily turned toward the comfort of the familiar.

Sabrina slammed the book shut, a tear splashing against the cover. What did she know? It was easy to think this way when you're seventeen and your life is going according to your master game plan.

She tossed the book on her bed and walked out of the room. As she started down the stairs, the warm, greasy smell of bacon lofted up to greet her. And pancakes, too, if she didn't miss her guess.

Inside the kitchen, she found Nana busy at work over the stove. She didn't turn, but in her typical all-knowing way, she said,

"Good morning, Sabrina. Would you be a dear and pour the milk? Cakes will be up in just a minute."

"Nana, you know you're not supposed to do this kind of thing. That was part of the agreement when I moved in here, that you wouldn't put yourself out trying to do stuff for me all the time."

"I think you and I both know that I do not do anything for you 'all the time.' But I know this weekend was hard on you and I know Mondays are busy days for you. If a grandmother can't do something a little extra special every now and then for her granddaughter, then something's just not right with this world."

"You are the best." Sabrina poured them both a glass of milk and carried them over to the table.

"You seem like you're hobbling this morning. You okay?"

"Yeah, just a little extra stiff. Probably because I slept funny or something."

Nana set a plate of pancakes and another plate of bacon on the already set table. "I wish I could take your pain away from you, Sabrina. I'd take it on myself in a heartbeat if the good Lord would give it to me instead of you."

Sabrina reached out and squeezed her grandmother's hand. "I know you would." It was true. Nana would do anything for her and Sabrina knew it.

A short time later, Sabrina stood in her room, punching numbers on her cell phone, her hands suddenly clammy. She listened to two rings on the other end.

"Grace Rose Public Relations, this is Naomi. How may I assist you today?"

"Hello, Naomi. My name is Sabrina Rice, and I am returning a call to Candace Davenport."

"Yes. She is expecting your call. One moment, please." The line clicked and some soothing orchestra music filled Sabrina's ear for about three beats.

"Sabrina, so glad to hear back from you. I'm assuming you got my message on Friday?"

"Yes. I'm sorry I missed your calls. I was in class and then at work."

"Now, that's what I like to hear. Someone who doesn't talk on her cell phone while at work. Yet another reason I am certain we made the right decision. I've got to tell you, Sabrina, I had to fight for you, so I need you to make me look good."

"Fight for me?"

"Yes. When we were narrowing it down to the final candidates, there was the feeling among some of the decision makers that although you are obviously a self-motivated person, you might not have enough killer instinct to be truly successful in our highly competitive field."

"Really?" A shiver ran through Sabrina, cold and prickly. "So . . . you convinced them otherwise?"

"Yes, I did, and I believe you'll make me proud. You'll be receiving a packet of paper work in the mail in the next week or so. Make sure you get it all filled out and returned as soon as possible. We can't finalize everything until all the paper work is turned in and slots assigned. I think I mentioned earlier there is a slight chance of another round of interviews, but I don't expect that to be the case this year, since we are firm on this year's choices. I'm looking forward to our future partnership. Welcome aboard."

"Thank you. I'm glad to be here." Sabrina hung up the phone with a few more misgivings than she'd had before, but realized that she'd just affirmed her plan to take the offer. A decision that she wasn't certain she had intended to make.

30

Sabrina thought her Monday afternoon shift would never end. She still felt achy, and tired, and just plain foggy. When five o'clock came at last, she retrieved her backpack and walked from behind the counter just in time to see Koen entering. He smiled when he saw her. "Hey there."

"Hey." It hurt to look at him, but there was no reason not to be friendly. She'd always known he was out of her league.

"If I didn't know better, I would say that you have been avoiding me today. I do know better, right?" He leaned against the wall, his head tilted to the left.

"Of course. Why would I be avoiding you?"

"No reason that I can think of." He continued to watch her closely, his expression serious. "But it did seem odd to me that you sat across the room in psych this morning and wouldn't even glance my way."

Sabrina adjusted her backpack on her shoulders and noticed a couple enter the snack shop hand in hand, smiling at each other and laughing. They looked so happy. And uncomplicated. She envied them more than she could say. "I needed to talk to Rosalia about something, so I sat with her."

"Sabrina, why are you always so closed off? Something's obviously wrong. When are you going to tell me what it is?"

"What makes you say that?" She turned her attention back to Koen, but didn't quite look him in the eye.

"You haven't answered any of my phone calls or responded to any of my texts since Saturday afternoon. I gather things didn't go so well at the race, but I'm not sure why that would make you mad at me."

"It wouldn't, of course, so see, you're imagining things. What did you do for the rest of the weekend?" She asked the question in the most upbeat and conversational tone she could muster.

He shrugged. "Not much. Hung out with the gang, you know, I invited you to play tennis with us."

"Which gang was that again?"

"You know, Jared and the group. The usual."

"Just the usual?"

His eyes narrowed. "What is it that you think you know?"

"The correct question might be, 'What is it that you think you saw?'"

"All right then, what do you think you saw?"

"I saw—" she paused—"the gang—" another pause for emphasis—"at the tennis courts."

Koen looked directly at her face. "And it bothers you because Lindy was there?"

Sabrina looked away. "I have no right to be bothered, do I? I mean, it's not like we agreed that we weren't going to see other people, right? What you do on your own time is your business."

"Sabrina, we *played tennis*. Period. There was a whole group of us. If you saw us, you know that."

"I know that Lindy has had her eye on you for this entire

semester. And from what I saw Saturday night, there might have been a whole group, but I'm not sure Lindy was aware of anyone but you. And you didn't seem to mind."

"You're being unreasonable. Lindy was with Emma, who happens to be dating Eric. I had nothing to do with inviting her to be there—they were just in the group at Jared's when the decision was made to play tennis. What was I supposed to do, sit at home all weekend because you're having a bad weekend with your parents in town?"

"Koen, like I said, you're free to do whatever you want to do. Since it looks like I'm going to be really busy for the rest of the semester, I'm glad that you've found someone who has more available time than I do."

He shook his head. "I give up. Ever since we started seeing each other, it's almost as if you've been looking for an excuse to end it. Well, I can't fight it anymore. Good luck, Sabrina." He walked out of the snack shop, still shaking his head from side to side.

Her ribs seemed to contract around her middle and squeezed so tight that it hurt to breathe. She wrapped her arms around herself, feeling as if she might implode.

This was a good thing, really, to get this over and done with. It had been a lovely dream while it lasted, but one that was certain to end. Now it was back to reality. Back where things made sense, were well controlled and comfortable. A place like . . .

Egypt.

The thought continued to plague her for the entire ride home. When she reached the house, she climbed the stairs and threw herself across the bed. For the first time in a long time, she allowed herself a good long, gut-wrenching cry.

31

Tuesday night, as usual, Sabrina sat in Campus Eats studying. Try as she might to focus on her work, the pain over Koen's parting created a low hum inside her head that dueled in distraction with the high-pitched voice of guilt about Brandy. The two had grown so loud that she couldn't even hear her own thoughts. It was useless to try and concentrate.

She rubbed her forehead with both hands. Surely there must be some way to get back on track, to move forward without all this pain and regret. But how?

Tomorrow was a training day—perhaps that was why the guilt weighed so heavy tonight. Still, no one could possibly expect her to keep putting in the same kind of effort as before after last weekend's debacle.

That was the problem. It wasn't so much guilt that she wouldn't be working with Brandy anymore—Brandy had more than brought that on herself. No, it was the unknown of what might happen with her in court because of Sabrina's decision. Maybe Brandy was getting what she deserved. But her poor grandmother, well . . . Sabrina couldn't stand the thought of putting Maudie Jenkins through more pain than she'd already endured. She could still picture the deep worry lines across her forehead and the dark circles beneath her eyes on that day when Brandy had gone missing.

The day that Brandy had waited outside her mother's broken-down house to make certain she got some food.

What could Sabrina do, though? She really didn't have the time to do this anymore, even if she wanted to—and she certainly didn't want to. Still, the nagging guilt would not relent.

An idea cut through the fog. A "next step" in Brandy's development, she would call it. She would write up an email now, for reporting purposes. She would declare this an experiment so it didn't sound like the permanent arrangement it really was. She could use phrases like "to help Brandy prepare for independent success" and "learning exercise in self-motivation." Yes. That's what she could do.

She spent the next hour writing it out as concisely and clearly as possible, then emailed it to Brandy, Mrs. Jenkins, and Mrs. Lauderdale, hoping the legal system would buy off on it. She knew the judge had been a bit of a stickler in the past, but even if Mrs. Lauderdale decided to put up a fight, in all likelihood, juvenile court was so overwhelmed and backlogged, it might be a while before she could do much about it. Especially since Sabrina had been so meticulous about filling out the necessary paper work since this all started.

Finally, she was able to return to her schoolwork, with that persistent voice of guilt quieted. At least slightly.

32

Sabrina jerked awake knowing that she was going to be late for class. Why hadn't her alarm gone off? She looked at the clock, her heart pounding.

Four thirty.

Thank goodness. It must have been a dream, or just a random jolt of adrenaline. Whatever the cause, it wasn't real. A long deep breath and slow exhale served to ease some of the tension. She double-checked that the alarm was indeed set for six thirty and turned to the "on" position, then fell back against her pillows. Two more hours of blessed sleep. She rolled over and pulled the cover up tight against her chin.

Her bed was so warm and soft and comfy. Soon she felt herself floating in the haze of a peaceful breeze.

And then she was running.

Feet pounding against the pavement as she moved up a steep hill. She could hear her coach's voice yelling down toward her, "Surge. Surge." She paid attention to the lift of her knees, the straight pump of her arms, and the position of her head. Form matters most when you're tired. Concentrate. Now's when champions are made. *She repeated those words over and over in her head as she made her way to the top of the hill, which she couldn't quite see because it was covered in fog. Still, she pushed to the end, knowing as she reached the top that she'd given it everything she had.*

As she broke through the fog layer, she looked toward her coach, hoping for confirmation that she'd done well, already smiling because she was certain that she had. And then she saw her coach's face and stopped running.

The woman she saw . . . was herself.

Sabrina the coach was smiling and clapping, seemingly oblivious to the fact that she was cheering for herself. "I'm so proud of you. You gave it everything you had. Way to stick with it."

Sabrina jerked awake. The dream had been so vivid, so real, that she couldn't shake it. She kept seeing her face, hearing her voice of encouragement, and remembering how much her real coach's words had meant to her as a runner.

She stared at the ceiling, which was little more than a gray presence in the predawn. The dream may have been gone, but all sorts of emotions still surged within her—hope, confusion, and anger. Sabrina flipped over, buried her head in her pillow, and screamed.

Why was this happening to her? Even as she asked the question she already knew its answer. She was supposed to be helping Brandy now. She felt it as strongly and with as much certainty as she'd ever felt anything. Yet just the thought of putting herself back into it, knowing how much of a risk it was, how foolish she'd look, felt impossible. Every time she had a dream, a calling—or at least the belief that it was a calling—she was eventually made to realize that she'd been wrong about the whole thing and ultimately embarrassed by the disastrous results.

She shook her head and stared at the ceiling. *God, why don't I ever hear you correctly? I always try to follow in faith, and things always fall apart. What am I doing wrong?*

For the first time in a long time, she allowed herself to go back and fully remember. The dream of running, the years and years of hard work, the constant striving to be better and do better because of the call. She remembered the girl she had been back then. Full of absolute and unwavering faith. So convinced of her call and the strength of her God that she'd never questioned any of it. That strength of faith had long since disappeared behind a cloud of reality.

Really? Was it a cloud of reality or was it the difficulties of the wilderness that turned your heart back toward Egypt?

Sabrina shook her head as she tried to shake off the thought that had surfaced, unsolicited and unwanted. She was not turning away from God's call on her life; she'd simply realized that she'd misunderstood the call.

Really?

Is that what it was?

The thought dug deep into places that Sabrina did not want to visit. This was crazy, because she knew that the voice was wrong, anyway. She looked toward the clock.

Five fifteen.

Brandy probably wasn't even out there. Without someone there to hold her accountable, she would blow the whole thing off.

Still, in spite of what she believed, Sabrina pulled on a pair of sweats and headed for the door, having no idea what she would find—or what she would do in any case.

Brandy rounded the corner for another lap, but her feet and legs were in full rebellion. Heavy. Tired. Not like the other time when Sabrina had told her to take it easy. No, this was a full body, no energy, emotional drain kind of exhaustion. Why was she here, anyway? It's not like anyone would know the difference, or even care.

She wouldn't allow herself to stop yet, but the consideration was gaining ground. It's not like it mattered anymore.

"Is that all you've got?" Sabrina's voice came from the general direction of the front porch.

Brandy turned and jogged back toward it. "What are you doing out here?"

"Watching a slacker, apparently." Sabrina walked across the lawn and sat on her usual spot on the retaining wall. "Hopefully, this next lap will prove me wrong."

Brandy jogged directly up in front of Sabrina. "Listen, I want to say—" she took a couple of deep breaths—"about the other day—"

"Say it after your workout. Right now, I want to see some effort."

"But I—"

"I came out to watch you run. Get moving." Sabrina's tone was as gruff as Brandy had ever heard. Apparently this was not going to be a quick makeup scene.

Brandy made for the far corner, moving faster than she had been just a few minutes ago. Hopefully Sabrina noticed. If Sabrina was outside, it meant she had changed her mind and was going to keep training her. Right? Or maybe she had gone back into the house by now and that was the end of it. Who knew?

Wanting to know the answer to that question pushed her to move a little faster than usual around the block. She turned the final corner, her eyes straining to see the retaining wall. A dark silhouette sat framed in the streetlight. She was still there. Brandy ran a little faster but moved past Sabrina without daring to look at her.

Three laps later, she finally chanced a glance toward Sabrina. She had her knees pulled up to her chin, her arms wrapped around her legs, apparently trying to keep warm. She seemed to be staring at the house across the street, giving no indication that she even knew Brandy was passing her.

By the end of the workout, Brandy had crafted a nice long apology. She'd thought out each word carefully, prepared to do what she could to defuse the situation. She rounded the corner from her cooldown lap to find the wall empty. Sabrina had gone inside.

Conversation over.

Friday morning, Sabrina's alarm sounded at four forty-five. Although she hadn't spoken with Brandy since Wednesday, she'd planned to at least go sit outside again today. This morning, however, she just couldn't do it. She turned off the alarm and rolled over. It required too much energy to get out of bed. Maybe it would do Brandy some good to work alone.

Several hours later, when she finally did get up, it took about ten minutes before the guilt set in. That little inner voice kept saying that she should have gotten up. A second voice was quick to respond that she had not committed to anyone that she would return to training and was under no compulsion to do so.

It was a cop-out and she knew it. She needed to make a decision and stick with it. Even when times got hard.

That was something she would think about later. When she was more awake and had time. For now, she needed to hurry and get ready for class. And she had another doctor's appointment this afternoon. These were things she needed to think about now.

Later that day, she sat in the waiting room of the school clinic. Again. This was her third visit in the past week and a half. Hopefully they would find the right antibiotic this time and get this nose thing cleared up. Her entire nose was puffy now, with red crusty scabs covering most of the left side. It was disgusting.

It was bad enough to watch Lindy Stewart in all her glory prancing around after Koen without having to look like a freak in the meantime. Sabrina was almost certain she'd heard her snickering behind her just this morning outside of psych class. To Koen's credit, he didn't seem to be giving Lindy anything more than polite attention, and he always smiled and said hello to Sabrina. Maybe she had been too quick to judge him. If only . . .

"Sabrina, come on back."

Sabrina followed the aide back through the doors, had her weight and blood pressure taken, and then walked through the back into an exam room. She sat on the paper-sheeted exam table and wished the doctor would hurry up.

A scuffling sound came from the back side of the door. After so many trips here, Sabrina knew what that sound meant. The doctor had picked up her chart from the shelf outside. At least she wouldn't have to wait long to be seen today.

The doctor of the day was young, maybe thirty or so, and pretty. She had shoulder-length brown hair, deep hazel eyes that seemed to light up her entire face, and a spring in her step—which was amazing considering the fact that she appeared to be about eight months pregnant. She stuck out her hand. "Hello, Sabrina, I'm Dr. Strohm."

Sabrina shook her hand. "Nice to meet you."

Dr. Strohm wasted no more time on niceties. Instead, she immediately leaned forward, squinted her eyes, and began to check out Sabrina's nose. "Tell me again what it is you're taking for your arthritis?"

"Naproxen, methotrexate, leucovorin, and adalimumab are the medications specific for my arthritis, plus there are a few others I take to manage the side effects of those."

"I see." She nodded. "And we've had you on three different antibiotic ointments, plus an oral cephalasporin and a sulfa antibiotic with no improvement. Right?"

"Right."

"I'm concerned that you have a resistant staph infection. I'm going to put in a call to your rheumatologist to discuss this, then I'll be right back."

"Okay." Sabrina picked up a magazine from the basket in the room. Apparently Costa Rica would be a nice place to spend a vacation. She flipped through page after page of beach photos and rain forest, paying very little attention to any of it.

Her phone vibrated in the side pocket of her purse, so she picked it up. *New email* flashed on the screen. She clicked the icon.

Sabrina,

Under no circumstances does this so-called "independent study" plan in any way fit the court-appointed mandate for Brandy's scheduled training. I need immediate confirmation that you will return to the schedule already agreed upon or I will be forced to take further action. Your prompt reply is expected.

Nancy Lauderdale

Sabrina rolled her eyes. That woman was wound way too tight. Truth was, Sabrina had indeed been present at Wednesday's session, so other than Friday, things had gone more or less according to plan. Since the paper work wasn't due until Monday, she saw no reason to send "immediate" confirmation. Let Mrs. Lauderdale stew for the weekend—maybe it would do her some good.

The door opened. "Your rheumatologist and I are in complete agreement as to the next course of your treatment. We're putting all of your arthritis meds on hold. We don't want anything to suppress your immune system right now. And, while there is another oral antibiotic we could try, given the fact that your immune system is already suppressed due to what you've been taking, I'm making the call to hospitalize you for a couple of days so you can get some IV antibiotics."

"Hospital?" This thought had never crossed Sabrina's mind. "Other than a cold I can't seem to kick, and this rash, I feel fine."

Dr. Strohm shook her head. "And I'd like to keep it that way, so I think it's time we erred on the side of caution. Now, here's the good news: it's Friday morning. I'll talk to the folks over at General and ask them to admit you this evening. After forty-eight hours you should be on the road to recovery, so you won't have to miss any classes. Not so bad, huh?"

"I guess not." Sabrina sat numbly while the doctor made the appropriate calls. She came back and said, "They want you to check in tonight at seven thirty. That is right after shift change, and things will be slower up on the floors by then. Sound good?"

"Uh, sure. Thanks."

Sabrina walked out of the doctor's office, too stunned to think. By the time she got to her car, she had at least thought to call her mother's cell phone and explained to her what was going on.

"So, you feel okay?"

"Yes."

"But you'll be in the hospital for a couple of days?"

"Sounds like it."

"I'll be there in a couple of hours."

"Mom, I'm fine. You don't have to come, really. It's just some silly meds."

"Silly meds or not, no daughter of mine is going to be in the hospital for two days while I'm lollygagging around in the comfort of my own home. Of course I'll be there. We're going to make the best of it, you wait and see. It'll be like a girls' weekend away—only in this particular instance the away part will be a hospital room. I'll take care of everything, don't you worry."

"I wouldn't dare."

"That's my girl. I've taught you well."

Sabrina hung up and couldn't help but smile. She wondered what kind of crazy scheme her mother would concoct to make the best of this weekend.

The local hospital was less than a year old. The hallways were lined with gleaming tile, and the pale green walls were sparkling clean and loaded with beautiful landscapes painted by local artists. It would have been a lovely place except for the whole sick and dying thing.

A heavyset woman wearing a green volunteer jacket led Sabrina and her mother up the elevator and through a set of corridors until they arrived at room 263. "Here's the closet and a couple of drawers where you can unload your stuff. Bathroom's here, of course," she said, pushing the door to the bathroom open a little wider. She walked over to the bed and picked up the remote. "Nurse's call button is right here, and these buttons work the TV and DVD player. Thermostat's on the wall. Get yourself settled, honey. The nurse'll be with you in just a few minutes. Is there anything you need in the meantime?"

"No, thank you."

"I wish you the best." She closed the door behind her, leaving Sabrina and her mother standing in the middle of the room.

"Well, let's get unpacked, shall we?" Mom went to the closet and hung up a couple of shirts she'd carried in on hangers. Then she turned her attention to a medium-sized red duffle that looked as though it might split at the seams.

"Mom, that bag looks pretty full. How many outfits do you think you're going to need for this little hospital excursion?"

"Well, a couple of changes of clothes, of course, but mostly this bag is full of contraband."

"Contraband? Like what?"

Mom smiled and reached inside her bag. In a matter of seconds she had removed bags of popcorn, gummy bears, and chocolate-covered peanuts.

Sabrina laughed out loud. "I don't ever remember seeing you in possession of quite that much junk food."

"It's not junk food—well, not exactly. In this particular case, it's theater food, which we need because—" she reached inside her bag and pulled out four plastic cases and held them over her head—"we are having a *Pirates of the Caribbean* movie marathon this weekend."

"*Pirates* marathon, huh? Now, that's what I call making the best out of a bad situation."

"My point exactly." Her mother's smile lit up her face and shone out through her eyes. "Might as well have a little bit of fun with this detour."

It was over an hour later and well into the adventures of Captain Jack Sparrow before the attending physician made it into the room. Mom hit the Pause button on the DVD and came to stand at Sabrina's side.

The doctor was in his early thirties, nice looking, and mostly well dressed. Except everything about his starched shirt and pressed khakis looked just a little askew, giving the impression of a neat freak who had just endured a really rough day. He ran his fingers through his hair and shook his head as he looked through Sabrina's chart. "I'm just going to be honest with you: I think this is a waste of all of our time for you to be here. If you were my patient I would put you on oral clindamycin for a few days and this would likely clear up. I called your doctor but she was adamant that this is what she wanted to do. I apologize that you are being inconvenienced like this."

"I don't consider it an inconvenience to get my daughter the best treatment for an infection." Mom sounded downright offended. "I'm sorry if this feels like a waste of time for you, but I suppose you should have considered that before you went to medical school."

That was about as blunt as Sabrina had ever heard her mom. She could only look on in stunned silence and wonder where this person had been lurking all these years.

The doctor glanced up at her, his eyes rolling as he turned his attention back to the chart, where he was scribbling orders. "I've ordered the Vanco. They should be in soon to set up your IV." With that, he walked from the room without another word.

"My, my, someone's having a hard day." Mom stared at the door, her mouth open. Finally she stood up and said, "I'll be right back."

33

For some reason Brandy couldn't think of starting her training anywhere else but here, in front of Sabrina's house. Even now, when Sabrina wasn't even here, this was the only place that felt right. Maybe because, for just a little while, she'd learned to give her best and had felt as though someone might care whether or not she should succeed.

She took her place at the "starting line," leaned slightly forward, then looked toward the house. "This one's for you, Sabrina."

Today was going to be interval training. It was the hardest, least enjoyable, and most downright painful of anything Sabrina had made her do. She would sprint all out, as fast as she could possibly go, for the first half of the block, then change to a slower jog to complete the circuit.

This was the type of training where, in the past, Brandy had been most prone to cheat. Push not quite as hard as she could during the first half, try to save a little something for later. Because, as she knew, later was going to be downright painful, even if she did hold back.

Not today. Today she was going to give everything she had. Maybe if she endured enough pain she could at some point forgive herself, at some point quit kicking herself for throwing away the closest thing to a friend she'd had in a long time. The same friend who was in the hospital, but who Brandy wouldn't visit because she was sure her presence would just make things worse. She needed Sabrina; Sabrina didn't need her.

On the first circuit, she blasted around the one corner and then the next, not allowing herself to slack off even a tiny bit until she'd completely crossed the driveway of the big blue house that marked the slowing point. When she switched into jog mode, she forced herself to move at a faster pace than normal for intervals. She took deep breaths, trying her best to quench her hunger for more air. By the time she reached the starting line again, she was still breathing hard but it was manageable. She took off again as hard as she could go. It hurt more than the last time, burning her lungs, her legs, her shoulders, but she refused to allow herself the luxury of easing up. She would take her punishment.

By the fifth lap, her legs had taken on something of a numbness, if something that hurt as much as this could be called numb. Her lungs, on the other hand, burned—screaming for more oxygen with every single breath she took, demanding that she stop.

At the end of the hour, she was barely upright. She rounded the corner in a jog, seeing the finish line fifty feet in front of her. She knew that she could stop now, with a clear conscience. She had pushed herself hard, until there was nothing left inside of her to push.

Yet when she approached the line, without ever consciously making the decision to do so, she began again at an all-out sprint. She tried to focus on something else besides the pain, but her mind was locked as tight as her muscles. The world around her blurred, and the sidewalk seemed to move in waves around her burning calves. Burning calves . . . what was it Sabrina called this? There was a word . . . some kind of acid, wasn't it? Lactic acid, yes, that's what it was called. Yes, there was definitely acid inside her muscles at this point, and there had been for a long time now.

When she reached the blue house's driveway, she could hear her wheezing breaths, and so could anyone on this half of the block, she was more than certain. She reached up to wipe her face with the hem of her shirt, but realized it was no good, her shirt was soaked through. She almost cried with relief when she reached the jog stage. Just half a block to go and she could stop and walk it out. That thought alone kept her going one step after the other.

She turned the corner and saw the starting line ahead of her, the finish line this time. Her legs were reduced to quivering mush, making her feel shaky all over. Looking back on it, she could never understand why it was she broke into a full run once she reached what should have been that blessed spot of relief.

A half-dozen laps later, Brandy dove across the finish line and simply lay in a quivering mass on the sidewalk. She stared up into the white fluffiness in the sky above her and wished that she could fly.

34

"Good morning, I'm from the lab. I'm here to draw some blood."

Sabrina opened her eyes to a still-dark room to find a sympathetic-looking woman standing beside the bed, a cart of tubes and syringes at her side.

"Huh?"

"Sorry to have to wake you. Can you give me your right arm?"

Sabrina extended her arm and watched as the all too familiar needle found its way into a vein—at least it didn't roll this time, as they often did. Needles were a familiar sight to most RA patients. Tests to check disease activity, tests to confirm her meds weren't damaging her liver or kidneys.

The lab tech changed vial after vial. Sabrina counted five before she fell back into an exhausted sleep.

When Sabrina opened her eyes again, her mother was up and dressed. Her Hide-a-Bed had been folded away and she was sitting by the window, reading by the light streaming through the slats in the blinds. There were dark circles under her eyes. Poor thing probably hadn't really slept at all, which wasn't surprising considering all the interruptions of IV changes and vital sign checks and blood draws—way too much disruption for any sort of meaningful rest. Sabrina would insist that she head over to Nana's for a nap today.

Her cell phone vibrated across her bedside table. She saw Koen's name on the text message. She took a deep breath and opened it. Hoping for . . . for . . . to be honest, she wasn't certain what she was hoping for.

Hey. I heard you were in the hospital. Is everything ok?

Yeah. Getting some IVs for a little infection. Nothing major.

OK, good. Is there anything I can do for you?

Sabrina thought about the answer to that one for a minute. There were so many things she could say: give me another chance, look at me the way you used to, forgive me. But she wouldn't say any of those things to him. He deserved better than her, and she knew it.

Don't think so. Thanks, though.

She set the phone down, willing him to reply. Begging it not to remain silent, to shut her out. But it didn't move. Finally, she pulled up her nerve and decided she would put herself out on a limb for a change.

We've got a Pirates of the Caribbean marathon going in my room. If you get bored, you can stop by.

She'd no sooner hit Send than she wished she could take it back. It sounded lame and pathetic and desperate.

She stared at the phone for what seemed like forever, but it didn't move. Not a single vibration.

The door pushed open and a nice-looking man, maybe forty but probably younger, with wavy blond hair came into the room. His smile was genuine and happy, as if there wasn't anywhere he'd rather be right then than in that very hospital room.

"Good morning, ladies. I'm Dr. Sorenson and I'll be looking after you today and tomorrow. How was your night?"

Sabrina nodded. "Good."

The doctor looked at the chart in his hand for just a second, then glanced briefly at Mom before he turned back toward Sabrina. He leaned closer, taking a look at her nose, then looked back toward Mom. "Is there any improvement that you can tell?"

Mom shook her head. "No, in fact, those spots on the right side of her nose are new since yesterday. Before that, it was all on the left side."

He nodded. "Okay. Well, it's early in her treatment course yet." He did the usual series of checks, spending extra time listening to Sabrina's lungs. He glanced toward Mom again. "I've talked with Sabrina's regular physician, and I see the note where you talked to Dr. French last night. I ordered some extra blood work this morning and based on those results, I've now ordered a chest X ray."

Sabrina's mother looked . . . relieved, but Sabrina didn't understand. "What? A chest X ray? Why?"

"There is some concern about the fact that you've had so many colds and flulike symptoms over the past few months. Given the nature of the medications you've been on, we just want to be certain we're not missing something. This morning's blood work came back a little . . . puzzling. Not completely indicative of infection, but something does seem to be out of whack."

Dr. Sorenson asked some questions, made some notes, then

walked out just as the morning nurse was making her appearance. She looked back toward the door as it pulled closed. "Don't you just love Dr. Sorenson? He has got to be one of the nicest people I've ever met. I wish he worked here all the time."

"Doesn't he?" Mom's voice held evident concern. Sabrina could hear the rest of the thought as clearly as if it had been spoken out loud. *If he doesn't work here all the time, is he a good enough doctor to be taking care of my baby?*

"No, he works in one of the big teaching hospitals up in Nashville, but he has family down this way. Every now and then when we need some added coverage, he comes down and puts in a day or two. One of the hospitalists is getting married this afternoon, and the entire team wanted to go to the wedding, so . . . Dr. Sorenson to the rescue."

"Well then, he sounds like a good man to have around." Sabrina's mother returned to her earlier state of high cheer, humming as she put her book inside her purse.

"My name is Jessica, by the way." Jessica wrote her name on the white board on the wall across from Sabrina's bed. "And my aide today will be Kaitlin." She walked over to the IV pump and checked the bag. "I'll be back in another hour to change out your fluid bag. In the meantime, let us know if you need anything, okay?"

Sabrina waited until Jessica left the room before she turned to her mother. "What did Dr. Sorenson mean when he said that you talked to Dr. French last night? What did you talk about?"

Sabrina's mother shrugged and her face turned pink. "I just asked him if he would run some tests while you're here. You've been sick so much this semester, I've been concerned that something was wrong for a while now."

"What makes you think I've been sick?" Sabrina had made a point not to tell either her mother or her grandmother when she'd felt bad.

Her mother smiled and kissed her forehead. "You put on a brave front, but your grandmother is one of the most intuitive people I know. She's been concerned."

"And when you talked to Dr. French last night, he didn't want to do any detective work?"

"No, he didn't. As I'm sure you recall, he didn't really even want you in this hospital." She shook her head, lips pressed together tight. When she looked over at Sabrina, she seemed to remember herself. "Shall we watch the next *Pirates*?"

"Sure."

Somewhere in the middle of Captain Jack Sparrow crowing about having a jar of dirt, a radiographer entered the room with a portable X-ray machine, and almost as quickly, disappeared out the door.

It wasn't long before Dr. Sorenson made an appearance. "Good morning again, ladies. I just got a call from the radiologist. There are a couple of areas they want to examine more closely, so we're going to get you in for a CT. Looks like it'll happen in the next couple of hours."

"What do you see?" Mom's face had gone just a bit pale.

"It's unclear. Maybe just mucous, but it could also be a nodule. After we get a clearer picture, we'll decide the next steps."

Sabrina looked toward her mother and couldn't help but notice the grim satisfaction on her face. "I told him something was wrong." She said this more to herself than anyone, shaking her head as she said it.

And for the first time, Sabrina felt a shiver of worry.

35

I'm telling you, you should have seen it. That girl was moving like a creature possessed. I don't think I've ever seen anything like it. Well, I take that back. I've seen it before—in you. Back when you were going crazy trying to get ready for your first year of college. I thought you were going to push yourself so hard you'd lose your mind in the midst of it."

Sabrina listened to Nana's story of Brandy's training run that morning. Apparently, Nana had watched the entire thing out the window in equal parts amusement and concern.

"When she finally fell over on the sidewalk, I wanted to run out there. It took everything I had to stay inside. But I could see that she was just recovering—as you used to call it—and I thought it might embarrass her to have an old lady hovering over her."

"Good thinking, Nana. Not to mention, if you let on that you'd seen the entire two-hour session, she might have decided that you were somewhat of a snoop."

Nana's eyes widened in angelic innocence. "Who, me? I wasn't snooping at all. Went outside to get my paper and saw her disappearing around the corner. Of course, then I looked at my watch and realized it was your usual training time, so I just peeked to see what she would do. After it became apparent she was running like a crazy person, I was just plain curious to see how far she'd push it. I must say, she surprised me with the answer to that one." Nana shook her head. "I worry about that girl."

Maybe Sabrina really had dismissed Brandy too quickly. The same way people had dismissed her when she first started having joint problems. "Maybe I—"

The door swung open and Dr. Sorenson entered the room. He looked different than he had that morning. Tired, maybe. The sparkle was missing from his eyes, his smile mostly absent. "Hello, ladies." He nodded around the room. "I come bearing test results, so . . . ." He let his voice fade out, an obvious hint that this was private.

"I'd like Mom and Nana to stay. I tell them everything anyway."

He nodded. "Of course. Who hears your medical information is entirely up to you."

Sabrina nodded, her stomach tightening up just a little. Why was he so solemn? This was the same expression she'd seen on her doctors' faces before they realized she did indeed have arthritis. It was the "according to all our tests there is absolutely nothing wrong and you are such a terrible hypochondriac that it caused a rash to break out on your nose" kind of look.

He looked at Sabrina. "The CT scan confirmed a couple of nodules in your lungs. Have you traveled anywhere in the western United States recently?"

"Yes, over the holidays."

He shook his head. "I think you picked up a fungal infection that is prevalent in Arizona and certain parts of California known as coccidioidomycosis. The spores are in the air, and if you breathe them in, you can be infected. It's sort of like tuberculosis, it usually infects the lungs. Given your immune-suppressed state, of course you were an easy target. In fact, I am more than a little relieved they didn't find any nodules outside your lungs, but they seem to be contained."

"What do we do now?" Mom was chewing on her fingernails, her eyes wide and focused.

"Assuming the blood tests confirm my suspicion, we'll switch her over to a different medication. It'll likely mean a few more days in the hospital, just until we get it all dialed in. This infection can be very serious if not caught early. It's a good thing she came in when she did. The nose is one of the first places these types of infection often manifest themselves outwardly, so your rash has been a nice diagnostic tool for us."

"All things work together for good," Nana said, nodding her head slowly, "even nose rashes, apparently."

Dr. Sorenson smiled. "That certainly seems to be true in this case."

"Thank you, Dr. Sorenson. Thank you so much for ordering those tests." Mom's voice was firm, in control.

He nodded toward her. "You were right in pushing for them."

"All things work together for good." Nana repeated the words even softer this time. "All things."

Sabrina was just now beginning to remember how strongly she used to hold to those words. Somehow, over the course of the last few years and all their hardships, that conviction had faded.

Sort of like the Israelites in the wilderness. Maybe it was time to quit looking at her circumstances and start believing God would show her the way to her Promised Land.

Sabrina tried her hardest to focus on her textbook, but there were too many distractions vying for her attention. Brandy's morning run, earlier conversations with Rita Leyva about Bridges, Koen's lack of response to her text, and visions of what might be lurking in her lungs filled every available space in her mind, leaving no room for thoughts of anything else.

She looked over at her mom, who was staring silently at the wall. Sabrina knew that she, too, was overwhelmed—more with worry for Sabrina than anything else. Perhaps a distraction would be good for them both. "Shall we put in the next movie?"

Her mother looked over at her. "Are you sure?"

"Yeah. I think distraction might be a good thing at this point."

"I know what you mean." She reached into her bag and removed a DVD, still nodding. "I sure, sure do." She had just reached up to insert the movie when her hand dropped and she turned her full attention out into the hallway, leaning forward to get a better view. "You know, I'm thinking before we start this, I might run downstairs and get a quick bite of dinner."

"But I thought—"

Sabrina's mother was smiling and waving toward the door. "Hello. Please come in, come in."

A handful of flowers came slowly into view, followed by their owner. Koen smiled nervously toward her, then her mother, then walked on into the room. "Hey." He looked nervously back toward Sabrina's mom. "I hope I'm not interrupting anything."

"Not at all. I was just telling Sabrina I was hungry and about to go down for dinner. Have a seat and keep her entertained for me, okay?"

"Sure."

"I'll be back in a bit. Call my cell if you need anything." Mom exited the room with an amazing blast of speed, leaving Sabrina and Koen to look at each other in awkward silence.

"You said it was okay if I stopped by, right?"

"Uh, yes. Yes I did. Please, have a seat." She motioned toward the chair her mother had just vacated.

He moved toward it, then stopped. "I brought these for you." He lifted the flowers just slightly.

"They're beautiful." Sabrina took them, drew in a deep breath of the rosy fragrance, then set them right beside her on the tray.

Koen looked down at her, taking in her T-shirt and pajama pants, the messy ponytail, and the sparkle slipper socks. "I wanted you to be more laid back, but this seems kind of extreme."

He smiled and Sabrina burst out laughing. "Yeah, you won."

"Even without this, it was a foregone conclusion. I didn't exactly ace the last psych test."

It felt so good to be near him again. So right. More than anything, Sabrina wanted that part of her life back. Time to use some courage and do what she should have done a long time ago. "I'm really sorry about what happened. You were always nothing but good to me, and I shouldn't have—"

He put his fingers to her lips. "Not another word. Apology accepted." He smoothed her hair back from her forehead. "How you doing, really?"

"Fine." Fact was, she felt all right—there wasn't any reason to bore him with medical details. Besides that, having him near, things suddenly seemed a lot better. "So, what's new with you?"

"Not much. The usual."

She nodded. "Me too." She looked at his face, and how she longed to touch it. Well, she supposed now was her last chance. "My usual isn't as much fun as it used to be. I . . . uh . . . miss you."

He reached over and squeezed her hand. "Maybe we should see what we can do about that."

"I'd like that."

"Me too."

The room grew quiet. Too quiet. Koen shifted and took to examining Sabrina's IV pump. "This is quite the gadget."

"Yeah, pretty high tech, I guess."

He nodded. "Well, I can't stay long, I promised Jared I'd help man the grill tonight. He's hosting one of his famous burger busts."

"Sounds fun." She tried to seem more upbeat than she felt. Fact was, she was more than certain who else would be at the burger bust. "Hopefully I'll see you at school sometime later in the week."

"Looking forward to it." He stood, gave her hand one last squeeze, and walked from the room. Sabrina watched the door close and the room suddenly felt so much darker and emptier.

"Please come back." She whispered the words to no one but herself, knowing that she was talking about so much more than just this hospital room.

"Okay, intermission." Mom ejected the DVD from the back of the TV. "Before we start another one, I say let's go for a little walk."

Sabrina looked at the door. Half of her wanted to get out of there and walk around, because in truth she was going a little stir crazy. The other half just felt like lying in bed and, for lack of a better word, wallowing. But she knew her mother well enough to know that she sensed this, and would not rest until she believed Sabrina sufficiently cheered up. "A walk sounds good." If she put on a good show of happiness, they could keep it short.

"They've got a lovely garden patio, not to mention the gift shop has a complete selection of every type of candy known to man."

"Now, that sounds promising." A quick trip to the gift shop would satisfy her mother that all was well, and they could come back soon and maybe get a little treat in the deal. "I'm looking for some gum."

"All right then, let's do it." Her mom put on her perkiest face, the one she reserved for emergency situations. "A girls' shopping expedition, right here in the hospital."

They checked with the nurse, then rode the elevator to the main floor. Sabrina knew she looked a mess, but since she was rolling an IV pole alongside her, she supposed it didn't much matter. She put on her own perky saved-for-emergencies face, determined to convince her mother that all was well in the shortest amount of time possible.

The gift shop was actually a nice little store. There were snacks, trinkets, stuffed animals, and even shirts. Sabrina picked up a hot pink Southern Tennessee General Hospital T-shirt. "This is kind of cute. Who knew hospital fashion was even possible?"

Her mother walked over, the gleam in her eye showing that she was pleased about how this outing was going. "Yes, you're right. It is cute."

"Sabrina?"

Sabrina turned at the sound of her name to find Cassie Ardito, one of Lindy Stewart's friends from school, standing behind her. "Cassie, hi. How are you?"

"I'm thinking I should be asking you that question. Are you a patient here?" Her gaze roamed from Sabrina's pajama pants to the IV pole at her side.

Sabrina didn't know Cassie well enough that she wanted to go into details, so she simply said, "Yes. It's nothing major though, just getting some IV meds for an infection."

Cassie looked at Sabrina's nose for just a split second. "I'm sorry to hear that."

"What are you doing here?"

"My mom's a nurse up on the fourth floor. I'm meeting her for dinner."

"Sounds good. Well, we're about to head back upstairs, so nice seeing you."

"You too."

Sabrina started toward the door, thankful to have made such an easy escape, when Cassie's words stopped her. "I heard you got offered an internship at Grace Rose. Congratulations."

"How did you hear about that?" She couldn't imagine the answer. Sabrina hadn't talked about it much, and she was certain Koen and Lindy hadn't exactly been discussing Sabrina's professional future.

"My sister-in-law works there as a personal assistant. When she found out they were hiring an intern from Southern Tennessee State, she called and asked me if I knew you."

"Oh, great. How does she like it there?"

"I think the hours are a little long, but she seems to enjoy it."

"Good to know. Well, nice seeing you."

"Get well."

"Thanks, I plan to." Sabrina made her way over to her mom. "Ready to go finish the movie?"

"Sure. Do you want to go check out the garden first?"

"No. I think I've had enough excitement for one outing."

They got back into the elevator. After the door closed and they were alone, her mother said, "That was someone you know from school?"

"Yes."

"She seemed like a nice girl."

"She is." And in truth, Cassie was a nice girl. But somehow Sabrina felt very vulnerable about running into her today. She shook her head. She was just being paranoid.

36

Brandy made her way up the hospital stairs. The morning's workout barked at her with each step, her quads and calves already growing sore. But because Sabrina had called and asked if she would come over, none of that mattered. She'd hurried over, a little afraid of what she was going to hear, but more relieved that Sabrina wanted to talk.

A half-dozen gadgets littered the hallway. Poles with some sort of mechanical boxes on them and IV bags hanging above, large rolling cabinets, wheelchairs, and at the far end of the hall a stretcher sat outside a room. She stood outside Sabrina's door for just a moment, trying to decide if she should knock or just walk in.

She knocked softly but didn't hear any kind of response. Then she knocked a little louder. Finally, she pushed at the door and knocked at the same time. "Oh, come in, come in." Sabrina's mother was rearranging some clothes in the little closet, but she leaned out and smiled. "Brandy, I'm glad you could come. I know Sabrina is anxious to talk to you."

"Where is she?" Brandy looked at the empty bed, confused.

"Oh, she's just in the bathroom. She'll be out any second, but it takes a lot longer to get around when you've got to drag an IV pole everywhere you go."

"Not to mention avoid getting tangled in any of the lines." Sabrina came through the bathroom door just then, pushing her IV pole in front of her.

"I'm going out to the lobby for a minute to make a few phone calls. You girls enjoy your visit." And just like that, Sabrina's mom disappeared out the door, leaving the two of them alone.

"Thanks for coming." Sabrina shuffled her way over to the wall beside her bed, where she plugged in a three-pronged extension cord that led to the box on her IV pole. She sat on the bed's edge, her feet dangling just above the floor. "So, as I recall, you had something you wanted to say to me on Wednesday morning."

"Yes, yes I did. I wanted to say that I am so sorry." And once Brandy started, the words just tumbled out of her mouth, out of control. "I should have come by your house, or called at least, that night after the race. But I just couldn't face you. I blew it, I know I did. There are lots of excuses I could give you, but the truth is, the pressure just got to me and I caved in. It was wrong. I'd give everything I have to go back and do things differently, but the fact is I can't. It was just so stupid, what I did."

"Yes. It was." Sabrina didn't seem angry, exactly, but her eyes looked so flat . . . hard, almost.

Brandy wasn't sure what else she should say. Her grandmother had told her that Sabrina had some weird kind of lung infection, but she wasn't sure if she was supposed to know about it. Still, she couldn't just ignore it. Finally, she settled for, "So . . . how are things going with you?"

Sabrina shrugged. "All right. I've got to stay in the hospital for a couple more days until some tests come back and they decide the best course of treatment. It'll put me behind at school, but I've got all my books here." She nodded toward a pile of thick textbooks. "What about you? How are things?"

"Good. Just the usual, you know. Hanging out." She paused for a second, not knowing why she had felt it necessary to try to play it cool in front of Sabrina. "I'm still running."

"So I heard." Sabrina shifted and looked out the window. "Nana told me you put in quite the workout this morning."

Brandy knew her mouth had dropped open. "Really? She saw that?"

"She saw enough to say that you almost killed yourself." Sabrina smiled and looked back toward her. "She said you reminded her of me in the old days."

It wasn't until that moment that the full force of what Sabrina had lost to arthritis truly hit her. To have worked that hard, to have endured so many long and painful workouts, years' worth, to have given up other opportunities . . . and then for it all to be taken away by something she couldn't control. Not because she wasn't good enough or didn't work hard enough, but just because. It was so unfair. "I wish you were still running." The words had no sooner left her mouth than Brandy realized how awful that might have sounded. "I mean . . . I wish you were still healthy." Urg! Could she dig herself any deeper into stupid?

"Me too." It was stated as a fact. Nothing more. Nothing less.

A beeping came from Sabrina's bedside, loud and high pitched. Sabrina reached for the mechanical box on her IV pole and pressed a button. "This thing drives me crazy."

"What does it mean?"

"The IV isn't flowing quite right for one reason or another. In a minute I'll call the nurse to look at it. But right now, I want to talk to you about a new training schedule."

Brandy waited for the rest of the sentence, the bad news. But Sabrina said nothing else. "You mean . . . you're going to help me again?"

"To tell you the truth, I'm not sure what I'm going to do. I didn't mean to, I'll tell you that, but for some reason I can't seem to help myself." She sort of smiled. "For now, I've revised your schedule, but obviously I'm not going to be there for the next few days. It's going to be up to you to push yourself. If you slack off on the back side of the block, I won't be there to call you on it."

"I won't, I promise."

"Good. Now let me find that chart I made for you." Sabrina opened the drawer on her bedside table and brought out a piece of paper with hand-drawn columns. "As soon as I get back home, I'll print out the official version, but this will have to do for now. This is your schedule for the next two weeks. After that, well . . . we'll see what happens."

Brandy's eyes burned, something totally uncharacteristic for her. Especially when it involved someone telling her what to do. "Thank you. For giving me another chance. I promise I won't let you down this time."

"I hope you won't. Your grandmother believes in you and in spite of myself, I believe in you, too. You've just got to believe in yourself enough to stick it out."

The IV started beeping again. Sabrina reached out and quieted it, then pushed the nurse's call button.

A voice came from the speaker just above her bed. "Can I help you?"

"My IV is beeping."

"I'll let your nurse know."

"Thanks." Sabrina turned back to Brandy now. "All right, you've got some training to do. And take good care of your grandmother, too. She deserves it."

"I know. I will."

As Brandy walked out to the parking lot, and even long after that, Sabrina's words rang through her mind over and over again. "I believe in you."

37

Monday evening, Sabrina's father arrived with a worried look on his face. He'd been in the room only a few minutes when the door swung open and Dr. Freeman, the infectious disease specialist, came to stand at the end of Sabrina's bed. "We've got a definitive diagnosis. I have just spoken with the pathologist and we are ready to move forward with treatment."

"Thank goodness. Will I be able to go home now?"

"Maybe by the end of the week. We want to start you out on IV treatment before we switch you over to oral meds." She looked down at the chart.

"Couldn't we just begin with the oral stuff? I really need to get back to class this week."

Dr. Freeman nodded. "You really need to get this infection under control, too. It has the potential to be very serious, especially given your immune-suppressed state. We are going to treat you especially aggressively."

"Great, just great." Sabrina sighed, then looked toward Dr.

Freeman. "Sorry, didn't mean to whine. What's the plan and how soon can we get this started?"

"I'm starting the paper work now, but it will take a while to get it in motion. The plan, first off, is to keep you off your arthritis meds other than naproxen for pain and inflammation. We absolutely cannot afford to suppress your immune system right now. We are going to start you out on an IV medication that has the broadest range of coverage for this type of disease. The drug is called amphotericin, but I must be honest. Among the medical community, it is known as ampho-terrible."

"I don't like the sound of that." Mom's eyes were huge with worry.

"Do whatever you have to do. Let's just get this show on the road." Sabrina would take anything just to get her treatment started and to get out of this place.

It was five hours later before all the procedures had been met and the nurse brought in the first bottle of IV medication. "There are lots of side effects with this one. I know we've gone over all of them with you, but push your call button and we'll help you with what we can. I'm going to stay in here with you for the first few minutes and make sure everything is okay."

"Sure." A minute later what felt like fire entered Sabrina's arm. She reached up and put her hand just below her IV line out of instinct, taking a deep breath. She supposed there was nothing to do but withstand it, but this hurt.

"Is it burning?"

"Yes."

The nurse pulled out a plastic pack, bent it to break something inside, and put it on Sabrina's arm. "Try this. Heat usually helps."

And it did. To some degree.

Then the shakes started. Whole body, uncontrollable shakes. Somewhere during the six-hour long ordeal, Sabrina's father took a seat right beside the bed, and every few minutes he would jump up to get a new heating pack for her arm in an effort to stop the burning.

Though she'd long ago let herself get lost in the pain and fire and shaking, she could feel him beside her. He'd put his head on the side of the bed and rubbed Sabrina's arms, and she swore she heard him mumbling the words "I'm sorry. I'm so sorry."

38

A couple of days later, Sabrina's stomach began to cramp as she tried to eat her lunch. She stopped eating and lay back on her bed, wondering when all this was going to be over. In the last twenty-four hours, a rash had begun to creep up her neck and across her face. The doctor said it was a drug reaction—not an allergy, just a side effect. Now it looked as if they could add upset stomach to the list. She pushed the tray away from her and closed her eyes. Her bedside phone rang, as it did almost constantly. She didn't even open her eyes, but said to her mother, "Will you tell everyone I don't feel like company today?"

"Of course I will." The phone scraped across the tray. "Hello."

There was a pause for a moment and then her mother explained to whoever it was that Sabrina wasn't feeling well and that it probably wouldn't be a good time to come by. "Yes, I'll tell her you called. I know she'll be glad to see you when she's feeling better."

"Who was it?" Sabrina never bothered to open her eyes.

"Koen."

Koen. He'd been by every day since that first visit. He'd brought assignment lists for her classes and he'd brought his own books, too, although he had yet to open one. Mostly, he'd chatted and worked on keeping things upbeat, in spite of the side effects Sabrina was muddling through. It was just as well he wasn't coming today. She certainly wasn't up to being anything close to charming, and to say that she looked a complete wreck was beyond an understatement. How she wanted her old life back, to be out of here and in her normal routine.

For the first time since this all started, Sabrina had no intention of doing homework today. She felt weak. Her stomach hurt. Finally, she opened her eyes and switched on the television. After flipping through the channels, she settled on a *Say Yes to the Dress* marathon. Her mother sat beside her in her chair and watched silently. She reached over to put her hand on Sabrina's arm and the two of them simply sat, unmoving.

They were halfway through the third episode, one where the bride loved a dress, but her overbearing maid of honor was being really rude in her voicing of her dislike, when Dr. Freeman came into the room. "How are you feeling, Sabrina?"

"Fine." There was no reason to complain.

"I heard you didn't eat much lunch."

She shrugged. "I've got a stomachache."

Dr. Freeman nodded. "I see." She came over and began poking and prodding Sabrina's abdomen. "Does this hurt? Does this?"

After a few minutes, she seemed convinced that it was nothing more than a routine stomachache. "Your last set of labs just came back. Your serum creatinine has been climbing every day since we started amphotericin. Today, I have no choice but to make the decision to discontinue the drug."

Sabrina's mother scooted to the edge of her chair. "What does that mean? It's kidney function, right?"

"Yes."

"So, does this mean permanent damage, or will her kidneys get back to normal? What about the infection?"

"As far as her kidneys go, it is likely that they will recover. Only time will tell for sure, but I'm optimistic. As for her treatment, I'm going to change her to the oral medication that I had planned to put her on when we discharged her. This is a little sooner than I'd hoped, but at this point there's just no choice."

"Can't say I'm sorry to see that one stopped." Sabrina could almost cry with relief at the thought of not having to put up with the excruciating burning in her veins during tonight's amphotericin infusion. Still, the rash that now covered her neck and back was there to let her know that she was not going to be completely free of its side effects for a while yet. "Let's get rolling on the new med so we can take this party back to Nana's house—not that the accommodations here aren't fabulous, mind you." She used every bit of energy she possessed to make a believable expression of bravado as she pumped her fist in the air.

The doctor reached down and squeezed Sabrina's foot. "You've always got such a positive attitude." She made some notes on the chart. "The good news is, you should experience significantly less side effects on the new medication."

"I'm all for that." Sabrina watched her walk from the room, then turned the sound back up on the TV. By now, the bridal shop owner had stepped in and helped the bride shut down her bossy maid of honor. The dress had been decided upon and everyone was going home happy.

Sabrina was tired—tired of trying to smile through the pain and tired of putting on a happy face for everyone. She was glad that it was just her and Mom, and she didn't have to pretend to be anything for the rest of the day.

A soft knock sounded at the door. Sabrina tried not to groan, wondering whether it was another lab tech looking to draw blood, or perhaps the pharmacy coming to check the IV levels in the current drip going into her arms.

Koen peeked around the doorframe. "I know you don't feel like entertaining, but I just had to come see you." He grinned nervously as he looked back and forth between Sabrina and her mother.

Sabrina realized how happy she was he'd dared to come. "Come on in, if you're feeling brave. I warn you, though, it's not pretty in here." She waved her hand over her cheek, game-show style, highlighting the increased rash since yesterday.

He walked closer and bent over to look at her, seemingly holding his breath. After a few seconds, he nodded his head a single time. "I'm saying that shade of red blotch looks good on you."

Sabrina actually laughed. A true, happy, not forced laugh. "Have a seat if you're not afraid to stay a while."

"Wait, I brought you something." He put his backpack on the floor and pulled out a stuffed polar bear. The bear had a ribbon around his neck, which Koen proceeded to use to hang him on the IV pole. "He's a 'pole-r bear,' get it?"

Sabrina groaned. "Don't make me ask you to leave. I think I'll call him . . ." She paused, looked at Koen, then worked up a grin, "Frederick."

"Tough crowd." He looked up at the TV and said, "Sorry, I didn't mean to interrupt. I'll be quiet."

Without another word he came to sit in the chair on the opposite side of the bed from her mother. He leaned over and took Sabrina's hand, and for the next two hours, sat in complete silence and simply watched TV with her.

Sabrina felt the soft pressure of his hand on hers, thought about how completely bored he must be, and marveled at how he had the sensitivity to just sit quietly and be with her.

When the attendant arrived with her dinner tray, Koen stood

up, kissed Sabrina on the forehead, and said, "I'll see you tomorrow."

"Thank you." Never in her life had those words meant more.

He stopped at the door and turned back to look at her. Just for a moment their eyes met. He blinked once and looked away. "You're welcome." And then he was gone.

39

Sabrina climbed into the passenger seat of her mother's car, stealing a glance at the clutter in the back seat of flower vases, balloons, and assorted posters her friends had brought to her over the course of the last six days. Frederick the polar bear, though, he'd stay in the front with her.

"Are you sure you don't want to go home, I mean to your real home, instead of going back to Nana's?" Mom had asked this same question, worded in various ways, several times throughout the morning.

Sabrina shook her head. "I've missed so much class already. I can't afford to miss any more."

"All right, ladies, let's get this show on the road." Sabrina's father closed the passenger side door behind Sabrina, then held open the back door. Mom could barely fit. He gently closed the door behind her, taking care not to bang her shoulder, then came around to the driver's side and started the car. He looked toward Sabrina. "I bet it feels pretty good to be getting out of that place, hmm?"

"You have no idea." Sabrina rested her head back against the seat, thankful that they had chosen to bring Mom's roomier SUV instead of her father's smaller sedan. Much roomier. She looked toward her father. "What would you say are the possibilities of stopping at Sonic for a quick burger?"

Her mother leaned forward. "It's nice to hear there is something that can stimulate your appetite, as sick as you've been. Does a Sonic burger sound good to you?"

"Yeah." Sabrina sighed and closed her eyes. "The food at General is not bad as far as hospital food goes, but I am so ready for something different."

"I really think we should go to Nana's and fix something a little healthier. Burgers don't exactly sound like the best thing for you right now. Don't you agree?"

Sabrina closed her eyes tight in an effort to hold the frustration inside her. Why did he never lighten up?

"Bill, the poor thing has had such an upset stomach for the last few days. If something sounds good to her, I think we ought to let her try it, don't you? I don't think one cheeseburger is going to greatly wreck her health."

"My daughter just spent six days in the hospital because her immune system can't fight an infection. I'm saying I want to do everything in my power to give her body the strength it needs to fight back, because I don't ever want to go through this again."

"*You* don't want to go through this again?" Sabrina's eyes flew open at the same time her mouth did. "I'm sorry that I've been an inconvenience for you, Dad."

"That's not what I meant, and you know it. This is about doing what is best for you."

Sabrina didn't say anything else, she simply nodded. It seemed her father was somehow once again blaming her for getting sick.

"Bill, she has barely kept five hundred calories' worth of anything down in the last week. I've always heard that if someone is having stomach trouble and they start craving something, it's something that will settle her stomach. Don't you think we should give it a try?" Mom's voice was calm, but it was also firm. She rarely stood up to Dad without backing down, but Sabrina was more than certain that this was going to be one of those times.

Apparently Dad realized this, too. He glanced once toward Sabrina and shook his head almost imperceptibly. "I guess it won't hurt. But I'm saying we need to make sure she's on a healthy living regimen once she gets settled."

"Sure, Dad, sounds good."

Brandy knocked softly. She knew that Sabrina still did not feel well, and she didn't want to wake her if she was sleeping. Mrs. Springer answered the door. She looked tired, but she smiled her welcoming smile.

"Brandy, it's so good to see you. Sabrina's just sitting at the kitchen table doing some schoolwork. Come on in. I know she's been looking forward to seeing you." She led Brandy into the kitchen. "Can I get you something to drink? Some water or soda or anything?"

"No, ma'am. Thank you."

"I'll leave you two young'uns to talk, then." She left the room, but not before she cast a worried glance in Sabrina's direction.

Sabrina was sitting with her head supported by one hand, elbow on the table. There was a thick book opened in front of her on the table, but she looked up and smiled at Brandy. "Hey there, slacker."

"Hey, yourself. And the only slacker around here is you. I've been running my legs off, thanks to that torture chamber you have the nerve to call a training schedule. You've been home from the hospital for three days now—time to look for a new excuse for sleeping in on training mornings."

Sabrina leaned back in her chair, a huge smile across her face. "That's more like it. I've got enough people trying to baby me around here."

"So I figured. It's time for some tough love, and I'm just the person to bring it."

"I don't doubt that at all. How's training?"

"Pretty decent." Brandy nodded. "I'm still pushing. I haven't missed a single thing on your list. Usually I try to do just a little something more."

"Good for you. It's that extra push that will see you through when you think there's nothing left." Sabrina's short sleeves revealed pale, skinny arms covered by a red rash. Brandy couldn't help but wonder if that's how Sabrina was getting by now. Just pushing past what would be expected of most people.

"And I'm thinking you're right about my slacking. Tomorrow morning I plan to come out and see for myself. Don't let me down."

"Really? Are you sure you're up for it?" She was still so pale.

"Don't tell me you're going to back off now. I've been pushing you hard all this time. It's time for you to start returning the favor. Besides, Mrs. Lauderdale is about to blow a gasket because I'm not, and I quote, 'living up to my end of the bargain.' That woman is something else."

"Tell me about it." Brandy rolled her eyes in agreement, with no intention of telling Sabrina that Mrs. Lauderdale had called their house a couple of times, too. Her talk of calling the judge had so far been just empty threats, and while that could change at any time, Brandy would not add to Sabrina's burden. Instead, she did what Sabrina had asked her to do and pushed. "I'm thinking we should start a little extra early tomorrow. Four forty-five-ish."

Sabrina looked at her without changing expression. No laugh, not even a smile. Of course, it was obvious by looking at her she did not feel well. "Or maybe a little later would be fine, too."

Sabrina rolled her eyes. "You backed down from that one way too easy. Let me see . . ." She made a pretext of looking at the calendar on her smartphone. "I already had you penciled in for five o'clock tomorrow morning. Since my social calendar is so completely overbooked, let's just stick with that."

A person couldn't help but admire Sabrina's show of bravado, even at times like this. It gave Brandy the odd need to cry, which she had no intention of doing. Time for a change in subject. "There's a big 5K in Nashville at the end of the month. I've entered it."

"Oh right, the Music City Run. I'd had that one on my radar, but then got distracted and forgot to mention it to you."

Distracted. Right. Brandy looked at Sabrina, a new determination burning inside her chest. "I'm going to win it. For my age group at least."

Sabrina smiled. "That's the fighting spirit. It's that kind of thinking that separates the good from the great."

Good and great occurred in a lot more places than running. Brandy knew that she was looking at a rarer form of great right now. "I learned it from you." She hated it when her voice cracked, but this was one of those times when she just couldn't help it. "I wish there was something I could do to help you."

Sabrina waved her hand dismissively. "I'm fine, really, just a little tired."

"You can try selling that to someone who will actually buy it."

"We're a lot alike, the two of us, when you get right down to it. Neither one of us likes other people's pity. Maybe that's why we understand each other so well in spite of our differences."

Brandy nodded. "I guess you're right about that."

"Of course I'm right. I'm your coach, I'm always right." Her attempt at humor was as feeble as she looked, but Brandy made a point of tossing her head back to honor the attempt at smack talk.

"'Course you are." She stood up, with every bit of her heart breaking for Sabrina, but determined to do what it was she thought Sabrina needed. "See you in the morning, if you're not too busy sleeping in."

Sabrina's smile was genuine then. "I'll try to work you into my busy schedule."

Brandy somehow managed to make it to the sidewalk before she burst into tears.

40

At four forty-five, the sound of pseudo ocean slowly filtered into Sabrina's consciousness. Ugh. Why had she been so quick to say she would be at this morning's workout?

She rolled over and sat up, rubbing the sleep out of her eyes, using every bit of her inner strength to fight the urge to roll over and go back to sleep. And *that* was the reason she'd agreed to this. Inner weakness was not to be indulged. It was that kind of thing that lost championships. Or internships. Or stellar grade point averages.

Somehow she managed to pull on some sweats, splash water on her face, and brush her teeth with one minute to spare. When she walked down to the sidewalk, Brandy was already there, pacing.

"So you did make it." Brandy made a show of looking at her watch. "Barely."

"Did you doubt me?" Sabrina meant it as a flip question, but instead of a quick, snarky response, Brandy simply looked at her long and hard.

"No." She grabbed her left foot behind her to stretch out her quads. "I guess I didn't."

The weight of responsibility pressed down on Sabrina's shoulders. It was more than a little uncomfortable. "What's on your spreadsheet for today?"

"Distance."

"Better get moving, then." She flipped open her laptop, ready to think about something else. "I'm expecting to see some progress since the last time I watched you."

Brandy took off in the usual direction without another word. For just a moment Sabrina watched, noting that her form did look better. Well, it was early in the run yet. Five miles had a way of showing what was ingrained and what was just for show.

Sabrina turned her attention back to her laptop. Her brain cells were not sufficiently engaged to do any sort of meaningful work at this point. Might as well check her email. She opened Outlook, thankful for the nice range of Nana's Wi-Fi.

She did a quick preliminary scan and noticed one from Candace Davenport. It had been received late yesterday afternoon. She scrolled down and read it first.

Sabrina,

We received your paper work in our office yesterday. Thank you for the promptness of your reply. Before processing this any further, however, we have decided to do one more round of interviews. I believe I told you this was a possibility when we talked before. Please call my secretary as soon as possible so we can schedule this in a timely manner.

I look forward to meeting with you again.

Sincerely,
Candace Davenport

Another interview?

An uneasiness settled on her that only grew worse the more she tried to talk herself out of it. Of course, they had said this was a possibility all along, but it seemed a little too convenient that this "unlikely" event occurred right after her hospitalization. What if Cassie had told her sister-in-law about the rash-covered girl she'd seen in the gift shop? Or worse, what if her mother had accessed her medical records and shared even more than that? Were they concerned that she wouldn't have what it took to do the job?

Either way, she planned to go into this interview prepared to show them that she was not only able, but was the best person for the job.

The sound of rubber slapping against concrete pulled her back into the current. Brandy was almost back from her first lap. Sabrina looked down at the stopwatch. "Three minutes. Not bad, but you'd better be back here before it gets to six."

Brandy huffed past her, shaking her head. "Now I remember why I liked training alone."

I like that better, too. The thought came with a fierceness that almost took her breath away. It was more than a random thought, it was an anger so deeply embedded she'd been able to ignore it most of the time. But not now. Not when another gross unfairness was staring her in the face. Why would God allow this to happen? Sabrina had done everything right. She had followed the rules, worked hard—she *deserved* to be out there running. She deserved to get the internship she'd earned on merit.

It wasn't her fault that her body had rebelled. It wasn't her fault even now, when her dream internship was being threatened, probably because of that same unfair disease.

She was good at designing publicity campaigns. That was something that neither arthritis nor her immune system could take from her. No. She was going to fight for this.

Hard.

Koen was sitting at the corner table, and even though his psych book was open in front of him, the movement of thumb against phone dispelled any thought that he was actually studying. As Sabrina moved toward him, she wasn't sure which made her happier—Koen's presence or the prospect of the nice padded chair beside him. She dropped into it, rubbed her right knee, then propped her feet on the chair across from her. "I'm glad that shift's over."

"Me too. Studying, in and of itself, is a horror, but having to do it alone, well, that's downright torturous."

"Like you've been studying. You've been texting the entire time you were in here."

"No I wasn't, I was . . ." He paused for a moment and then leaned closer. "Hey, I think I like knowing that you've been watching me." He leaned closer for the shortest of kisses. His lips felt so warm and soft. "What do you say we blow off studying altogether?"

It was so tempting, or at least it would have been if there wasn't another trip to Atlanta, another interview looming. "Next week, after I get back, I promise I'll relax a little."

He nodded slowly. "I'm going to hold you to that." He kissed her on the cheek. "You're limping today. You feeling all right?"

"I'm fine." Sabrina repeated the same answer she'd given her grandmother while standing in the kitchen that very morning, and on the phone with her mother repeatedly throughout the week. Fact was, the absence of her strongest arthritis meds was taking a toll on her knees. She knew that she couldn't afford to show any kind of weakness in Atlanta on Monday, because she was not going to give them any excuse, any indication that she was not fully up to the job.

"Have you tried icing your knees?"

Normally, this kind of comment would put Sabrina into a "mind your own business" frame of mind. With a busy week looming ahead, she thought now might be a good time to swallow her pride. "That's probably a good idea. Hold on a second, I'm going to get some ice from behind the counter before we get started."

"Would you be more comfortable if we went back to your house to study?"

"More comfortable, probably, but not worth the added worry it would give to my grandmother, and hence my parents."

"You really don't like people to worry about you, do you?"

"No, I don't. And I like pity even less."

And, more than that, I hate that this disease is able to take away everything that matters to me, one dream at a time.

41

Brandy stumbled into the house from her Friday evening training run. As she walked inside on spaghetti legs, she heard Mrs. Springer's voice coming from the kitchen. She rushed forward in spite of her wobbling. "Hi, Mrs. Springer. Is everything all right?"

"About as all right as it can be right now. Sabrina's getting ready to go back to Atlanta on Sunday for another interview Monday morning, and she's worrying herself to death over it."

Brandy crumpled into a chair between the two older women. "She never seems to catch a break, does she."

Mrs. Springer shook her head. "She's had a rough road, there's no doubt about it."

Brandy looked at Mrs. Springer and her grandmother, who she knew shared the same deep faith. "Can I ask a question—without being rude, I mean?"

Mrs. Springer leaned forward and squeezed Brandy's hand. "Of course you can—you're among family here."

"Why is it that someone like Kayla Ratcliff is so convinced God blessed her hard work and dedication, and eventually showed the world that she was superior to Sabrina, that lazy pretender? I mean, we all know better—Sabrina wasn't slacking. Yet Kayla goes around everywhere giving her talk, dissing Sabrina, and she makes it sound like she and God are real tight, but I know part of what she's saying is not really the truth. How can she be so convinced she's got God on her side?"

Mrs. Springer nodded her head slowly, thoughtfully. "I think about things like that a lot. The only thing I can figure is that's what happens when we try to take our own ideas about the way things should work out and make 'em God's. I don't doubt that she has a real desire to know God and that she's doing her best to follow Him. Seems to me, she let herself become so convinced that God was going to give her a scholarship, she stopped listening for His voice about anything else along the way."

She took a sip of the iced tea on the table in front of her. "I imagine she knew how she thought things should work, and when God didn't work that way, she looked for someone to blame. Sabrina was the easy target."

"That makes sense, I guess." Brandy shook her head. "But why doesn't God just shut Kayla up—at least where Sabrina's concerned?"

"Those are the kinds of answers I don't suppose we'll ever get this side of glory."

"I guess not."

"Truth be told, I'm not sure but that Sabrina has made a bit of the same error. After she lost her running, well, she gave up the call to do mission work. She assumed how God was going to work things out, and He had other ideas about how things should go." Mrs. Springer's voice grew quiet. "I've always thought she was missing something there, but she doesn't see it that way."

Grandma, who had been sitting silently, nodded. "Maybe this

is part of God's plan to make her see it, then—her getting called back to Atlanta, I mean."

"I think you may be right, but to tell you the truth, I'm hoping if that's the case, He'll show Sabrina the truth and let her come to the same conclusion. It feels like so many things have been taken out of her control. I'm praying that He'll show her the right path, but give her the option of whether or not to choose it." She took another sip of iced tea. "And I'm praying like crazy that she makes the right choice when the time comes."

The sunset reflected red and pink against the windows of downtown Atlanta. One look at the sky said this wouldn't last long—a thick mass of dark clouds hovered nearby.

Sabrina hung up her clothes for tomorrow, then spent a few minutes settling in for her brief stay. After that, there was nothing left to do but think. And wonder.

This did nothing to settle her already raw nerves, so she turned on the television in an attempt at distraction. The local anchorwoman was talking about plans for lengthening the northbound MARTA line further into the suburbs. Try as she might to pay attention to the story, Sabrina could not stay focused.

The first flash of lightning was followed quickly by a second and a condo-rattling peal of thunder. That got her attention. Sabrina watched the lightning zigzag a random pattern through the black sky. It felt so out of control, so random. Just like her life.

"Stop it. Quit being a whiner and get to work." She shook her head hard, then went in search of her Grace Rose file. For the past year, she'd been collecting all sorts of information about them. There were clippings, articles, and links to publicity campaigns they had created. Top-notch work, all of it. As she had long ago memorized all the pertinent details, there was little to keep her attention.

She reassembled the paper work and thumped the edge a couple of times on the coffee table to line it all up before sliding it back into the file. Then she opened her backpack, considering to which school project she might devote some time.

The pink edge of a small book caught her attention. Her old journal. She'd thrown it in on a whim. She pulled it out. "Okay, naïve Sabrina who knew nothing about the harsh realities of life, let's see what else you have to say."

She pulled it open where the satin bookmark noted her last stopping point. What she found was more notes about the children of Israel leaving Egypt. "I was really stuck on a theme."

> *Seems to me, the people of Israel were too quick to look at their circumstances and come to an assumption on what that meant. Thing is, they never knew beforehand how God was planning to work on their behalf. Who would have ever thought He'd part the Red Sea? Or bring water from a rock? Or send something unheard of, like manna, to feed them? This is a good reminder to avoid letting circumstances alone direct my life. God may have bigger or better plans for me.*

Sabrina closed the book and shook her head. A heavy, guilty kind of feeling pressed against her stomach, but she refused to allow it. "The person who wrote that had never lived through having her entire life plan taken away from her, by something far beyond her control." She tossed the book onto the bed. "You thought you were so smart back then. So full of faith."

She stood up and began to pace around the apartment again, trying to clear her head of the unpleasant thoughts that burned inside her. Try as she might, she couldn't, because a single word had solidified into a chant that would not be quieted.

Faith.

Faith.

Faith.

She turned on the television and flipped through the channels. *The Biggest Loser* finale was just wrapping up, so Sabrina stopped to watch. The woman who won was crying. As they showed her before and after pictures, it was an astounding difference. The hostess asked her what she had learned this season. "When things are at their hardest, that's when you stop looking at the hard things and keep your focus on your goal."

Sabrina thought that sounded a little too similar to the thought she was trying to escape. She took a quick shower and climbed into bed, setting ice packs on her knees, knowing that she needed to be well rested for tomorrow.

Sometime in the middle of the night, she woke up, wide awake, and could not get back to sleep. In desperation she reached for the little journal, still on the bedside table.

Like the Israelites when God called them to the Promised Land. They finally made it where they were supposed to be, but they saw how big the people were who lived in the land and they didn't want to go to war against them. They made the assumption that somewhere along the way Moses had messed up—they were talking about killing him. Now, these same people had been following God all through the desert, they had followed God back when they were slaves, but they had maybe assumed they would just walk in and take the land easily. Their assumption cost them forty years in the desert.

Don't assume.

"Okay, God, if there is something I've been assuming, then please show me what it is. I think I've done everything I'm supposed to and more, but if you see it differently, then I'd like to know about it."

It was said as more of a challenge than a prayer. But after she said the words aloud, she turned out the light and fell back into a deep sleep.

42

The elevator of the Kershaw Building was packed full this morning. It seemed to stop at every other floor, making the trip up excruciatingly slow. Still, after alternating ice and heat all night long, Sabrina's knees felt better than they'd felt in over a week—something for which she was truly grateful. At least she wouldn't be hobbling through her interviews.

As the crowd thinned, Sabrina noticed another young woman about her age. She was dressed in a perfectly fitted blue dress and designer heels, and her hair could have been a photo taken straight from the pages of *Vogue*. Everything about her reverberated confidence, poise, and success.

At each stop, more people left the elevator, but the young woman made no move to do so. At the twenty-first floor, everyone got out but the two of them. The only remaining lit button on the elevator panel was twenty-five. She looked at Sabrina and smiled. "Looks like we're both on our way to Grace Rose."

"Yes." It was bad enough that Sabrina suddenly felt underdressed and dumpy, but why couldn't she think of one intelligent response? She finally managed to blurt, "Do you work there?"

"Not yet, but that's my plan. What about you?"

Just then the elevator doors opened, relieving Sabrina from having to give a firm answer. She mumbled something about this summer then made for the woman at the desk. She looked up.

"Good morning, Ms. Rice, so good to see you again. Ms. Davenport is expecting you. Right this way please."

As she walked away, Sabrina heard the other young woman say, "I'm Tessa Roseman, here about the intern position." Sabrina cast one more sideways glance before following the receptionist down the hall to Candace Davenport's office. Had all the interns been called back in for an interview? Or was this girl a possible replacement for her slot?

Somehow, she knew in the back of her mind that the answer was the latter. Had they decided that she didn't have enough killer instinct after all? Or were they concerned about her health? Either way, Sabrina was not going to let one bit of a limp be apparent today. This was one thing her arthritis was not going to take from her.

The receptionist knocked once on the office door and then opened it. Candace was on the phone, but she waved for Sabrina to come inside and take a seat, holding up one finger to indicate she would be done with the call soon.

"As I explained to Mr. Sumners yesterday, in spite of the fact that he may consider *Noonday With Leslie Franks* less exciting than the Jerry Litton show, *Noonday* appeals to his target market. The majority of Leslie's viewers are young mothers, which is obviously your chief demographic. I believe that you will all be more than pleased with the response."

She went silent for a few seconds, occasionally nodding her agreement with whatever it was that was being said on the other end of the line. "Exactly. I'm so glad we are in complete agreement on this. Rosalee will call you back with the final numbers this afternoon." She pressed the button on the phone, stood from behind her desk, and leaned forward to offer her hand. "Sabrina, so good to see you again."

"It's nice to see you, as well."

"So, I hope we didn't throw you for too much of a loop with this second interview process. Occasionally it happens when there are changes with our clientele or our needs, so we have to redouble our efforts to make sure our interns are exactly what we need for an upcoming season. This year especially, our choices were particularly difficult, so we thought it wise to look at things with laser focus."

"Not a problem at all." Sabrina thought about the healing but still present sores on her nose. She thought about Tessa Roseman in all her perfection. Was she her direct competition? Well, she was here to make certain that whatever it took, she would retain her intern slot. "I'm thrilled to be back here." *And no one is going to take the right away from me. I'll see to it this time.*

Brandy groaned when she saw the name on the caller ID. "Grandma, it's Mrs. Lauderdale calling again."

"Well, answer it." Grandma sounded as irritated as Brandy felt.

"Good afternoon, Mrs. Lauderdale. And how are you today?" Brandy used her best smart-aleck voice, adding an equally fake smile, even though it was a phone call.

"I would be much better if I had your mandatory paper work sitting on my desk in front of me. There are several weeks' worth of reports that are missing."

"Sabrina would be better if you had all those, too, because it would mean that she hadn't been sick and in the hospital. Which, unfortunately, she was. You'll get the new stuff, 'cause she's out and coaching me again."

"So you've said before. I need to speak with your grandmother."

By this time, Grandma had made it into the living room and was standing at the ready. Brandy handed her the phone, rolling her eyes in the process.

"Mrs. Lauderdale, what can I do for you?" Grandma listened for only a few seconds. "No, my granddaughter is not making up stories. That poor girl spent almost a week in the hospital and was sick as could be for a long time after that. She's still not up to full speed. Now, you listen to me. I don't ever want to hear you accuse my granddaughter of lying again, and especially about something like that. She's been worried sick about Sabrina, and for you to even insinuate . . ."

Listening to her grandmother, Brandy's fake smile turned real and it took every bit of strength not to reach over and hug the woman. Instead, she simply thought about the warm feeling she had inside her chest. It felt good.

Grandma shook her head as she listened to what was being said on the other end of the phone. "That's because Sabrina is out of town right now. She'll be back late tonight and I'm sure you'll be able to reach her at her grandmother's house tomorrow." She paused for a moment. "You wouldn't dare." Grandma listened for another few seconds and then hung up the phone. "That lady is just looking for a fight, is what she is. I think she's just mad that she's actually having to do something."

"What wouldn't she dare?"

Grandma shook her head. "Don't you worry about it. She's doing nothing but blowing a bunch of hot air. No judge in the world would blame you because your coach got sick and then got a little behind on mindless paper work."

"I hope not." Brandy toyed with a button at the hem of her shirt. "Thanks, Grandma. For standing up for me like that."

"Well, of course I'm going to stand up for you. I'm your grandmother and I love you to pieces."

Brandy's eyes stung, but she was certainly not going to succumb to any sort of sniveling. "I'm glad you're on my side."

"'Course I am. So are lots of people."

Brandy started to say something like *Yeah, right*, but she didn't. Instead, she choked out, "Like Sabrina."

"Yep. And Louise Springer, too."

"I guess so." She paused, then said, "Sabrina is such a strong person."

"You're right. She has overcome so much and yet she still remains upbeat and positive, when it would out and out crush most people. You know what, though? I know Sabrina would say the same about you."

Late that night, Brandy tossed and turned for as long as she could stand it. With less than a week to go before the Nashville race, her nerves were on edge. Now, even more than the last time, she knew she needed to succeed for Sabrina. After all she'd been through she couldn't bear the thought of letting her down. Not this time.

She climbed out of bed, made quick work of getting dressed in her running gear, and slid open her window. Just a quick run. She knew if she woke up her grandmother she would be worried, or more likely all-out forbid it, but Brandy had to do something. She wouldn't be gone long.

Instead of heading toward Sabrina's house as usual, she turned toward town. She took off in a slow jog, picking random streets without giving it much thought. At least she didn't give it much thought until she heard the car slowing behind her.

What were the odds that once again Janie would be out and about on the same street at the same time Brandy was running off some nerves? She forced herself to turn, preparing herself to face this challenge head on.

But this time, she didn't see Janie's car behind her. It was a family sedan that had pulled into the driveway just behind her.

She exhaled a sigh of relief and took off at a slightly faster pace. As her feet moved her forward, she couldn't help but ask herself the question, *What would I have done?*

Resisted, of course. That's exactly what she would have done. But then again, she'd done that the last time—at first. When it came right down to it, when it was time for the final decision, would she have held firm, or would she have caved in to pressure again? In fact, was that what this run was all about? Was she hoping for the small chance that she would once again run into Janie?

In that moment, she knew that she was. That's why she'd come out tonight. The search for something that would, for just a little while, relieve her of the pressure.

She turned the next corner to move her closer to town, closer to any action that might attract one of her friends. They were likely around here somewhere. All she had to do was keep running and she'd find them. As she made the turn toward McDonald's she saw several cars she recognized in the parking lot. A good time was less than a half block away. It would feel so good to— Stop!

Brandy locked her feet in place, refusing to take even one more step forward. Up ahead of her was the promise of almost instant relief. But she knew now that it came with too high a price. She pivoted and ran back the other way. With each step that hit the pavement, she reflected on the hard workouts she had put in, all the times she had wanted to quit, and all the sacrifices so many people had made to help her with her running. She would not take all that and make it nothing by throwing it away on a quick but temporary fix.

Just to remind herself, she aimed toward Sabrina's house. That would keep her focused.

When she jogged past, all the lights were off and Sabrina's car was back in the driveway. She had made it home from Atlanta, then. She'd already made some excuse about not coming to the race this weekend, probably afraid to.

This time, though, Brandy was going to prove herself worthy of sticking around for.

43

Well, my darling, how did the interview go?" Nana had a full pancake breakfast on the table by the time Sabrina made her way downstairs.

Sabrina shrugged. "I wish I knew for sure. It seemed like it went well, but I can't help but think that part of what prompted this second round of interviews is my illness. Whether or not they think I can handle the job, I can't say."

"Isn't there some kind of antidiscrimination laws for that kind of thing?"

"Probably, but I certainly don't want to start out my career with a legal fight. I want to be hired because I'm the best one for the job. Period. Not because my lawyer forced them to take me."

"Yes, but it seemed like they wanted you just fine back when they thought you were healthy."

"True enough." Sabrina poured syrup over her pancakes. "Luckily I wasn't limping much yesterday, which is more than I can say today. And my nose is looking better, so . . . I guess we'll just have to wait and see."

"Will your heart be truly broken if you don't get the job?"

Sabrina started to give the flip answer, but then paused to actually think about it. Finally, she shrugged. "I don't know, Nana. I mean, no one wants to be rejected, right? Especially if the reason for the rejection is not my fault. And this job is such an amazing opportunity. To begin my career there would give me the experience I need to go anywhere and do anything."

"Where would you want to go and what would you want to do?"

Sabrina took a bite of pancakes, more to give herself time to think than because she was actually hungry. "I don't know, but having lots of choices available is always a good thing, right?"

"Sure enough. I'm just thinking, though, it seems to me that one choice is enough, if that's the choice you want to make."

"You've been talking to Mom, haven't you?"

Nana smiled. "Maybe a little. And I'm afraid she might be right. But"— she reached for the butter and put a sliver on top of her pancake—"it's your life. You're the one who is going to have to figure all that out."

"Mom is so convinced that I'm supposed to be doing some other kind of work, I know she is. But the thing is, by beginning my career at somewhere like Grace Rose it gives me the background I need to work somewhere else eventually."

"I'm thinking beginning your career at the place you're supposed to be would be even better. Don't you?"

"I think more options are better. I really, really want this job."

"Sabrina, if that's the case then I hope you get the job of your dreams. You know what my biggest concern is?"

"What?"

"You have such a competitive spirit, I'm afraid that you want this job so badly because you think you might not be able to have it. It's sort of like that silly show on TV . . . what's it called, where all those girls try to get that guy to propose to them?"

"*The Bachelor.*"

"That's it. Thing is, if most of those girls met that same guy at work, or church or wherever, they would all think he was nice looking most likely, but after a date or two, probably half of them wouldn't want to keep seeing him. Yet, when they get put in this high pressure situation pitted against other girls, it becomes more about *winning* than actually finding a person they want to spend the rest of their lives with. You know what I mean?"

"I guess so. But that's not the case with me."

Nana nodded. "Good, I'm glad to hear it."

The two of them finished the rest of their breakfast in silence. Sabrina picked up her plate and carried it over to the sink. She rinsed it and then loaded it in the dishwasher. "I'm going to go over to the campus to study."

"All righty." Nana stood up with her own plate in hand. "Oh, I almost forgot. You got some mail yesterday. I never did make it up to your room to put it on your desk. I've got it right here." Nana picked up a large envelope from the far counter and brought it to Sabrina.

Sabrina looked at the return address. Rita Leyva.

Out of curiosity, she opened the envelope. Inside was a calendar for the current year, each month showing the smiling face of another orphan who was being helped through the Bridges program. One picture, a small girl with braided pigtails, seemed to look right at Sabrina. She did not want to admit to herself how much it moved her.

She finally slid the calendar back inside the envelope. "I've already got a calendar for this year."

44

Brandy drank the last of her yogurt and fruit smoothie, hoping she could keep it down. That would be ironic, she supposed, if she hurled today simply due to nerves. At least no one would be there to see it. With one exception. "You ready to go, Grandma?"

"Good and ready. How about you? You okay?"

"I think so. A little nervous."

Grandma waved her hand. "Nothing to be nervous about. I can practically guarantee that you'll do better than you did at the last race." She winked. "Don't you think so?"

"At this point, I wish I was more sure of that. What if I don't?"

"Oh, honey, you're working yourself all up into a tizzy. You are a very good runner. You've put in the work. You will do just fine."

"Well," Brandy said as she reached down and picked up her purse, "let's get moving. I want to be there on time to warm up and stretch out."

"I wish Sabrina was going to be there to watch."

"Personally, I'm relieved she had other things she had to do today." Brandy tried to use her brave voice, the one she used when she was trying to sound tougher than she felt. Because, in truth, she wished Sabrina wanted to be there today.

She had come up with some lame excuse about a paper due and that she couldn't take the time to drive all the way to Nashville and back. And knowing Sabrina, she would actually use most of that time to work on her paper. But that wasn't the reason, and Brandy wasn't so stupid that she believed that it was.

They made the drive mostly in silence. As they neared the race area, Brandy turned on some hip-hop music, trying to get pumped up. To Grandma's credit, she didn't say a word about it, just let Brandy do her thing.

Brandy went to the staging area and signed in, then did some warm-ups and stretched. Erin Methvin was out of town this weekend, and Brandy had to admit that she missed having her there. A couple of kids that she knew from the track team were gathered together, but she'd never really talked to any of them, so she stayed in her own little space.

Across the way, the Samson Academy kids were all gathered in a group doing their routines. Their faces were focused, yet not stressed. This was the group that knew they were going to do well, that they would likely win the race, and then they would move on to win the next. What must it be like to have that kind of confidence?

Brandy crossed her right leg over her left, then bent forward to touch the ground. She was more than stretched out by now, but had to do anything to keep busy. And to keep her mind off the red shirts and black shorts just across the way.

"Runners, approach the starting line, please." The announcement moved the herd together toward the starting area.

Brandy's stomach roiled just a little, but it was becoming more the buzz of adrenaline than the nausea of fear. She positioned herself directly behind one of the Samson Academy boys. *You*

*can do this. Pace yourself. Remember your form. Pace yourself,
remember your form. Pace yourself, remember your form.*

"Runners, take your mark."

Brandy took a deep breath, a complete determination welling
up inside her. She was going to beat these girls, she had to.

"Get set."

"Go."

With a blast of the air horn, the line surged forward and Brandy
kept herself in the front of the group so as not to get blocked. The
Samson boys took off at a blistering pace, and she controlled the
temptation to try and keep up with them. Today, she was going
to run her race. The very best race that she could run.

People lined the sides of the race course, shouting encouragement as the runners passed. For the shortest period of time, the
absence of Sabrina burned its way across her chest, but she forced
herself to ignore it.

The only thing she could do now was to win this race and
show them all that she was worthy of being there. And maybe
someday she'd get in the face of that Kayla Ratcliff and tell her
just how mixed up she was about some things.

The first mile was always the hardest for her, so she concentrated
on keeping a nice steady pace and keeping good form. Two of the
Samson Academy girls were a fair distance ahead of her, but hadn't
pulled completely away. Still, she would not use up all her energy
now trying to catch up to them. She would run her own race.

The second mile meant pushing through the heaviness that
wanted to settle in her legs. She'd burned her adrenaline and now
her muscles knew it was their turn. But the weather was perfect
and her breathing was steady and she was more determined than
ever to run her own race.

Up and down the biggest of the hills, there was less than a
mile to go now. Brandy had already caught one of the Samson

Academy girls and they were running mostly shoulder to shoulder. The other remained a good distance ahead. Her brain told her to be logical at this point. A second place finish was plenty respectable, admirable even. The thing to do now was to keep running at her own pace and beat her closest opponent. To push too hard would risk burning up all her energy and placing behind both of them. Better to beat one than none.

But then there was another voice. It started out small, but grew louder and louder. *Beat her. Beat her. Give it all you've got and beat her.*

Her body seemed to make the decision before her brain fully agreed, but Brandy pushed harder and began closing in on the short black curls in front of her. Just to gain an inch cost more pain and energy than she had bargained for, but she kept pushing for the next step and the next, until her legs and lungs were both consumed by fire.

With a quarter mile to go, Brandy realized that she had made a mistake. She could not continue at this pace, and now the runners behind her would get the chance to catch her. Why couldn't she ever listen to the voice of calm and reason in her brain during a race, instead of doing something stupid like this?

"Go Brandy, push. You can do it. *Dig deep!*" The voice came from somewhere to her right. Brandy's eyes flicked over just in time to catch a glimpse of Sabrina and Koen standing on the sidelines. Sabrina was jumping up and down, and frantically waving her arms toward the finish line.

The smallest bit of leftover adrenaline coursed through her body. Not enough, not nearly enough. Brandy knew there was no way she was going to make it, but she decided to push herself so hard that she at least passed out and lost the thing in a spectacular fashion.

Come on, Brandy. Let's see what you've got left.

45

Sabrina hadn't meant to be there. Had done everything in her power to make certain that she would not, in fact, come. But here she stood, the finish line in sight, watching Brandy struggle to keep herself upright and moving.

This morning Sabrina had begun the day early and according to her plans—until she paused to eat some breakfast and Nana said, "I feel like there's something I'm supposed to be doing today. I just can't remember what it was."

Sabrina took another bite of Cheerios. "I hate that kind of feeling."

"Me too." Nana looked at Sabrina, head tilted to the side, as if she expected to find her answer.

Sabrina took another bite and then another, still feeling her grandmother's gaze locked onto her face. Finally, Nana shook her head slowly and stood up. "Guess not." She wandered out of the room, leaving nothing but a gnawing, guilty feeling behind.

By the time Sabrina took her bowl to the sink, her focus had been replaced by a growing sense of guilt. Today was Brandy's race. But why should she feel guilty about not being there? It wasn't like she could do anything to help Brandy during the race. And she knew Kayla and company would be there. Why subject herself to more of that? She was doing what was required of her. She was coaching Brandy three days a week, just like the courts had asked her to. They never said anything about driving up to Nashville to stand on a sideline during a race.

She turned toward her room. She needed to get started on her paper—that was her job for today. Somehow she would just have to focus hard enough to get past any inner voice that said otherwise.

Half an hour later, she was pacing her room in frustration.

When her phone vibrated, she picked it up, welcoming the distraction. It was a text message from Koen.

You ready to go?

Go where?

The race of course.

I'm not going. I told you that, remember?

You told me that, but I know you better. Shall I pick you up in 5?

Sabrina stared at the words across the screen, then walked over to look out the window. She looked down at the very sidewalk where Brandy had been putting in mile after mile, and at the retaining wall where she had sat and coached. Those were the things that were required of her. Nothing more.

She walked back over to her phone, picked it up, and typed her answer.

Sounds great.

Why had she replied that way, when she'd just spent so much time convincing herself she didn't need to? Whatever the reason, after she sent the text her guilt vanished and for a second she felt happy. Only a second. What would she find when she got to the race? Would they drive all the way up there just to watch another debacle? It was possible. Almost likely. But in the moment, Sabrina knew that her mother was right. Brandy was part of her new calling, and that meant being there at the darkest of times.

They had arrived at the race just at the start. Just in time to see Brandy pass. She looked focused and healthy. And she was pacing herself. Maybe, just maybe, today might be a good day.

They'd moved to a stretch of course near the finish and waited, the silence and calm somehow worse for not knowing what was happening. But soon enough the runners appeared, blasting toward the finish line, and Sabrina could hardly believe her eyes. One of the Samson Academy girls was the first woman to appear, but only five yards back, there was Brandy. Sprinting. But her face was bright red and her arms were not pumping quite as hard as they should be.

Sabrina knew what had happened. The girl had pushed herself. She'd decided to give chase, but now, with a quarter mile left, she'd run out of everything. The expression on Brandy's face said that she knew it, too. Catching the leader seemed unlikely. And worse, the third-place runner, another Samson girl, was closing in. If Brandy totally crashed, she'd be caught.

Then, somewhere in the back of her mind, Sabrina heard her mother's voice. *"Brandy needs you. Encourage her."* Sabrina cupped her hands around her mouth and screamed as loud as she could. "Go Brandy, push. You can do it. *Dig deep!*"

Brandy's face flicked in her direction for just a moment, but the instant their eyes locked, Sabrina saw the girl's expression change. It went from the "beat down, about to give up" look to a clenched-teeth determination. She straightened and leaned forward, and her arms began to pump a little harder, her legs continuing to keep the pace. Five yards to the leader became four. "Go, Brandy, go. *You can do it!*"

"Go, Shelby, go. Push! Push!" Kayla Ratcliff's voice came from just a few feet before the finish line. She was leaning forward, clapping and motioning toward her runner.

"Go, Brandy. You can do it!" Sabrina just kept shouting the words over and over and over. "You can do it, you can do it!" She couldn't seem to stop herself.

Koen was shouting at the top of his lungs, too. "Push! Keep pushing!"

Brandy seemed to stumble but regained her footing yet a little bit further behind her competitor. And then she did something that Sabrina had never seen her do before. Something she'd never seen anyone do, other than the footage she'd seen of Eric Liddell. She threw her head back, face to the sky, and surged forward with one last burst of speed. She leaned forward at the finish line, falling forward on the asphalt in the split second after she crossed.

The first woman.

The world around Brandy blurred in clear waves and a sort of milky haze. She was unable to move, unable to think. There were only three words that her mind could fathom at that moment. *I. Did. It. I did it.*

Somewhere in the deep recesses of her brain, there was enough conscious thought left to remind her that she needed to get out of the way before she got trampled, but there was no way she could stand up. She just couldn't move. That's when she felt strong arms lifting her and she found herself floating off the race course.

The movement made her nauseous and she thought for a moment she might vomit. She looked toward the source of her forward progression and saw a cute guy smiling down at her, a really huge smile. It didn't make sense. Then slowly she realized who was carrying her. Koen.

As her brain cleared, she noticed the bouncing head at his shoulder and began to hear and understand the words that had been only unintelligible noise until now. "You did it. You did it. I knew you could. I knew you could." Sabrina had tears flowing down her face.

As soon as Koen set Brandy on a bench, Sabrina was sitting beside her with her arms around her. She was sobbing. And then Brandy started crying, too, although she couldn't remember why.

"Oh my sweet darling, you won. You won!" Grandma's voice came from somewhere nearby. Brandy reached out her arms and hugged her grandmother around the waist, since she still didn't trust herself to stand. She was taking huge gulping breaths, but her body couldn't seem to get enough air.

Then little by little, her mind began to function and her breathing began to slow. She looked over at Sabrina, who by now had calmed down, but still had tears running down her cheeks.

"I didn't think you were going to come."

Sabrina shook her head. "I was wrong. And I'm so glad I changed my mind so I could see this. You are amazing."

"You told me to plan my race so that when I crossed the finish line I didn't have even one ounce of energy left. Nailed that one to perfection today."

Sabrina laughed. "Maybe a little too perfect."

Brandy took a sip of water and looked around her. She could see the Samson Academy contingent gathering nearby. She nodded her head toward them. "How'd they do?"

"Second and third in the girls, first and fourth in the boys," Koen said.

"I think I'll go over there and congratulate them." Brandy stood up and tested her legs. She made her way over to find the girl that she'd barely beat out at the finish and extended her hand. "Good race."

"Thanks." The girl shook her hand, but scowled as she did so.

Brandy shook the hand of the other three girls in the group, as well. Then she came to Kayla Ratcliff. "I heard you speak at our school."

Kayla smiled. "I hope I was an inspiration to you."

"Maybe you might have been." She paused long enough to see the surprise register on Kayla's face. "Before you tell people your story for inspiration, you might want to check your facts. I can't be inspired by someone who tells people she lost her scholarship to a slacker, when I happen to know that you lost your scholarship to a person with a lifelong, crippling disease. Thing is, she's the one with the lifetime problem, but you're the one so bitter you can't even see the truth about what happened. Maybe you should think about that before your next talk."

Brandy turned and walked back to her group, which had expanded. A man and woman were talking to Sabrina. They didn't look familiar, but Sabrina seemed happy enough to see them. They were smiling and talking and gesturing. When Brandy approached, Sabrina said, "Here she is. Allow me to introduce Brandy Philip. Brandy, this is Coach Watkins and Coach Sheridan, from the University of Tennessee track team. They came to see the young talent at the race and wanted to meet you."

"Young lady, that was an amazing race you ran out there today."

"Thank you."

"We were just telling Sabrina we'd love to have her come back and visit sometime. It would be great if you came with her. We could show you around the facilities and talk about what your college aspirations might be."

College aspirations? Until this very moment, Brandy had never had any. "Really? Uh . . ." Brandy looked at the pride on her grandmother's face and the peace on Sabrina's. "That sounds good. I'd like that."

"Good." Coach Watkins reached into his wallet and pulled out a business card. "You feel free to call or email with any questions, and we'll be in touch soon."

"Sounds good." And it did. Who would have guessed that one?

Sabrina rummaged through the back of her closet until she found what she was looking for. The brown box had been stuck back in the corner, undisturbed, for the past three years. She wasn't sure why she'd even brought it here, because she had never planned to open it. Just as she'd never planned to remove her journals, she supposed. She pulled it out, opened the lid, and removed the contents.

"I know you must be proud of Brandy's finish today." Nana came into the room, all smiles.

"I am. I can't believe that she pulled it out the way she did."

"What are you getting into over there?" She moved closer. When she saw the contents of the box, she smiled. "Reminiscing?"

"More like remembering." She unfurled her favorite poster of Eric Liddell. It was black and white, and showed him head thrown back and arms outstretched, the number 451 across his chest. Just the sight of it again after these past few years brought tears to her eyes. But they weren't tears of sadness, not completely anyway. They were so much more than that.

"Would you mind if I hung a couple of posters on the wall in here? I'll use some of that tape that doesn't damage walls."

"I've been waiting for you to do that for the last three years."

Sabrina smiled at her. "I hate to admit it, but maybe you and Mom have been right about a few things."

"Ha. At least a couple, I'd say."

Sabrina rummaged through the box and found the DVD at the bottom. "Hey, Nana, would you mind if I invited Brandy over to watch *Chariots of Fire* after dinner tonight?"

"I can't think of anything I'd like better."

"She'll probably hate the movie, but she needs to see it. At least once."

46

S o why is it you like this movie so much? It doesn't look all that exciting to me." Brandy held the DVD case at arm's length, as if afraid of standing too close.

"It was kind of *my* movie when I was growing up. Until . . . well, until it wasn't anymore."

"Why did it change? Because of your arthritis?"

"Yes. No. Sort of." Truth was, Sabrina wasn't sure of all the reasons. It had just become too painful to watch.

"Makes perfect sense to me."

"I guess so." Sabrina laughed and put the disc into the DVD player.

Two hours later, Brandy said, "That was pretty good, I guess." She stuck some popcorn in her mouth but couldn't quite hide her smile.

Sabrina wiped her eyes. "It's only the best movie ever. That's all."

"I mean, I get it, it's about running and all, and the characters are interesting enough. What hits you so hard about it?"

Sabrina thought about what the true answer might be. "It's just that I always thought I was going to be a runner and then do work that really changed people's lives."

"Like that Eric Liddell guy?"

"Exactly."

Brandy shook her head. "It seems like an odd combination to me. I doubt there are many Olympian missionaries. Why did you have to give up both?"

Brandy's question sounded more than a little like the ones Sabrina had heard from her mother. They never ceased to sting. "The two things had always been lumped together into one big dream in what I understood to be my call. It was the running that gave me the . . . I don't know . . . clout, maybe, to do something really special."

"Because you would be a hero, people would listen to you?"

"I guess so."

"And Eric Liddell was a hero because he won a gold medal?"

"To a lot of people, yes. They came to hear him when they wouldn't have given most speakers the time of day."

"You know, for someone with such good grades, you're not very smart."

"What do you mean?"

"Seems to me this Eric Liddell person didn't succeed in exactly the way he thought he would. Seems to me what makes a hero is someone who gets knocked down but gets back up and looks for what it is they're supposed to be doing now that things didn't work out quite like they planned.

"And to be perfectly honest, while I think Olympic athletes— and especially runners—are totally cool and all, I can't think of a better hero than someone who has been through all you have and come through the other end bigger and stronger. Like you keep doing. And then you put all that aside and pour all your time into helping someone like me.

"If it's the hero part that's holding you back from being the missionary you always wanted to be, then I think you've missed the fact that you already are one."

Monday morning, Sabrina woke up with Brandy's words still ringing through her mind, as they had been since Saturday night.

She picked up her phone and pressed the numbers. "Good morning, this is Sabrina Rice. May I please speak with Candace Davenport?"

"I'll see if she is available. Just one moment, please." Violin music filled the phone line, but it did nothing to calm Sabrina's nerves.

"Sabrina. So good to hear from you, as I was planning to call you later today. Listen, good news. After the last round of interviews, we have decided to make you a firm offer for the intern position. You wowed us on the second interview and we know how hard that must have been with your recent health concerns. With that kind of perseverance and drive, I expect nothing but good things from you."

The job was hers! Sabrina hadn't expected to hear those words when she called. She hesitated, her conviction suddenly less firm than it had been only moments ago. "Uh, well thank you so much for saying that, Candace. And I can't tell you how much I appreciate all that you've done for me. I know you've gone out of your way to help me."

"I expect repayment in full, because I see lots of potential in you."

Potential. Recent health concerns. So they did know about her hospitalization. "Listen, I've been thinking a lot about that in the last few days. My potential. And I've come to the conclusion that . . ." The words froze in her throat. The clear answer was suddenly so foggy in her mind. Was she crazy? What would make her even consider doing what she was thinking of doing? "I've come to the conclusion that there's no need for you to hold that position for me. I think my path lies in a different direction."

The silence lasted long enough that Sabrina had begun to wonder if they'd been cut off. "What?" Candace almost whispered the word. "But I thought you were so committed."

"I was. And I am. I've just come to realize that I didn't want to commit to the wrong thing. Once again, I can't begin to tell you how much I appreciate all you've done for me." *I hope I'm doing the right thing, I hope I'm doing the right thing.*

"Sabrina, I want you to really think about this before we end this phone call. After that, if you change your mind you will not get a second chance. This is it."

Deep breath. Move forward. "I know. And I don't expect to."

"You're making a mistake, but I wish you all the best." A click sounded on the other end of the line, and just like that it was over.

Sabrina reached in the drawer for the phone book because she had one more call to make. She punched in the numbers and waited until a receptionist's voice came on the line. "Yes, I'd like to make an appointment to speak with Judge McGuire." It was time to shut down Mrs. Lauderdale and her threatening phone calls once and for all.

47

The front porch at Mrs. Springer's house looked the same as it always had—a couple of wicker chairs, a small round table, and off to the right, a porch swing suspended by long chains. Yet, Brandy realized as she walked up to it, this place *felt* different now.

The first time she'd come up here, it had been against her will to have dinner with one of Grandma's friends and her snobby granddaughter. In times after that, it had been a place where her overly demanding coach would disappear after doling out Brandy's workload for the day. Then it became a place of hope. A place where maybe, just maybe, there was the slightest glimpse of some sort of bright future waiting for her.

Now, as Brandy reached up to knock on the door, the place seemed full of strength. She doubted Sabrina saw it for what it was, but it could be nothing else.

Mrs. Springer opened the door. "Hello, Brandy."

"Hi, Mrs. Springer. I've got a graduation present for Sabrina I wanted to bring by." Brandy extended the wrapped box, somehow feeling as though she had to prove her words.

"Come on in. Sabrina and her mom are upstairs packing up her stuff. I know she'd love to see you."

Brandy climbed the stairs to Sabrina's room and found the door was open. Cookie was standing at the closet, door open, holding up a handful of shirts on hangers. "What about these?"

"Uh, sure." Sabrina was sitting at the little wooden desk near the window, loading some books into a box at her feet.

"Hi." Brandy walked up to the doorway, wondering if maybe it had been a mistake to come over.

"Hi, Brandy. Come on in." Sabrina wiped her forehead. "How was your run this morning?"

"Good. I did a long one out toward the old Stewart place. Nice day, lots of flowers, cows mooing, the usual."

"You are working so hard. I think you are going to be amazing." Cookie held up a couple of shirts. "Keep?"

"Sure." Sabrina nodded. "She already is." She spoke the words quietly, but with clear conviction in her voice.

"What did you say, dear?" Cookie looked up at her.

"I said she already is. Amazing." Sabrina smiled toward Brandy now, who had never felt more unworthy in her life.

She shook her head and walked over and sank down onto the bed. "This is wrong. So much of this is so wrong. It should have been you."

The words hung in the silent room for what seemed like forever. Finally Cookie said, "I've heard rumors that there are several college coaches following your progress. I am so proud of you." Cookie said this as she laid out some shirts on the bed, beside an already foot-high pile of other clothes on hangers. "Do you have any thoughts about where you'd like to go?"

"I'm hoping for Tennessee. I'd like to finish what Sabrina started."

Cookie came over and put her arms around Brandy, squeezing her tight. "You really are an amazing girl." She pulled away and wiped at her eyes. "I'm going downstairs to check Mom's progress with dinner. Brandy, can you join us?"

"No, thanks. Grandma was in the middle of making a big pot of chicken and dumplings when I left."

"That sounds good." Cookie sniffled as she disappeared out the door.

"When do you start work for Bridges?"

"Next week. I'm spending a couple of weeks in California at their main office, then they're sending me to Africa for three weeks so I can experience the work there firsthand. This is not my original plan, or at least not the way I thought my original plan would play out. But I've come to realize this was my 'promised land' all along. I was just expecting the journey to look a little different so I kept turning back."

"Those are some lucky orphans, to have you on their side."

"Not lucky. Blessed."

"Yes, blessed. We all are, because of you. Because you fought your way through your wilderness, as you call it, and didn't give up."

"I came close a few times, but I'm glad God didn't give up on me."

"So am I. So am I."

She was running.

Feet pounding against the pavement as she moved up a steep hill. She could hear her coach's voice yelling down toward her, "Surge. Surge." She paid attention to the lift of her knees, the straight pump of her arms, and the position of her head. Form matters most when you're tired. Concentrate. Now's when cham- pions are made. *She repeated those words over and over in her head as she made her way to the top of the hill, which she couldn't quite see because it was covered in fog. Still, she pushed to the end, knowing as she reached the top that she'd given it every- thing she had.*

As she broke through the fog layer, she looked toward her coach, hoping for confirmation that she'd done well, already smiling because she knew that she had. And then she saw her coach's face and stopped running.

The woman she saw . . . was Brandy. She was surrounded by an entire group of African orphans who were all smiling, and clapping, and dancing with joy. "You made it, you did it!" They were all shouting and singing at once.

Then he *stepped from the crowd. Sabrina would know his face anywhere. He came up to her, took her hand, and shook it hard. "I'm so proud of you. You gave it everything you had. Way to stick with it, even when times got hard, even when you wanted to quit. Well done." And just like that, Eric Liddell vanished into the mist.*

Sabrina jerked awake, her heart pounding, her breath coming in short gasps. But this time, she wasn't drenched in sweat and tears. This time she was . . . smiling.

Thank you, dear Father. Thank you.

EPILOGUE

Everyone please welcome Miss Brandy Philip."

Everyone in the audience applauded. Well, almost every-one. Not Tansy Rhoades. She would not give her mother the satisfaction. Her friends were all at the mall this afternoon, trying on bathing suits and shorts in preparation for next week's trip to the lake, and she was stuck here listening to some speaker she couldn't care less about.

The lady looked like any other athlete, except that her hair was died pink with blue on the tips, and she had a nose ring. "Thank you, Coach Thompson. Thank you, everyone, for coming. I know there is one particular thing that you all are here to hear about." She paused and the audience made an idiotic giggling sound. How lame could this get? "But first, I thought I'd give you a little background on how it all came to be. Lights, please."

The lights dimmed and this Brandy Philip lady turned on the PowerPoint. The first picture was a black and white of some weird-looking guy running. Yeah, this was going to be bad, all right.

But the pictures went on, and so did the story, and it wasn't long before Tansy found herself leaning forward in her seat, squeezing her chair handles. This was an amazing story. And it was in that moment that Tansy found her. Her hero.

"Here I am at the age of sixteen, when I first got to know the woman who changed my life forever. This is my coach and friend, Sabrina Conner—she was Sabrina Rice back in these days." The audience had gone dead still, enthralled as the story continued to unfold of training, arguments, hangovers, illness, and eventually scholarships and triumphs.

The last picture showed the two of them together, arms around each other's shoulders, with two gold medals hanging around Brandy's neck. "And this is how it all ended up just a few months ago. But this isn't the end, it's still only the beginning. Sabrina continues to help people all around the world with her work as a spokesperson for Bridges. We're fortunate to have her with us today, her and her husband, Koen. Will the two of you please stand?" A dark-headed woman and a pale blond man stood and gave a quick wave to the audience, then quietly took their seats.

"And as for me, I'm still taking my training runs, making plans for the next Olympics, but there is so much more. Running is a God-given talent, one that I may or may not be able to continue to use. His timing is better than my best plans, so I can only trust Him. In addition to running, my heart's call is to help inner-city kids find mentors who are willing to show them a better way."

That's when Tansy knew. With absolute certainty she knew what she wanted to do with the rest of her life. As she walked from the auditorium, she turned to her mother. "I'm going to be a runner, and I'm going to work with kids who have cancer. That's my call."

Mom threw back her head and laughed. It wasn't one of those grown-up kinds of laughs that let a kid know how stupid they were. No, this was one of those "I'm so completely happy I can't hold it in" kinds of things. She reached down and scooped Tansy into her arms and spun around in a circle. "Sounds terrific."

Tansy was so happy with her newfound purpose that she wasn't really too embarrassed by her mother's public display of affection—thankfully none of the kids from school were anywhere near this place. "Can we start training now? You want to go for a run when we get home?"

"I think that's a grand idea." And just like that, they became running partners.

Every single day.

At five in the morning.

Rain or shine.

"Go through the camp and tell the people, 'Get your provisions ready. Three days from now you will cross the Jordan here to go in and take possession of the land the Lord your God is giving you for your own.'"

Joshua 1:11

ACKNOWLEDGMENTS

Heavenly Father—*For your great love in all circumstances.*

Lee Cushman—*For standing by me in all things. Your strength and support are unwavering. I love you.*

Melanie Cushman—*For setting an example for us all with your strength, and for agreeing to let me use parts of your story to tell this one.*

Caroline Cushman—*For being the family cheerleader in all things—including my writing and my (often annoying and inconvenient) research on running.*

Ora Parrish—*Your love and support go well beyond a mother's love. You are amazing.*

Carl, Alisa, Katy, and Lisa—*The best family ever!*

Brenna, Judy, Kristyn, Denice, Kathleen, Gary, Carolyn, and Lori—*great friends and supporters*

Dave Long—*It is such an amazing privilege to work with you.*

Carrie Padgett—*Not only a writing friend, but a true friend*

Kelli Standish—*For always "cheering me on"*

To all the runners, past and present, whom I have hounded endlessly for coaching tidbits and personal experiences—Gary Brown, Emily Turvey, Liam Cetti, Kyle Krutenat, Garrett Iverson, Nate Fearer, Jansen Dahill, and many, many others

QUESTIONS
for
CONVERSATION

1. Have you ever run a distance event or trained for an athletic competition? How did it impact your life and did it teach you anything about yourself?

2. Sabrina acts as both coach and mentor for Brandy. Is there someone in your life who needs you in the same way Brandy needed Sabrina? How is your situation different?

3. Sabrina has a challenging relationship with her father. In what ways do you think it helped her? It what ways did it hurt her? Do you have a similarly challenging relationship with a family member or friend?

4. Both Sabrina and Brandy had very supportive grandmothers. Did any of your grandparents play a significant role in your childhood or in your life as a young adult? What is the difference between the relationship a person has with her grandparent and her relationship with a parent?

5. Sabrina deals with very difficult physical challenges. Have you or someone you love dealt with a chronic health issue? How does a person's physical body affect both their mental and spiritual lives?

6. Running is a physical gift for both Sabrina and Brandy. What do you see as some talents or gifts you've been given and how do you use them in thanks to God?

7. Do you have a Kayla in your life? How do you deal with it? Why do you think God allows Kayla-type misunderstandings between believers?

8. Do you have a hero? What is it about that person that makes you admire him or her? What heroic qualities do you think others might see in you?

9. Sabrina and Brandy both had life situations that were "not fair." In your own life, do you feel that your circumstances are fair, unfair, or unfairly blessed? How do you feel about people who fall into the other categories?

10. Have you ever felt called to do something or go somewhere—your "promised land"—and then when things didn't happen as you expected, you began to doubt your call? Was your faith strengthened or weakened as a result?

Kathryn Cushman is a graduate of Samford University with a degree in pharmacy. She is the author of six previous novels, including *Leaving Yesterday* and *A Promise to Remember*, which were both finalists for the Carol Award in Women's Fiction. Kathryn and her family live in Santa Barbara, California.